Praise for *The Heavens*

A *New York Times Book Review* Editors' Choice
A *Guardian* Best Book of the Year So Far
A Tor.com Best Book of the Year So Far

"We're in New York in the summer of 2000, at a spacious apartment where a gorgeous young couple fall in love. But both harbor secrets, and one seems to be losing her grip on reality."

—*Entertainment Weekly*

"In [*The Heavens*] Newman's sparky sensibility is given the grandest of backdrops . . . Newman's genius lies in balancing these time-lines and world so finely that the whole thing is seamless—not to mention lots of fun . . . A study of creativity—its importance and worth, but also how it separates creators from their loved ones."

—*Guardian*

"Intriguing . . . The surreal comic tone has a lot in common with Elif Batuman, Patrick deWitt, and Ottessa Moshfegh."

—*Times* (UK)

"An exquisitely calibrated strangeness . . . The calamities of our age, in this novel, are also an intricate drama of moral philosophy. Like all dramas, it has a resolution, and one of such eye-popping metaphysi-cal grandeur that I couldn't spoil it even if I wanted to."

—*Irish Times*

"A compelling and complex critique of our current times."

"We're introduced to a world that feels like first love, as hopeful and beautiful. Unsurprisingly, and just like in a love affair, in a plot halfway between science fiction and magical realism, things quickly begin to go wrong. Every one of *The Heavens*'s pages feels like that first shuddering spark of attraction—the potential for great joy, and terrible pain. *The Heavens* gives us both."

"A daring and brilliant piece of speculative literary fiction, and a thoughtful, timely, and unnerving meditation on what it means to hope against hope."

"[A] changeling of a novel."

"Stellar . . . Newman's novel expertly marries historical and contemporary, plumbing the rich, all-too-human depths of present-day New York and early modern England, and racing toward a well-executed peak . . . A fantastic, ingenious novel."

"A thought-provoking, head-spinning fever dream of a novel; highly recommended."

"Smart and terrifying and delicious literary storytelling."

"I was bewitched by the ambition and charge of Sandra Newman's time-slip narrative, which is at once troubling and beautiful, emotionally resonant and fantastically strange."

—Olivia Laing, author of *Crudo*

"I fell into *The Heavens* and it was not unlike falling in love: effortless, magical, seductive, humming with beauty and possible danger . . . Sandra Newman has created a fictional world that was a frightening pleasure to inhabit, one in which the realm of dreams and its mysteries were as compelling as waking life."

—Fatima Farheen Mirza, *New York Times* bestselling author of *A Place for Us*

"What a wonderful, strange, terrifying, brilliant novel this is."

—Kamila Shamsie, author of *Home Fire*

"Reading Sandra Newman's *The Heavens* is like falling up a brilliant flight of stairs. Inventive and moving and surprising on every level, it's a novel that doesn't just play with time and history and certainty: it turns those things inside out. I've been haunted by its characters and ideas ever since I reluctantly finished it."

—Elizabeth McCracken, author of *Thunderstruck & Other Stories* and *Bowlaway*

"An elegant and untamed novel that illuminates the soft edges between love, madness, idealism, and the narrative power of the unconscious mind." —Catherine Lacey, author of *The Answers* and *Certain American States*

"Unique and brilliant, I tore through *The Heavens* and I loved it. It is a house made of trapdoors, where dreams are real and reality a dream. Through this strange labyrinth of 21st century New York and Renaissance England, it is love which deftly, movingly, finds the way." —Adam Foulds, author of *The Quickening Maze*

"*The Heavens*, shifting restlessly between worlds, gently encouraging Elizabethan England into eccentric New York, rolling everything into a dreamy, desperate new reality, is everything we expect from Sandra Newman. It's strange but focused, beautifully written and put together, dangerously benign, comic and clever, bright as a knife." —M. John Harrison, author of *Light* and *You Should Come with Me Now*

THE
HEAVENS

Also by Sandra Newman

The Only Good Thing Anyone Has Ever Done

Cake

How Not to Write a Novel

Changeling

Read This Next

The Western Lit Survival Kit

The Country of Ice Cream Star

THE HEAVENS

SANDRA NEWMAN

Grove Press
New York

Published simultaneously in Canada
Printed in the United States of America

First Grove Atlantic hardcover edition: February 2019
First Grove Atlantic paperback edition: November 2019

This book was set in 11.5-pt. Scala LF with Fournier MT
by Alpha Design & Composition of Pittsfield, NH.

Library of Congress Cataloging-in-Publication data is available for this title.

ISBN 978-0-8021-4797-4
eISBN 978-0-8021-4683-0

Grove Press
an imprint of Grove Atlantic
154 West 14th Street
New York, NY 10011

Distributed by Publishers Group West

groveatlantic.com

19 20 21 22   10 9 8 7 6 5 4 3 2 1

To Howard

THE
HEAVENS

I

1

Ben met Kate at a rich girl's party. He didn't know the rich girl personally; it was one of those parties where no one knew the hostess. He'd come with the rich girl's cousin's co-worker, whom he instantly lost in the crowd. It had started out as a dinner party, but the invitations proliferated, spreading epidemically through friends of friends until it turned into a hundred people. So the rich girl opened up both floors, made punch instead of risotto, and ordered a thousand dumplings from a Chinese restaurant. It was August and you had to let things happen the way they wanted to happen. Everyone was in their twenties then, anyway, so that was how they thought.

It turned out to be a mostly francophone party, conversational and quiet; a party with the windows open to the night, a party where people sat talking on the floor. Most of the illumination was from solar-powered tea lights, which the rich girl had hung on the fire escapes all day to charge, then pasted along the walls. That light reflected softly from the heavy glass tumblers into which wine was poured. There wasn't even music playing. The rich girl said it gave her bad dreams. New York City, so everyone was interning at a Condé Nast publication or a television program or the UN. Everyone a little in love with each other; the year 2000 in the affluent West.

Ben talked to a dozen girls that night. He wasn't seriously looking for a girlfriend. He was working and doing his PhD then, so there wasn't time for emotional investment. Still, it was pleasant to flirt with just anyone, to feel the power of being attractive and six feet tall. A night of receptive postures and parted lips; such an easy blessedness, like ascending a staircase into the air.

At 1:00 a.m. he went down in the elevator to buy cigarettes. Kate was outside on Eighty-Sixth Street with the rich girl's dog, which had needed to pee. She wore a loose dress that didn't look like party attire; at first he wasn't sure she was from the party. Then he recognized the dog, a terrier mutt with a soupçon of dachshund, elongated and shaggy. Cute. Ben stopped to pat the dog.

He went and bought his cigarettes. When he came back, Kate was still there. He paused to smoke. They talked desultorily for five minutes, then something shifted. The traffic fell quiet. They were smiling at each other and not saying anything. Already it felt strange.

Kate said, "What's your name?"

"Pedro," Ben said.

She laughed. "No, I already asked you, didn't I? You said you were something else."

"No." He was smiling foolishly. "I don't think you asked me."

"I did, but I don't remember what you said." She nodded at the dog. "I've forgotten her name too. So if we left town now and went someplace where nobody knows us, you two wouldn't have names."

"I could be Pedro."

"No, I know you aren't Pedro."

"I could be Rumpelstiltskin."

"Done."

He laughed, but she didn't. She just stood there, smiling her liking at him. He finished his cigarette. Then he should have gone back to the party, but he couldn't. It was strange.

And they talked for a while about taking the dog and running off to a town in South America, about the boat they would live on and the smugglers they would meet and the sunsets over the turquoise sea, where blue crabs would scuttle over the beach, and it felt as if they were even younger than they were, as if they didn't yet have jobs.

Kate was Hungarian-Turkish-Persian: three romantic, impractical strains, three peoples who had thrown away their empires. Her ancestors wore jewels in their beards; they galloped on horses, waving swords. With them, it was opium dens or Stalinism, no middle ground; so Kate said, laughing at herself. She was talking obliquely about herself.

Ben was half Bengali, half Jewish. That could be interesting, but it was sedate. He came from a line of rabbis, shopkeepers, lawyers; there was a feeling that he might be uncool by comparison, a feeling Ben had to consciously suppress. He said, "My family didn't wave swords, but I'm always willing to try."

Both Ben and Kate were tawny, black eyed, and aquiline; they looked like members of the same indeterminate race. They commented on this likeness, using self-deprecating terms like "beige" and "beaky," and became so happy at this—at nothing—that they started to walk the dog downtown. The dog was beige, too, Ben pointed out, and they paused and crouched to compare their arms to the dog's coat; that was how they first touched. The dog was licking their hands and confusing the issue. Still there was a definite spark.

Walking back toward the apartment, they traded the information that goes in dating profiles, with the feeling of belatedly completing the paperwork for something they'd already done under the table. Then up in the elevator, where they were alone, and in which he suffered and wanted to kiss her. She smiled forward at the doors, unkissable, glowing with the idea of sex. They came out, and she unleashed the dog and slung the leash onto a branch of the coat rack. Without discussion, they headed to the balcony.

There was someone already there, the rich girl's houseguest, an older New Zealander whom Kate knew and who would later figure prominently in their lives. Ben didn't think much about him then. All he meant was that Ben wasn't alone with Kate. The New Zealander talked about a garden he was working on; he was a garden designer, in New York to create a rich person's garden. Ben listened to his accent and mainly considered him a useful pause, a device that would ease them more gently to the next stage.

So it was the windy balcony, the lights of New York a nether starscape. The actual stars were dull and few. From this perspective, the city was brighter and more complex than the cosmos; the cosmos in fact seemed rote, like a framed print hung on a wall solely because the wall would look wrong without pictures. There have to be pictures and there has to be a cosmos, even if no one looks at them. And Ben looked at Kate surreptitiously, wishing he could tell her this, convinced that she would understand.

She had a long nose and long black humorous eyes, a full, red-lipsticked mouth. *Persian*, his mind said besottedly, *Persian*. In heels, she was as tall as he was. Full and rounded, like a cat with a lot of fur. She stood uncannily straight, as if she'd never ever slouched, never hunched over work. She didn't even lean on the balcony's railing but stood with her arms loose at her sides. Weightless. A queenly bearing. *Persian*.

Outside, she'd told him she was an artist—"works on paper"—who'd given up on her BFA at Pratt. She had suddenly not seen the point. "If it were something like geology, maybe," she'd said (because he'd told her he had a degree in geology, although he was also a poet—*published,* he had hastily added. She'd volunteered, in a helpful tone: "Well, *I* read poetry." He'd said, "Really?" She'd said, "I'm on Apollinaire right now," and quoted some Apollinaire in French, as if that were a normal ability for a failed art student. She'd added, "My French is awful, sorry," and he'd said stupidly, "Me neither," because he was powerfully distracted, he was suddenly thinking in terms of love.

Then she'd said, "We should get back to the party," and the world turned cold. How had he got to that point so quickly?)

Now the windy balcony, the obsolete stars, the city a mystery of glittering towers. Kate and the New Zealander were talking about the Great Man theory of history, according to which human progress was driven by superlative people like Socrates or Muhammad, who single-handedly changed the world. Kate defended this idea, while the New

Zealander pooh-poohed it and refused to believe she was serious. He said, "How could anyone be *that* much better? We all have such similar biologies."

"They wouldn't have to be that much better," said Kate. "It would be all the circumstances lining up, like with any unusual event, like a supervolcano or a major earthquake." She looked at Ben.

Ben said, "Major earthquakes aren't that unusual."

"Ben's a geologist," Kate told the New Zealander.

"But is he a great geologist?" the New Zealander said.

Kate laughed. Ben laughed, too, although he also wondered if this was a slight that might diminish him in Kate's eyes. The New Zealander said he was going to get another drink and left. Ben's heart was suddenly racing. Scraps from the Apollinaire she'd quoted surfaced in his mind: *mon beau membre asinin . . . le sacré bordel entre tes cuisses* (my stupid beautiful dick . . . the sacred bordello between your thighs). When she'd said it, it had certainly seemed like flirting. But it might have just been the only Apollinaire she could call to mind.

Now Kate smiled at him vaguely and looked back at the French doors. Her face caught the light and her smooth cheek shone. Some new intention appeared in her eyes—a bad moment, where he thought she was about to ditch him. But she turned to him again, smiling wonderfully, and said, "I've got the key to the roof deck. I'm sleeping on the roof, if that sounds like something you might want to do."

He was nodding, breathless, while she explained that Sabine (the rich girl) was her good friend. Kate often slept on the roof. She had an inflatable bed up there. "It blows up with a mechanism," Kate said, making a mechanism gesture in the air.

He laughed, he was light-headed. He made the mechanism gesture back, and Kate took him by the sleeve, just like that, and led him back to the party. She said, "I'd better ask Sabine, but she'll say yes."

It was breezy and wonderful in the apartment, which had two floors and twelve rooms and belonged to the rich girl's uncle; it hosted his collection of African drums, and for this reason (somehow this knowledge had filtered through to everyone) the air-conditioning was meant to be always on and the windows closed. The drum skins would perish in humidity. Presumably they were from a dry part of Africa or were meant to be re-skinned periodically by a caste of craftsmen who had died out, whose descendants had become engineers and postal workers. In any case, the windows were open, the air-conditioning was off, and everyone kept looking at the drums, discussing them, aware that this party was subtracting from the drums' life span. Likewise, Ben now imagined the drums as sacrifices to whatever this was.

They found Sabine, the rich girl, talking to three men, who were all much taller than she was, so she appeared to be standing in a grove of men. They were speaking French and making what Ben thought of as French gesticulations. Sabine was very blond and as heavy as Kate, though on her it was not provocative but pudgy. She didn't look rich. She looked unhappy and intelligent. When Kate made her request, Sabine frowned, displeased, as if this were only the most recent in a series of Kate's unreasonable demands, and said, "Fine. Do whatever."

"It's not whatever," Kate said, but didn't pursue it. She just smiled at Sabine, at Ben, at the three tall men who smiled back conspiratorially.

9

"I don't want to cause problems," Ben said.

At this, Sabine suddenly changed. She grinned and tousled Kate's hair, saying to Ben: "You won't need to cause problems if you're sleeping with this one. She'll take care of that."

Kate laughed delightedly and looked at Ben as if she were being complimented. The three men were all looking at Kate, looking wistfully at three different parts of Kate's body. Sabine said, "Enjoy," and turned back to the men in a peremptory manner, mustering them back to their earlier conversation. They took their eyes off Kate reluctantly.

So Ben bore her away like a prize he had won by defeating those three men or—looked at another way—he followed her obediently up the stairs, in her absolute and permanent thrall.

The roof had a deck of solid blond wood, with a plain iron railing around the edge. There was a grill, a picnic table, Adirondack chairs. To Ben's eye, there were no apparent signs of wealth, though he wasn't sure what he'd expected. Fountains? There were gardening implements but no garden, only a row of potted plants along the railing—or really several of the same plant, a shaggy blond grass with overtones of purple. The inflatable mattress, a green canvas rectangle with no sheets or blanket, had been set beside these plants. It had already been inflated, and Kate went to it without hesitation and sat, looking back at Ben seriously, as if she were inviting him to something of great moment.

He came and sat. His immediate lust was gone. He was expecting thirty minutes of conversation, anyway, before anything could happen. And in fact, Kate began to talk about the potted grass—it was an endangered species, which was why the roof hadn't been opened up for the party and possibly why Sabine had chafed at letting Ben on the roof, because the grass was illegal. It had been smuggled in by a friend of the New Zealander, a mining executive, in his corporate jet. You weren't supposed to take the grass out of its homeland, although in this case it was intended to preserve the grass from becoming extinct, which it soon would be in the part of Argentina where it was native, an area now devastated by mining. The dirt in the pots was Argentine too. It was the sort of thing that happened to Sabine, that she ended up harboring smuggled grasses.

Ben looked dutifully at the grasses, which—he now noticed—were in two different kinds of pots. Some were standard clay pots; some were green celluloid pots that had been molded to imitate the shape of standard clay pots. He pointed this out to Kate, and she immediately frowned and expressed concern for the grasses in the celluloid pots.

"I don't think the grass cares," Ben said. "Grass isn't that sensitive to aesthetics."

"No, it must affect the soil."

"It would be such a tiny difference it wouldn't matter," Ben said with the air of a man with a degree in science.

"Even tiny differences matter. There could be a butterfly effect."

"Oh, no, not the butterfly effect," said Ben teasingly.

But she insisted that a plant is a complex system, just like weather; there could easily be a butterfly effect. He objected that a plant isn't very complex; a grass would have thousands of cells, not millions, and most of those cells would be exactly alike. She objected to *exactly*—they couldn't be *exactly* alike. He said, "Well, if you're going to be like that." They laughed. Then she reached out suddenly and took his hand, which sent a particular shock through him. He was tamed. He was impressed.

She said, "I wasn't inviting you up here to have sex. I hope you didn't get the wrong idea."

"Oh, no," he lied. "I didn't expect anything."

"Maybe we could have sex next time, though."

"Okay."

"I mean, I'm not rejecting you."

"Yes," he said, a little hoarse. "Don't reject me."

"I won't," she said. "I don't."

They were silent for a minute. He was wondering what the parameters of no sex were. He was thinking about the butterfly effect in the case of falling for people, the small differences between one girl and another creating a cascade of results that changed your life. He looked at the grasses and decided he shouldn't tell her this.

Then she said, sounding nervous for the first time, "Do you remember your dreams?"

That was the last important thing before he was kissing her. He stroked her cheek, her skin soft as powder, so wonderful it was bizarre. The whole world had gone to his head, with its purple-tinted grass and its black hair, in both of which the wind moved gracefully and smelled of sky. And when they lay down together, their bodies fit in an uncanny way, interlocked; however they moved, they fit together again, *plugged in,* and electricity flowed between them. Then he stayed awake for hours while Kate slept easily, naturally, in his arms. For the rest of his life, he would remember it: that intoxicated moment not only of first love but of universal hope, that summer when Chen swept the presidential primaries on a wave of utopian fervor, when carbon emissions had radically declined and the Jerusalem peace accords had been signed and the United Nations surpassed its millennium goals for eradicating poverty, when it felt as if everything might work out. He could conjure it all by harking back to that inflatable mattress with no sheets, the endangered grasses fluttering and springing above their heads, the stars like dusty candy. Without sheets, the wind blew directly on his body, on his bare arms. Far below was the sound of traffic, as quiet as a thought. Occasionally a siren rose, like a frail red line that scrolled across the sky and faded again. Kate muttered and kicked in her sleep. Every time, it was adorable and he was amazed. He fell asleep at dawn, still plotting how he would make her stay.

2

In the dream, Kate was asleep.

She was sleeping but not where she'd fallen asleep. It was a place distinct from any place she'd ever been, although in the dream she knew it well. She knew the bed, the house, the great city. She didn't have to wonder where they were. But it wasn't Kate who knew them. It was *the person she was sleeping as.*

Often, she dreamed in the dream—or *the person she was sleeping as* dreamed. These dreams were mostly of horses she was riding, which reared and threatened to throw her off or flew uncannily into the sky; or else she was playing a stringed instrument whose strings broke, lashing her fingers. Once she was conscious that a man in her dream-within-a-dream was her father, but his face remained vague; of course, she was supposed to already know what her father looked like. But since it wasn't *Kate's* father, she didn't. She never learned what he looked like; she only knew, vaguely and pitifully, that he was dead.

Other times she drifted toward waking as that other person in that other place, and was aware of lying nude under heavy layers, the air comfortably chilly on her face. Something itched. There was a closeness—the bed was enclosed somehow—and a variegated landscape of smells. Somewhere nearby, the alto hoots of doves made her idly, desultorily dream of pie. Kate would try to wake up further, but *the person* was tired, bone tired as if from manual labor, exhausted as Kate never was. So she always blissfully, helplessly, fell back into deeper sleep.

In the dream, Kate was magically happy. *The person* had fears and resentments and sorrows, but even these were a wonderland of sensation, like a series of beautiful colors. When Kate woke up, there would be a few minutes when she felt that way about real life.

Kate had started having the dream when she was a child. At first it only came a few times a year, but now she had it most nights. On mornings after she'd had the dream, she felt a particular, sublime importance—as if the dream were a secret mission, on which depended the fate of millions; as if it held the key to the salvation of the world.

3

Ben breakfasted with Sabine. Kate had vanished while he was asleep, although she was expected back any minute since the dog had likewise vanished, and presumably Kate was out walking, not stealing, the dog. The breakfast was made by a servant, a middle-aged woman with jet-black hair, to whom Sabine spoke companionably in French. When Ben listened in, the conversation was about the extinction of the [word he didn't understand] in the Mediterranean, which was being killed by pollution. The pollution caused algal blooms that suffocated the [word he didn't understand]. Agricultural runoff had been cut back, but it was too late for the [word he didn't understand]. *It's horrible,* the servant said, and Sabine repeated in the same aggrieved tone, *It's horrible.* Then Sabine said that her uncle—here she gestured vaguely around at the uncle's apartment—didn't believe in pollution. *He thinks all chemicals are the same,* said Sabine. *He says the air is made of chemicals.*

At this point, Sabine and the servant noticed Ben listening and smiled at him. He said in his careful French, *We are all made of chemicals too.*

They laughed in a friendly way, as if they wanted to make him feel good. Then the servant brought him a plate of scrambled eggs, said, "Bon appétit," and left.

Sabine said to Ben, "Kate shouldn't be long." Then she opened a *New York Times* and started to read. It was startling, both for its rudeness and because Ben hadn't noticed the *Times* there. Also the naked feeling of being left to eat without reading material while someone else was reading. It made him feel leaden and ridiculous, while at the same time he accepted it as part of this new world, the world with Kate. There were secrets to which he would not be privy. He would have to feel stupid because he cared too much.

Then just as suddenly, Sabine put down the *Times.* "Fuck. I just realized Kate could be a while."

Ben made an intelligent face, chewing eggs.

"I mean, I'm not throwing you out," said Sabine. "You can wait. But I'm thinking she took the dog to Nick's."

Ben swallowed awkwardly. "Nick's?"

"Nick's her ex. She didn't say about Nick?"

"No."

"I mean, don't worry. It's over with Nick. Nick left Kate for a mail-order bride. Somebody else's mail-order bride. I think she's Thai. But Kate brings the dog there because Nick's depressed and she thinks it cheers him up."

Ben smiled with forced casualness. "Nick stole someone's mail-order bride?"

"No, she'd already left her husband. She was a runaway mail-order bride. I know it sounds weird, but it's not that weird. We've got a lot of mail-order brides around, because a friend of ours started an organization to rescue them. I've got three living here now."

At that moment, a toilet flushed upstairs. Ben immediately pictured a mail-order bride, wan and homesick, turning away from a glugging toilet and straightening her traditional Thai garb.

"Well," he said. "That's got to be weird."

"Not really." Sabine shrugged. "Everyone stays here. Right now, I've got a congresswoman from Maine, plus two environmental activists, plus the mail-order brides and Martin and a couple other people. I'm the only person in left-wing politics who has spare rooms. I'm like the red hotel."

"You're in politics?"

Sabine made a stupid-questions face, then suddenly got up and went to the sink. She fetched a large metal pitcher from a shelf and started to fill it at the faucet. For a moment, Ben imagined she was preparing to pour cold water over his head. But when it was full, she carried the pitcher, ponderous and sloshing, to the windowsill, where Ben now noticed a gathering of elegant plants. They appeared to wait expectantly, bracing themselves to receive the water.

Sabine started to pour and said, "I shouldn't have mentioned Nick. That sucks. I can't stand people who gossip, but then I go and do it myself."

"It wasn't gossiping, exactly."

"Dude, please. It was gossiping. I mean, I'm not *out* to poison your mind against Kate. But I have to start in about Nick or some fucking thing. It's like a compulsion."

Then, as if to prove her point, she launched into another story about Kate, often forgetting to water the plants and simply standing there talking with the heavy pitcher trembling in her small hands. The story began with Sabine meeting Kate when they were twelve, at the American International School in Budapest. At that time, the thing about Kate was that she believed, or said she believed, she was from another world. Kate fashioned odd headdresses from towels and said it was what the women wore there; she once made a castle from bread that was supposed to be like the castles in her world. She called it Albion. The Albionites sang beautifully; they liked to sing in four-part harmony, standing in courtyards full of otherworldly peacocks and flowering trees. Kate was a sleeping princess there, like Sleeping Beauty, only more serious. She'd been asleep for years and therefore knew little of her Albion life, except that in Albion she had a horse (as Sabine did in earthly Budapest).

Kate's fear was that our world was actually just Kate's dream, an enchanted dream she was having in Albion. This was what Sabine and Kate used to talk about in their sleepovers at the ambassador's residence (Sabine's father had been the American ambassador to Hungary). They lay in the dark and scintillatingly pondered: *If Kate woke up in Albion, would our world disappear, and everyone in it? Was it Kate's fault when Earth people died, because she'd dreamed their dying? Could Kate direct her dream and thereby bring about heaven on Earth?*

Soon other girls (the popular girls at school) were inducted into the secret, and they would gather conspiratorially to discuss their intuitions about the crisis, to draw pictures of Albion, and to speculate about whether they might also have sleeping Albion counterparts. On this point Kate was generous; when someone claimed to have had an

Albion dream, Kate never pooh-poohed but listened intently. She *wanted* to believe. Still, Kate was the official dreamer, and they would lock themselves in Sabine's bedroom, sit in a circle around Kate, and chant "inspirations" to help her dream a better world. Kate lay in the middle with her palms pressed to her eyes. She wished so hard her toes curled. A typical inspiration was: *Dream no cancer, dream no cancer—Albion!* There were other chants to end poverty, infidelity, and hurricanes. At the time, they found proof of their benevolent influence in the nightly news, though in retrospect, the news had mostly been terrible.

Then a difficult girl (the granddaughter of a Hungarian movie star) rebelled and said Kate was lying. She pointed out that "Albion" was just an old word for England; Kate hadn't even made up a new name! That girl was exiled from the group, but told the story of Albion far and wide. Then other kids (the unpopular kids at school) began to snigger—this was what Sabine remembered most: being laughed at, the topsy-turvy of popular/unpopular, and how it made her suddenly realize she'd never believed in Albion. It was just a game, a game of make-believe, like little kids played.

Next came an ugly scene where Sabine and the popular girls cornered Kate and hounded her to admit she'd been lying. When she resisted, they called her names and one of them began to tear up a sandwich she was eating and threw the fragments into Kate's long hair. Kate wept but refused to change her story. The panic mounted; it made the girls vicious. One girl threatened Kate with a lit cigarette. Another told Kate she was going to call an ambulance to take Kate to a mental hospital, where Kate would be kept tied to a bed. Sabine herself walked out instead of defending Kate—ran out, although they were at her house. She ran to her boyfriend's place and got drunk there for the first time, though that was another story.

Sabine had never really believed in Albion. Still, she felt the loss of it no less. It was as if they'd *almost* made it real; they had *almost* been the gods who determined history. Now the world was magicless, a dull, inanimate thing, and they were insignificant children.

Here Sabine stopped. By now, she'd set the watering pitcher down and was sitting on the windowsill. She said, "That's Kate."

"Okay," Ben said (and sickeningly wanted to protect Kate, tearstained preteen Kate; the story had made it ten times worse), "but what do you mean by that? *What's* Kate?"

Sabine paused, possibly biting her tongue. There was a gathering din upstairs, of footsteps and slamming doors and voices. A shower was running somewhere and a hair dryer somewhere else. Ben was trying to guess Sabine's point, but was distracted by images of mail-order brides in showers, of congresswomen drying their hair.

At last Sabine said slowly, deliberately, "I guess I'm saying Kate doesn't live in the real world, and ultimately people can't deal with it and then they end up hurting her? Like, Nick was crazy in love with Kate, but then he couldn't take it and he left her for Phuong. Now *Nick's* depressed, and Kate goes over there and comforts him like she ruined his life. And okay, she kind of ruined his life. Nick's fucked up. But."

"So you're warning me away from her?" Ben said, giving it an incredulous note.

"No," Sabine said. "I didn't mean to. Is that what I'm doing? Jesus Christ, I'm such an asshole."

* * *

That was the last real thing Sabine said, because the door banged open and the kitchen started to precipitously fill with houseguests. There was the garden designer from last night, the congresswoman from Maine, a Nigerian mail-order bride who was missing a tooth in front, and a diminutive, hirsute guy who looked like a little glum hamster and was never identified. Then more people. Most wore identical cashmere bathrobes, which Sabine presumably kept for guests, and they exuded a frowsy *bonheur*; they were pleased to be here. When the table filled, people sat on the floor or perched on the kitchen counters. The servant reappeared, a little flustered, and the egg routine began again, while the houseguests made a lot of noise and laughed. They argued about labor policy and baseball and whether the Antarctic was going to melt. They quoted nineteenth-century economists and added, "Which is horseshit straight from the horse." They told stories about President Chen's transition team and the fight for the universal basic income and how one staffer had threatened not just to quit, but to burn himself alive on the convention floor if the UBI wasn't in the party platform. One environmental activist demonstrated how she'd set a right-wing candidate's stump speech to the tune of "O Sole Mio," in a harsh histrionic soprano, and the Nigerian mail-order bride laughed so hard she snorted egg out of her nose. Meanwhile, others had side conversations about another right-winger's mistress's chlamydia; tickled each other and shouted "Revisionist!"; got up to interfere with the cooking, were threatened with a spatula, and slunk back to the table with comically chastened expressions.

And Ben was taken, buoyed, caught in a widening circle of infatuation. These were Kate's people, better than *people,* just as Kate was better than *women.* Even when they discussed the congresswoman's

haircut, the haircut chitchat was markedly superior: they made bo-
tanical allusions, called the haircut *anti-intellectual*, and laughed very
happily, enjoying each other. The glum hamster summed up, "It's a bit
shag carpet," and the congresswoman said, "Well, let's be honest, my
base is a bit shag carpet." Ben laughed and ate cold toast and imagined
himself in this jovial world—*with Kate*—and his suspicion that she
was his answer, his escape, became a conviction.

Then more footsteps came from the hallway, and Ben was caught
grinning as he looked back at the door, expecting more mail-order
brides. But when the door opened, it was Kate.

She was still in her rumpled dress from last night, but because she'd
come from outside and was entering a room of bathrobes and bare feet,
she seemed very poised and competent, as if she'd stolen a march on
everyone and taken possession of the day. The dog was trotting along-
side, looking up to her face with a worshipful air. Her hair was wild
and windblown. She was beautiful as she hadn't quite been last night,
conventionally beautiful in a way that made Ben feel wrong-footed.

She saw him there and balked. There was a pause of social embarrassment. It occurred to him for the first time that Kate had expected
him to leave. She'd ditched him. Her vanishing was a hint, not even a
particularly subtle hint. Sabine must have known, and that was why
she'd been trying to warn Ben off. He was an idiot.

There was a sickening moment of exile. He wanted to catch all the
things, to catch the morning and the careless laughter, Kate's windblown
hair that had been in his hands, that belonged to him, the halcyon
night where he had belonged. Even the dog, who was now looking
openmouthed at Ben, as if trying to place him.

Then Kate said, "Ben! Are you free today?"

For a moment, he was still preparing his exit. Then the penny dropped, clangorously, thrillingly. Ben stood up from his chair. The room fell silent as Kate came toward him, dropping the dog's leash on the floor. She put a hand familiarly on his chest and said, "I was thinking we could go to the movies."

"Movies," he said. "Yes, I suddenly really want to do that."

"Or we could do pretty much anything else."

"Yes, I really want to do that too."

Then they felt their audience and looked around at the table of houseguests, prepared to bask in implicit congratulations.

"Sweet," said Sabine behind them. "But Kate? You shouldn't just take my dog."

4

When Kate was in love, when a man was in love with Kate, the dream grew stronger. She was still asleep in the dream. *The person she was sleeping as* could not wake. But her oneiric world could be intuited; it grew into a city around her bed. There were fields beyond the city, with dream cattle shaking their horns at a dim dream sun; there were sailing ships that rode on a bright dream sea. The dream was strongest of all when Kate's heart was broken. Then she fell asleep as if falling out of life, and the dream became numinous as real things are numinous, vivid even as it blankly slept. She couldn't prove it even to her own satisfaction, but she felt the dream was quickened by love.

So after her first kiss, she dreamed the bed where her other self lay, the musty velvet curtains enclosing it. The night she first had sex with a man, she dreamed a cat that slept beside her, that stretched and poked her ribs with a small, distinct paw. When her first boyfriend cheated on her, she dreamed the bay-leaf scent of Christmas garlands and knew how she'd spent the long day making them; she felt her stiff, chafed hands. By the time Nick left her for Phuong, she anticipated that the dream would compensate his loss, and her sadness was an ecstasy, a guilt, an assignation.

In fact, in those weeks, the dream came closer. Names appeared, the fanciful names of dream locations and dream people. In her sleep, she heard the tolling of the bell at Saint Sepulchre, the bell that rang when a man had gone to hell. There was a band of actors ruled by a Lord Strange—once she'd ridden a black-maned horse to see the actors; she'd worn a velvet mask. And there was None-such Palace, where she'd sat at the feet of a queen and played an ivory flute. The queen had worn a cloak of silver lace, embroidered with enormous spiders; she was Cynthia, Sovereign of the Moon, and she had a toothache that swelled her face. All the nobles came with broths and potions, but nothing could ease her pain.

There was something Emilia had to do. (Emilia was Kate's dream name.) There was a quest or a message to deliver—Emilia had no time to spare in the dream. But Emilia could never wake up. Only Kate could wake up, wake up in New York, and that was neither here nor there. It was fiddling while Rome burned.

So Kate woke in New York and was meant to get up. She was meant to forget her dream, wash it off in the shower. She was meant to get a job.

She would think: *If I'd truly loved Nick, I could wake.* She would think: *If Nick were truly good.* She would think: *If he loved me.* She would also think that other people had recurring dreams, and it didn't have to mean anything. She thought this but didn't believe it. She believed in the dream.

And after all, belief was a beautiful thing. That was the trouble with atheists (Kate thought); they might be right, but their unbelief was utilitarian, bleak, like a Brutalist building. Nobody wanted to live there. No one could *want* them to be right.

She believed. And in the real night of New York, she would walk along the river and look at the moon. It was blank and real. A rock. It had no Cynthia who danced in the chilly air of None-such Palace, no argent queen whose spiders fluttered in the lunar air; no girl who sat on a floor strewn with straw and meadow flowers, in a wash of embroidered skirts, and played an ivory flute.

In the meantime, she didn't have a job. She hadn't finished college. Her life went nowhere. Still, there was nothing to be done, Kate thought. The dream was just what had happened to her. It was one of those things where the best you could do was to hide it from other people.

5

The first few weeks of being in love: what magic had meant to him when he was a child, what he'd wanted when he'd dreamed about riding a dragon. Everything was that different. Just Kate's face looking up and seeing him. He'd walk across a dive bar to her smile and then her hand in his that made his body ignite with pleasure. He felt it in his feet. On the wall behind her, a framed vintage advertisement for the Tour de France was blessed, was alive and significant. Sexual. Nothing could be this good again, and already the scrambling vertigo of that. Of clinging to this thin moment that wouldn't cling back.

The fear when he glanced at her casually and felt nothing. The relief when she smiled and was amazing again.

Or she might just leave you.

Ben had a job at an energy-industry journal, a job he downplayed and treated as a stopgap embarrassment but secretly liked. He rewrote press releases. He had spats with his editor and drank ten coffees. He attended conferences in Pittsburgh that were an ocean of suits in a Holiday Inn, where, at a certain hour of night, the suits started daring each other to look up strip clubs in the Yellow Pages. It was rote, it was soulless: a comfortable nothing, like going to an office to play cards all day.

What was important now: it was a job you could leave at five.

Kate was never doing anything. He picked her up at Sabine's, and they walked all through New York, creating a personal geography of train stations where they'd kissed and bars where they'd had break-through conversations, all through those last summer days that delicately chilled, became serious, became the first bright days of autumn. Everywhere, they were the couple in love. They were stars, cocooned, invulnerable; would be laughing happily on a jam-packed subway platform, in its tropical reek and heat, while the F train just didn't come and the other travelers endured a stifled misery that Ben now couldn't even imagine. How had that stuff ever mattered to him?

And back to Sabine's—it was always there. Ben's apartment was too grim; it had linoleum in the bedroom. Kate had a place—a shared house in Brooklyn—but somebody's brother was staying in her bedroom, and anyway, Kate didn't like bedrooms; they made her feel like a doll that had been put in a drawer. So it was Sabine's rooftop, where Kate was always stroking the endangered grass motherhennishly, worried that it missed the Andes, that it wouldn't like the local rain. When there *was* local rain, they went indoors to the uncle's library, where Kate was in the habit of sleeping on a sheepskin rug; it had a semicircle of rosy smudges where Kate's lipstick had come off on the wool. With the addition of Ben, she brought a futon out, and they had sex for hours beneath the books that filled the walls to the ceiling, books that seemed to solemnly think their thousand stories in the gloom beyond the light of the reading lamp, while Ben and Kate didn't think but moaned and felt and were animals in that light.

Outside the library door, it was politics. Sabine was the sort of rich girl who bankrolled left-wing political movements: squatters' rights and prison reform and open borders and just plain communism. Her apartment was a churn of left-wing activists and local politicians, of reporters whose stories Sabine dictated and moneyed friends who wrote her checks, of squatters and ex-convicts and refugees who came to her apartment in threadbare legations to second-guess everything she did. Often they stayed the night, and there were always staffers from Albany staying, who stank the place out with their cigarettes and shouted at the breakfast table, stabbing the air with a fork to make their points. There was also a shifting population of mail-order brides and miscellaneous penniless riffraff, plus Martin the New Zealander garden designer, who'd been grandfathered into the apartment as a condition of Sabine's own tenancy.

Every weekend, there was a party where these same people appeared in different clothes. There was one intimate party where everyone sat on the floor and told stories about times they'd been depressed; there was one uproarious party where the mail-order brides danced in bikini tops and a stringer from *La Prensa* put her foot through one of the African drums. One Saturday, there was an unplanned party because people kept turning up with wine, hoping there might be a party they hadn't heard about. At one presidential debate–watching party, a drunken state assemblyman told Sabine he wanted to leave his wife for her, and when Sabine turned him down, he locked himself in a bathroom and shaved his head.

Kate knew everyone. They knew Kate. Half the men carried a torch for her; women dragged her into bedrooms to tell her secrets. Ben was hers, so he was instantly A-list, included in kitchen powwows and treated to coke and offered jobs at the Jersey City mayor's office. It went to his head. He took sides. He cared. He became a fork-waving shouter at breakfast. He donated twenty-dollar bills and marched and went out knocking on doors in the Bronx. Just being in Sabine's crowd made him feel like a soldier in the good war; he was no longer just Ben for himself, but an invincible Ben for all mankind.

And after all, it was the year 2000—Chen's Year, the first year with no war at all, when you opened up the newspaper like opening a gift; a year of mass protests at which the same violin-playing blind girl would always appear and play the same Irish air; the year Les Girafes occupied the embassy of Germany and flew the anarchist flag and the Jolly Roger from its broken windows; that best-ever year when Ben was first in love.

And began to spy utopia. In bars and taquerías, in the inebriate dark of a much-used bed, on the rooftop, above/among the starry opulence of Upper Manhattan, he believed what Kate believed and was always (in his mind) in a wine haze, dancing in a jostling swarm of mail-order brides and political hacks, while the world became the something else of dreams, of books, of Kate.

The first wrong note came in the Debendranath Talk—the talk Ben had to have with all new people, in which he explained his first name was Debendranath, not Benjamin, as people assumed. It was at an early party, where Ben and Kate had crept off to be alone. They were hiding in a bedroom and smoking a joint there like (Kate said) two teenagers about to be dramatically caught smoking a joint by their strict parents.

Then he told her about being named Debendranath ("You see, it is basically Rumpelstiltskin") and Kate said she liked multisyllabic names, and it was nothing to a person who spoke Hungarian, and repeated, "Debendranath. Debendranath. Debendranath," making Ben laugh from stoned inconsequence.

This developed into the Parents Conversation, and Ben was taken aback to learn Kate thought of her parents as her best friends. Just loved them, zero problems, and went to have lunch with them every Sunday. They read newspapers together and ate Hungarian pastries and complained about contemporary art. Kate's mother was a professor of Hungarian, and her father was an artist, specializing in works on paper—just like Kate. And Ben's parents?

Then Ben had to confess he didn't like his parents. Well, everybody hated his mother. It was possible to pity Ben's mother, who'd spent half her life in mental institutions being hated by psychiatrists, but no one liked her. She was an extreme narcissist. If you weren't admiring her, she saw you as a persecutor and railed at you or threatened suicide. Even her sisters in Kolkata wouldn't speak to her, an astonishing feat if you knew Bengali families. Ben's father was okay. Or if he hadn't been so oppressed by Swati (Ben's mother), he would be okay. Ben could hardly meet Kate's eye while saying this: everyone knew that men with terrible mothers grew up hating women.

Kate apparently *didn't* know this, however, and reacted perfectly strangely by wondering aloud if there was any way to break up Ben's parents' marriage.

"If we did, my mother would kill herself," Ben said, annoyed. "That's why my dad doesn't leave."

"Did *he* say that?"

"He wouldn't say that to me. Come on."

"But what if she did kill herself? Would that really be worse?"

"Wow."

"No, but if she'd killed herself years ago, wouldn't you be happier now?"

"You really don't understand what it's like to have bad parents, do you?"

Kate frowned. Her face intensified, he wasn't sure how. A bad moment, when he thought *Kate* might be a narcissist and felt an acrophobic nausea. But her black eyes softened suddenly. It was as if she were about to cry, but instead she blushed and crossed her arms against herself.

"I'm sorry," she said. "I'm being an idiot. Sometimes I say really awful things."

There was nothing so wrong with that conversation. They'd both been wasted and Kate had apologized. In fact, whenever Ben thought about it, his worry would slowly evaporate. But when he didn't think about it, it niggled and made him need to think about it again. At last, he labeled it "the anomaly" and tried to put it out of his mind.

The next strange thing happened at the party where Ben first met Oksana, the Ukrainian mail-order bride.

He'd heard a lot about Oksana, partly because she was the one who ran the organization that rescued mail-order brides but also because she took her clothes off at parties. Therefore, at all Sabine's parties, men and lesbians would ask hopefully, "Is the naked girl coming?" and even some women and gay men would ask pruriently, "Is the naked girl here?" Then everyone would talk about how it changed the atmosphere to have a naked woman at a party, until someone mentioned the mail-order bride organization and someone else said, "I always forget that. I always just think of her as Naked Girl."

Because she was naked, Ben immediately recognized her. He watched her come into the room with a peculiar shock, because he'd been envisioning her as a centerfold type, even though he'd been told time and again she had an ordinary body. She did. She was flat chested, bottom heavy—duck shaped—and her skin was anemically white. Even her lips were off-white. At first glance, she seemed to have no nipples at all. Her hair was also pale, white blond, and so messy he assumed it was a feminist statement.

Oksana crossed the room, and no one stared, but everyone parted before her. She went to a bookcase and studied the spines. A man appeared at her side and talked, but she opened a book and leafed through the pages until he gave up and went away. Ben would have thought she wasn't interested in parties, except that she had a sprinkling of purple glitter across her broad white buttocks.

Soon after, Sabine introduced her to Ben. Oksana had in the meantime put on one of the house's signature cashmere bathrobes, presumably because it was October and chilly. There was a new man standing with her, proprietorially standing; he seemed to be angrily in love with her. This was one of Sabine's moneyed cousins, meaty and blond, with a yachting tan.

At first, Sabine was talking about her open borders organization and the crucial period coming up, for which she needed to fund new hires. No one listened, and yet it was clear the yacht man was going to write a check. Oksana smoked a cigarette, drawing Ben's attention to the fact that her lips were chapped and her teeth a little yellow.

When Sabine finished talking, Ben asked Oksana (because he'd always wondered, and he didn't want to be intimidated into *not* asking), "Why aren't you wearing any clothes?"

She said, "My clothes are bad. Not good enough for such a party here."

The yacht man laughed as if she'd hilariously put Ben in his place, while Oksana looked at her cigarette impartially. Her voice had been eerily sweet and high-pitched, a little reminiscent of the musical saw.

"You don't need good clothes here," Sabine said. "Look around you. *My* clothes aren't that great."

Oksana shrugged. "So maybe if you're naked, it's better."

"No," said Sabine. "That's what I'm telling you. It's really kind of gross if you sit on the furniture."

"Whoa!" The yacht man clawed the air. "Mee-ow!"

"Not meow," Sabine said. "This is physical reality. Cunts and assholes in contact with fabric."

"It isn't always about my body, please," said Oksana. "I'm actually tired of this."

Ben said, thinking to change the subject, "So what do you do, Oksana?"

She said, "I am a filmmaker."

"She's a *great* filmmaker," the yacht man said combatively. "And she runs a *great* organization. She's saved a lot of women from impossible situations, abusive situations." Then he lectured Ben for ten minutes about the mail-order brides Oksana had saved and the documentary films she made, as if he were making the point (Ben thought) that he didn't only love her because she was naked.

Something about this performance left Ben feeling shaken and sentimental. He detached himself from them and went looking for Kate.

He found her in the kitchen with some people who'd unearthed a waffle maker and were trying to remember how to make waffle batter, digging through the cupboards and naming ingredients. For a while, he endured their hubbub and delight, feeling like time was running out. In this interim period, he had the idea and believed in it immediately.

At last, he dragged Kate away to a bedroom—the garden designer's bedroom, which had clothes flung everywhere on the floor, so they were treading on a carpet of expensive pants. Ben was standing on some khakis and holding Kate, a familiar but mysterious thrill. Her back was plump and strong beneath his hands. He didn't know why it felt so great.

Kate confirmed to him that Oksana was a filmmaker. Had even been one in Ukraine, before. It was why she'd been a mail-order bride; it was too difficult to get films made in Ukraine. "I thought you knew," said Kate. "She was really poor in Ukraine, but she always made those films. I thought you knew."

"I *so* didn't know. And Sabine was being awful."

"She doesn't like Oksana. It was probably that."

"Oksana seemed okay. A little like a person on heroin, maybe."

"She isn't on heroin. She works about a thousand hours a day. I think Sabine hates her for being so pretentious. Once she broke her own toe to see what it was like."

They both looked down at their toes, then saw each other doing it and smiled. Ben said, a little unsteadily, "There was one of those rich guys there who was so obviously in love with her."

"I wonder if it was Paul."

"I don't know. It made me think how I'm in love with you."

"Oh!" Kate's hands softened on his back. "And I'm in love with *you*."

There was a pause while they appreciated that. Her black eyes were charged with the pleasure, so wild and outlandish, like a pleasure they were having on Neptune. His was magnified by hers. It went back and forth that way for a while, then he said, "When you were all making waffles . . . I was thinking we could move in together. I don't mean my place. We'd get a new place. I want to move out of my place anyway."

Then Kate subtly withdrew. Her hands were not quite holding him now; it was as if the embrace were diluted. She was thinking. (And there was the anomaly. A thing—he could have sworn—she decided not to tell him. It had a visage, a taste. It wasn't good.)

At last she said, "I can't pay rent."

"No, seriously?" He laughed with relief. "I know you don't have a job. I know all about it. Was that what was bothering you?"

She shrugged (that hadn't been it) but she was warm again. Was how Kate was.

"It's okay," said Ben. "I can take care of rent. It's fine."

"I could get a job. It's not that I couldn't get a job. But it would take time."

"Or we could just live somewhere cheap. Like Queens."

"Queens," she said. "Yes, I like Queens. Let's go get an apartment now."

They found Zazie (the dog) and took her out for a walk, pretending they were going out to get an apartment now, and walked in silence all the way down to Sixty-First, just happy. At Sixty-First, they stopped in front of a jewelry store that already had Christmas decorations up in October, and Ben was looking at the tinsel and lights and diamond rings and feeling a massive euphoria, believing in engagement rings for the first time, because if he had to buy Kate a diamond to prove his love, he'd buy the fucking diamond, even if it *was* a stupid waste of money and a relic of bride price. He'd buy it just to throw away the money for Kate. He'd buy a white elephant, just to say *This big!* Maybe he should buy her a literal elephant. Kate would probably prefer the elephant.

Kate turned to him and said, "I know what you're thinking."

"Really?" He laughed. "No way."

"Yes. But they didn't just put up the Christmas decorations. They left them up all year."

Ben laughed again and agreed he'd been thinking that. Then they walked a little farther and stopped at the first pet-friendly hotel they found. Their first real bed: and it was not so much the sex as the falling asleep, the drowsy wondering if he was making a mistake, the wanting to panic and enjoying it all so much.

She dropped off first, with a child's ease, like stepping through an open door, and he lay breathing into her hair and trying to believe it would all work out. If it was love, that happened to a lot of people. There was no reason for doubt. Still, the anomaly was there—like something heavy she had slipped into his hand, a stone he'd taken and put into his pocket without looking. As if she'd said, "Don't look at this, or you'll lose me forever." He had put it in his pocket. It was probably a stone.

6

Then in the dream, she was waking up. There was the weariness familiar from all her dreams; she was Emilia and she wanted to fall back asleep. Outside, a rooster was crowing, shrieking with a lunatic fervor, nagging her awake, though its voice came only dimly. The chickens were two streets away. They were the royal chickens at Whitehall Palace. In the distance, the bells of two different churches were ringing, tolling, on and on.

By stages, it ceased to be a dream. It was actual cold on her face, real morning light on her real eyelids. The moment was still and dull, as no dream was. She opened her eyes.

She was lying in a too-soft bed, walled in on all four sides by curtains. Close to her face, the curtains had a smell of dust and winter. She tugged them, and they opened easily to show a low plaster ceiling, a narrow brick hearth whose fire had died to ash. The floor was strewn with rushes: a shaggy carpet of pale dry grasses with a silvery sprinkling of lavender. Emilia saw them with a bodily satisfaction. She knew where the lavender was grown, the eastern garden where she'd first smoked a pipe of tobacco. She remembered sitting on the rushes, breaking them in her hands to help her think. She remembered a host of things she'd never known before, Emilia things from Emilia's head.

This is the dream, Kate thought. *This is me in the dream. This is why I've been so happy.*

She struggled to sit, and her breath squeezed thin. Her belly was stretched and squashed at once, the heft of it hot and alive against her arm. Then her insides *woke,* a kicking that snagged at her ribs, and made her want to argue with it. Her breasts sore and aware. She was pregnant. *This is why I've been so happy.*

Then she held still to know more: a snow of information that settled in important flakes and joined to form a new terrain. It wasn't the moon. It was Longditch, London. It was the new house, leased from a clothier, the fashionable house near Whitehall Palace. The Queen wasn't in London now; there was plague. That was why Emilia's husband was absent; he was traveling with the court. It wasn't fall, as it was in New York, but March. Anno Domini 1593. A misfortunate year, a plague year; all the places of entertainment closed and the gentlefolk frightened out of town, although by God's grace there was no war. Emilia let the news accumulate and was easy, the child inside her a lively ballast, the covers warm.

As she blinked and remembered, a mouse appeared on the floor by the hearth. Its movement startled her; then its existence startled her. It was jarringly identical to the mice that infested Kate's apartment in Brooklyn: a perfect twenty-first-century mouse. It nosed importantly among the strewn rushes, just as a Brooklyn mouse would nose importantly along the linoleum.

Then she was Kate, amazed. The mouse crept along the floor, undeniably alive. It was real. It was alive and real.

This had never been a dream. It was the past.

A step came in the hall outside, a slipper scuffing on wood. The mouse underwent a blinking paroxysm of fear and darted under a painted chest. Emilia sat forward, half understanding, half moved by habit. She called nervously (and felt the intention of it, felt it in her throat, was surprised by her grave and musical voice): "Is it Mary there?"

The step paused. For a breath, Emilia was self-consciously aware of not exactly being Emilia. Then she thought of what she needed to say. In the queer dream manner, she called, "Prithee, come and light the fire, child. 'Tis cold as the moon here."

There was the sound of a wooden pail being set down, the odd hollow resonance of its water. The door came open, squeaking. Mary appeared and was a tiny, pink-faced girl of about thirteen. She wore a grubby cap, but her dress was clean, full skirted, peacock blue. To Kate, she looked like a little girl in costume for a school play. To Emilia, the grubby cap was annoying, was an old, frustrating story. Mary fiddled with her cap and her hands all in soot; she was a dirty sort of housemaid.

Mary curtsied, so rapidly it looked like a missed step, then went to the hearth and took a poker to the ashes, rooting and uncovering a slurry of embers, orange and luminous, as startling as a snake. She planted a few twigs into the brightness with a delicate precision like legerdemain. Flames grew instantly along their flanks, and Mary hoisted and positioned two logs on top. There was the scent of heat but not the feel of it yet, Mary's lively stink within it; and now Emilia recognized her own body's smell, its tired perfumes complicated by sweat and the sourness of leaking breasts. All real.

And within it was a burgeoning importance, the tugging suggestion of a thing Emilia needed to do. It was something in the framing of the scene, in its shape. She was here to . . . it was on the tip of her tongue. It wasn't about the baby or the plague. It wasn't about the Queen. She felt she had known it all her life. It was . . . she almost knew.

Meanwhile, she gazed at Mary's smudged face with a proprietorial affection that was Emilia's, that wasn't like anything Kate ever felt. And now Mary looked back, raising her chin in preemptive stubbornness, and said, "If it please you, the moon's not cold."

For a moment, Emilia was caught off guard. She answered carefully, "How, the moon not cold?"

"Madam, you was saying, 'tis cold as the moon here. But the moon is closer to God. So 'twill be warm enough. I was thinking, madam."

"Ah, God is warm? He warms the moon?"

"To be sure. God's good. And very large He is. He can warm all the heavens."

Emilia laughed, surprised, and Mary glowed with intellectual satisfaction, rocking slightly on her heels. Mary was—Emilia now remembered—a great thinker of thoughts, who suffered when she wasn't allowed to hold forth. It was why she'd been sent here from Hunsdon's household, where her blather couldn't be tolerated.

Now Mary said, with growing importance, "'Tis hell, what's cold. My brother says hell is hot with hellfire, but I say it must be a cold flame in hell, what burns but cannot warm. I knew a priest said something like. So 'tisn't only my fancy. It is true teaching, madam."

"Melancholy thoughts," said Emilia. "What brings thee to such black musings, imp?"

"Faith, if the pestilence be not enough!"

Then Mary chattered on, describing hell and telling how her own mother died in sin; and Mary prayed that her mother be not in hell, but if she be there, 'twas a question to Mary if it be a daughter's duty to be good or sin wickedly and join her mother, for we are told we must honor our parents, and 'twould be poor honor to abandon them in hell. And 'twas a very present thought in this plaguey town, this town where only worms could smile. Why, even the cats had fled London's sickness. So Mary had heard, and she wouldn't wonder at it, for beasts were often wise when men were foolish. Mary talked on and Emilia listened, feeling nervously that a clue must emerge, while the fire rose bravely in the hearth, Mary plucked at her cap, the window rattled in and out in gusts of breeze. Some phrases in Mary's speech prickled at Emilia's mind and stuck like burrs: *my cousin . . . wiser that we flee . . . that she gave my father horns.* At last Mary fell silent, gazing at the fire reprovingly, gloomily, as if she saw her mother shivering there. She picked up the poker and jabbed a log resentfully, biting her lip.

"Yet why am I here?" said Emilia hoarsely. "Canst thou not tell me, imp?"

Mary scoffed. "Why we be here, 'tis for your belly being too great to travel. So you said. But I say 'twill be no favor to a baby if London's miasmas be his first breath. And my aunt once rode five days when her belly was greater than—"

Then Mary caught herself. She rose to her feet with the stiffness of any thirteen-year-old balked by adult stupidity and turned to set the poker back in its hook. Emilia now noticed the poker's handle, shaped like the head of a salamander but with human ears. And for a moment, the logs and flames behind Mary formed a ghastly skyline. It was a jagged city of fire and cinders, a writhing apparition of a dead world.

There was a stabbing lurch in Emilia's belly—the infant responding to her response before she knew what it was. It was fear. Outside, the rooster had given up crowing, but the bells tolled on and on. They were tolling for the dead of the plague. The fear became a clarion emotion, an imperative that held Emilia's breath. In the fire, the skyline blackened and clarified. It was real. It was a vision, but of something real. It was a city at the end of the world.

Then she felt what she needed to do. It was out there. She scented it like a hound.

She stood from the bed and said to Mary, "We were better out of London. Thou art wise to be afraid. We shall fly to my cousin at Horne."

The room dissipated and grayed. She lost the sense of it. She was falling asleep. She couldn't see. It went black.

She woke in Ben's arms—strange, cold, elated. The hotel room was there: its white, anonymous walls; the TV whose remote was on a chain so short you had to stand beside the set to use it; the notice reminding them not to waste electricity, with a cartoon of a smiling Earth. Kate was covered in sweat. The sheet was damp with it.

Oh no, she thought happily. *I have to go back. I'm no use here at all.*

7

The next day was Sunday, the day Kate saw her parents. Ben, as they'd decided the night before, would come and meet them for the first time.

The parents' apartment was in Low Droit, an immigrant enclave along the East River, dominated by fifties housing projects and overlooked by the blackened stacks of the Con Ed plant that had burned in the riots of '98. At eye level, every wall had the patchwork of politics typical of low-rent districts: flyers for political meetings, spray-painted Les Girafes graffiti—the phrase QUI VOIT, enigmatic and minatory, with the stenciled cartoon of the giraffe who sees farther with her uplofted head. All this was layered over older posters and scrawls, including a chapped mural in honor of the Mars landing, showing the three doomed astronauts planting a UN flag on a dull pink Mars. Walking from the subway, you only heard Arabic and French; all the people had a look of casual disrepair. Tides of children came and went, and the benches were occupied by clusters of women, mostly grandly fat, all smoking. Several passersby used canes or crutches; many people here had come to grief. Still, it was a peaceful scene. It had the laziness of any nice afternoon in a community that liked itself, whose people had food in the cupboard and weren't afraid.

Ben had woken up late, out of sorts, and needing time alone to process the decision to move in with Kate. Instead, he'd had to shower hurriedly and throw on last night's clothes. On the subway, he and Kate hadn't spoken at all—a terrible omen, a terrible feeling, that toothache light in the train. Now they walked down the street very slowly, dreadingly, holding hands with gloves on, while Ben kept wanting to free himself. He was thinking of excuses, ways of saying he couldn't do this today, ways of saying they should wait to move in together. But he loved Kate. Didn't he love Kate? Up to that moment, he had loved Kate.

They came to the courtyard of the building where Kate's parents lived, and found a woodwind quartet playing there, the music thinned, enfeebled, by the damp wind from the river. The musicians had been there long enough that leaves had drifted against their feet. Ben and Kate were fifteen minutes early, and they stopped in indecision and sat on a bench. Kate's face was bright from the cold, red-tinged. She was clean and beautiful.

And she said, carefully, gingerly, as if her long silence had been spent deliberating how to say this, "I had a dream last night."

In the dream, she'd been heavily pregnant and living in a plague-stricken sixteenth-century London. She knew she had a vital task to perform.

She'd been sent there for that purpose. And in the fire (there was a fireplace in the room) she'd seen the apocalypse that would result if she failed, an apparition of a burnt, dead world.

"You see, I was important in the dream," said Kate with a humorous wistfulness. "I was the most important person in the world."

"I used to have dreams like that," Ben said. "They were mostly based on comic books."

Kate laughed but looked a little estranged. The comic books weren't wanted now. She took the dream more seriously than she'd let on. She looked at the woodwind quartet, which had paused. They were flexing their cold hands. She said, "Well, I know it's not important to anyone else."

Then it was time to go to her parents; they now walked with their hands in their pockets. The building's elevator was broken, and they climbed the stairs, which were bleak and grimy. The parents' door was like the other doors: lumpy red paint, a dirty peephole, an advertising sticker from a locksmith. A murmur of voices came from behind the door, a foreign murmur that made Ben anxious. What if he didn't like her parents? He was in the wrong mood. This was a bad idea.

Then the doorbell, the parents themselves, and their apartment—a warmth impossibly charming, like the smell of the poppy seed cake that was baking in the oven, like the Persian rugs on the floor, whose corners had been visibly chewed by a dog. The dog in question, a pensive sheltie, regarded Ben dubiously from beneath a battered coffee table and was laughed at and cajoled to come out. ("Don't be foolish," Kate's mother, Ágota, told the dog. "You are really very brave.") The dog was named Dog-knees, a pun on Diogenes the Cynic—*cynic* meaning "doglike" in ancient Greek. She'd been named by Kate's little brother, who'd just moved away; he was a freshman at Penn State. "It was so very clever when he was twelve," said Ágota, "and now we are saddled with this terrible joke." Kate crouched down to stroke the dog's ears, smiling up at Ben, who loved the dog and the parents and her, and felt complicatedly relieved.

Kate's father, Salman, was extravagantly Persian somehow, although his accent was broad Bostonian and he wore a Red Sox sweatshirt. He gesticulated and was gorgeously physical; Kate was his female self. They had the same childlike seriousness, an ease in their bodies that was insistently *about* their bodies, a sexiness. While Salman talked and talked, Ágota kept wryly catching Ben's eye and once said, "I hope this is not all too ridiculous." She was delicate and mouse-like, pale, with salt-and-pepper hair and tiny hands poised in a manner that suggested gloves. She spoke with a slow Hungarian accent that seemed drenched in Eastern European folklore, pelagic and wise and good.

Kate's parents took to Ben immediately. While Kate set the table, they made him recite one of his poems, then called it *remarkable, intense, exquisite.* Ágota asked Ben about his PhD and seemed very interested in the issues arising in CO_2 sequestration in deep saline aquifers (his dissertation topic), even though it *wasn't* interesting; that was the reason it was taking so long to write up. Then Salman raved exuberantly about a Fra Angelico exhibition at the Met that was so amazing it had made him believe in God—the paintings were holy, Salman felt this, they had the unmistakable quality of truthful statements, statements about an experience of God—until Kate laughed and said, "But you *don't* believe in God, Dad," and Salman said without breaking stride, "Well, of course I don't," and they all laughed. Everything was good, maybe better than good. Ben felt he understood for the first time what it would be like to have a happy family.

Meanwhile, the poppy seed cake appeared. There was a pause to take first bites, to react, to give it appreciative room. Then Kate said, with an air of great moment, as if she'd convened them all here for this purpose, "I had a dream last night."

She told the dream again, adding details—she was pregnant by the Lord Chamberlain in the dream, Lord Hunsdon. She was his mistress. She had some different husband, though, a musician who played at court. He played the recorder, but was that really an instrument they played back then?

"In the dream, I decided to leave London with my servants. I had a hunch that was what I needed to do. It sounds really stupid now that I say it. If I was there to do something important, shouldn't I have tried to end the plague? But you'd have to manufacture antibiotics on a massive scale, so I can't see how you'd actually do it."

"Very interesting," said Ágota, in the tone of a person waiting to change the subject, and Salman got up and went into the kitchen to get more coffee. There was a change in the mood, a stiffness. Kate fell silent. She was staring into the middle distance, looking isolated and thwarted.

Ágota smiled at her worriedly and said to Ben, "Kitty dreams a great deal. I always say she's like the little boy lost in a dream. Do you know that story?"

"Of course he doesn't know it," Kate said absently. "No one in America knows it."

"I don't," Ben said.

"It's a story about a boy who takes a wrong turn in a dream," said Ágota. "He can't find his way back to his bed, so he travels through many countries and kills a dragon, and he becomes a prince, and he marries a princess. Very normal fairy-tale adventures. And the years pass, and he grows old in the dream, and he dies.

"Then he wakes up in his bed and he is a child again. But his father, who was very poor before, is a wealthy businessman; his mother, who was dying before, is now very fat and healthy. So we understand, this is because of what he accomplished in his dream. It's a Hungarian children's book," said Ágota. "Our old friend Gabor wrote it."

"Gabor really believes in that kind of thing," Salman said, coming back from the kitchen. "He's the one who fell in love in a dream."

"Oh, bullshit," Ágota said.

Salman set his coffee down and smiled at Ben. "Gabor left his wife for a woman he met in a dream."

"It wasn't a woman he met in a dream," said Ágota. "It was his student."

"He saw her first in a dream and fell in love," said Salman. "Then one day she walked into his class."

"Bullshit," said Ágota.

"Maybe it's true," Kate said.

Ben said, "I'm voting bullshit."

Everyone laughed but Kate. Salman said to Ágota, "You think he's lying? But why would he choose that lie?"

"I think he's a man who fell in love with a twenty-year-old girl," said Ágota. "It's not a mystery."

"That book used to frighten me," Kate said. "*The Boy Who Got Lost in a Dream*. It made me think it was going to happen to me."

"We know," said Ágota. "Don't get upset."

"I'm not upset." Kate looked to Ben. "Do I seem upset?"

"You *can* get upset," Salman said in a softer, be-fair tone.

Kate shrugged. "I'm only saying what I felt."

"Gabor is a pill addict," Ágota said. "You aren't like Gabor. What happens to Gabor won't happen to you."

"What if it's *already* happened to me?" said Kate.

"The man takes handfuls of pills every day." Ágota held out her cupped hands to show the handfuls.

Kate said, "He could be a pill addict *and* have dreams that affect real life. Correlation isn't causation."

"Please, Kitty," Ágota said. "This is not a realistic problem."

Suddenly Kate ducked under the table. She went down on all fours and was crawling around. Her parents frowned, bemused.

Salman said to Ben, "She doesn't usually do this. This isn't part of a family ritual."

"Kitty?" said Ágota. "What are you doing?"

Kate called from under the table, "I'm looking for the sigils me and Petey made. I want to show them to Ben."

"What are you talking about?" said Ágota.

"The sigils!" Kate said. "But I can't find them. The sigils me and Petey carved on the table legs?"

"You carved on the table legs?" said Ágota.

"You *know* we carved on the table legs. We used to carve things with that cloisonné pocketknife. The knife with the bluebirds on the handle."

"We have the knife," said Ágota. "But if you carved my furniture, I don't know about it."

Kate poked her head up next to Ben's knee, tousled and smiling. "I can't find them."

"What were they like?" said Ben.

"My brother, Petey, made a peace sign, and I was trying to carve a hawk, but it came out looking like a seal. We were making believe we were medieval lords. My sigil was a hawk and his was a peace sign."

"This never happened," Salman said smilingly to Ben.

"I remember the game, but I don't understand," said Ágota. "Did you and your brother really carve on the table legs?"

"*Yes,* we carved on the table legs," Kate said. "But it's gone. There's nothing there."

"Thank God," said Ágota.

Kate whispered to Ben: "We really did carve the sigils. It's making me feel a little crazy."

"This never happened," Salman said.

On the stairwell as they left, Ben said, "I *love* your parents."

She stopped on the stair below him. "So you're not going to leave me now?" He laughed and caught her in his arms. They kissed. The stairwell around them smelled of cold dust, and the window there was dirty, so the light looked dirty, but they glowed cleanly like a jewel within that light; it was far and near somehow. As a child, he'd seen the distant lights of towns from his parents' car at night, and the lights were colored and enchanted, delicious looking like fairy fruit. He'd imagined they were magical cities that could never be reached in his parents' car. Only Ben could reach them someday, if he were brave enough, if he believed.

Two weeks later, Ben and Kate moved in together. Everything was good between them for a very long time. It was a wonderful autumn.

8

Then the weeks when she couldn't get back to the dream. She woke up next to Ben and had almost been there. She woke up next to Ben. And again, with the nothing that had happened. With Ben.

(But once, it seemed she dreamed into a scene by an inn. She watched it darkly from above, like a bat—but at the same time she was Emilia, small below. It was night, and the sky spreading into a rain that fell like darkness visible, a glistering where there was no light. The windows of the inn were shuttered, blind. Its eaves noisily streamed. Half a dozen people were mounted on horses and mules in the flooded yard. Others walked around below. Emilia's horse shifted beneath her, finicky at the shouting voices.

It was an argument ongoing while her back ached unendurably; her servants yelling and banging the shutters because the innkeeper wouldn't open for them, afraid they'd brought the plague from London. There was Mary, shrieking as a servant never should, beating on the door with both small fists, swearing that if her mistress died for their strange uncharity, she would burn them all like sticks. Behind her, a manservant—Arthur—smiled in mortification and blinked the rain from his eyes. His hat was shapeless, sodden, a heap of drip.

Kate was speaking in her sleep. She was commanding and weeping beneath the silencing rain. They left . . .

going to, fleeing to—the place name, Horne, repeated in her head until she heard horns. Perhaps the horns were real. Horne, Surrey. Horns in the cold outdoors . . . hey, ho, the wind and the rain. So cold.)

(Then a long impression of riding in a rain that darkened the dawning morning, of a clenching that pinched until it flew)

(if her baby would live)

(a bed

and at her ear, Mary's scolding prayers that Saint Margaret not suffer Emilia to die, as Mary's good mother had been let to die, with the blood running all about the floor and the dreadful infant come dead and blue)

and Kate was trying to dream past her black sleep, and almost breaking through to the screams of childbirth that wrung and bled her, that sweated the blankets wet—but she never woke up, but to Ben and nothing. To the penetrating silence of no pain.

Then in waking life, she was dogged by anomalies, discrepancies, attacks of *jamais vu*. In every street, there were new stores and restaurants, appearing at a pace that seemed impossible even for New York. She didn't know most of the songs on the radio. She didn't know half of the movie stars. She went to get custard apples at the Co-op, and the people there had never heard of custard apples, though Kate had bought them there the week before. Sabine's friend the congresswoman from Maine, who'd had gray hair all the time Kate had known her, appeared on TV with a stiff blond bob, and when Kate mentioned it to Sabine, Sabine said, "She always had that weathergirl hair."

These were all things Kate could have missed somehow. She'd always been absentminded, unworldly. It would have been just like Kate.

But she knew. And she tried to tell Ben one night, when she was drunk enough to think he would see what it meant. They were on the subway coming home from a party, tipsy and tired and too happy to read, and Kate told Ben about the dream again. She said she knew it had no impact on reality. She hadn't really gone to the past—of course. And yet things had changed, just as if it were real, just as if she'd traveled to the sixteenth century and done something there that had altered history.

Ben said, "I've never heard of custard apples, either."

"I've been thinking . . . Do you remember the butterfly effect? That night?"

"Well, I know what it is."

"No, the night we first met, you teased me about it."

"I guess I don't remember."

Then Kate became maudlin and stared out the window. The train jolted through flashes of graffiti and darkness. Perhaps the graffiti had always been there. She'd never seen it before, but it could have been there.

"Are you okay?" Ben said.

"I'm just thinking, if you did something four hundred years ago, it would have some effect. It wouldn't matter how trivial a thing you did. That's the butterfly effect. That's what I think I might have done."

Ben laughed. "Go home, butterfly. You're drunk."

*　　*　　*

Kate had never blamed a man, and she didn't blame Ben. He couldn't know what only Kate had seen. But a magical idea that had attached to him began to dissipate about this time. She saw him for who he was: an ordinary man who needed things from her, and perhaps this was love. She still wanted him there. She reached for him when she woke and the contact comforted her. He was her earthly body.

She would hold him in the darkness, waiting to sleep, and think about the dream. She tried to guess its meaning and came up with teasing details: the fireplace poker in the shape of a salamander; the fire that had turned into a long-dead city; the date 1593, which felt significant, although she'd looked it up and couldn't find any important thing that had happened in that year. Then she would fall asleep and feel the dream there, alive, but couldn't wake there. She woke up next to Ben.

The rest of her life was inconsequential. She did nothing with her days. It was a time when she spent a lot of time on the phone or visiting people. She was mostly happy.

9

The baby entered the picture the day Ben and Kate had their first fight.

It was December, and the new apartment in Queens—already a Katified space, a place like her old room in Brooklyn, which Ben had seen in hurried passing when he helped her move. That meant drawings in colored pencil, which she made on paper of various sizes pinned to all the walls, and assorted Persian rugs with geometric patterns in crimson and teal, which Kate's father binge-bought in Iran and which dignified the plain pine furniture (Ben's contribution) that was all they otherwise had. It was a happy-looking place, both Spartan and luxurious. Friends stopped by to see the apartment and stayed for hours, sitting on the rugs (because there weren't any sofas or comfortable chairs) and chatting while idly tracing a woolen pattern with a finger; announcing they should leave, then drawing out the conversation in order to stay. The neighborhood was Astoria, and the building was named Stella Court:

Ben would repeat these starry names in his head and feel unreasonably good.

The morning of the fight was a workday. Ben had been getting ready while Kate lay reading in bed—as he'd conceived of it up until then, industrious Ben was preparing to go out to win bread for them both (because Kate scarcely worked; she made hand-painted tablecloths and napkins, which she sometimes sold to friends and for which she was always intending to create a website), and this happy notion played in his head like a song, until the moment he had to shave. It was a task he'd always hated. Then a thought appeared, a blot. It was like a little cockroach in a clean room.

He turned his shaver off and said, "Are you still thinking of getting a job?"

"I don't know," she said in a voice infused with sleep, a distant, desultory voice.

"I'm only saying, because you said you were going to look for a job."

"Okay."

"Okay?"

"I'll try to get a job, but I'm not good at getting jobs. Maybe I should get a cat instead."

"That's not funny," Ben said, and suddenly nothing in the world was funny. He turned away from Kate, turned the faucet on, and washed his face. Every movement was tiresome and intimate, a series of petty impositions. For the duration of this face washing, Ben was angrily thinking he would grow a beard—the patchy, indecorous beard Ben grew—if Kate wouldn't get a job, he would grow a beard.

When he'd finished, he said, "I just think you'd be happier if you were doing something."

"Okay," Kate said, now with trepidation. "Although I'm pretty happy now."

"But you can't go on like this forever. And anyway," he said, though he'd resolved not to say this, "it's unfair to me."

Then the fight really got started. He was explaining the unfairness, explaining at too much length, too loudly, and she was objecting faintly that Ben liked his job, he'd said he did. And Kate had been trying to figure things out; it felt important even if it wasn't visible to others. She added in a tight, defensive voice that she panicked when she did jobs, it gave her existential panic. She could do them for a while, but it felt like darning socks in a burning building. Time was running out and . . . Did he ever get that?

"So you won't get a job because it gives you bad feelings."

"I didn't say I wouldn't get a job. I'm only saying it's strange. I don't think life is exactly *real* when you're working for money."

"This is bullshit, Kate. You don't think my life is real?"

"I didn't say anything about your life," she said, and she was pleading now. "I can try to get a job. It's fine."

But he'd lost some kind of grip. He was seeing her as a weight, a parasitical weight that would ruin his life. He started to explain the unfairness again. She was weeping. It made her look distorted and alien. Her voice grew shrill. He didn't know her. He didn't understand why she wouldn't just admit she was wrong.

There was no time left. As he put on his coat, she was saying, "Don't go yet," and he was speechless with rage, he couldn't think. Now she wanted to make him lose his job. And no one was going to take care of Ben. He didn't have a Ben. He couldn't sit around all day and expect other people to pay the bills.

Then he was on the stairs alone. Deafeningly alone, and terrified because he'd just lost Kate. His footsteps sounded small and meaningless. The chipped tile and stained paint in the stairwells were signs of something rotten at the heart of things. Everything squalid: he was going in the wrong direction, away from what mattered. But he had to go to work. There had to be a bottom line.

When he got outside, the day was cold and practical, the sky a clear, no-nonsense blue. People went by in their ordinary moods. He walked behind a woman whose child was tugging urgently on her hand; the woman said amusedly, "You're pulling my mitten off," and the child said, "I *want* to pull your mitten off," and the woman said, "Well, you're succeeding." Everyone in bright winter coats and pom-pom hats; by the subway, there was a wall of Christmas trees for sale, at which people lingered as they passed. Nothing was wrong here. It was as if he'd stepped through a portal to a parallel universe where nothing was wrong.

He got on the subway and while he traveled in the morning crush, the fight reappeared in his head. He was angry again. It went and went. Everyone was pressing against him, nudging him with their elbows. They didn't care what he felt—like Kate. In flashes, he remembered her tearful face and hated himself, but the thoughts kept going. He couldn't go to work. He had to get off the train right now. He was going to lose his mind.

Another stop, another stop, and he was there. In the cold sunlight of Manhattan, he was immediately calm again, a feeling like collapsing to the ground after great exertion. He didn't know what all the drama had been about. She'd said she would try to get a job. He walked toward work, already knowing he wouldn't go in. No one would miss him this close to Christmas. Why had he thought it mattered so much? The facades of office buildings, which on this block were in the gargoyled, opulent style of the twenties French revival, passed in his peripheral vision with a tickling sort of disregarded beauty. Occasionally, the gilded letters of a building's name caught his eye, and he read without conscious thought: *Van Dusen Cooperative, American Uranium Building, Hotel Ariane.* Did he even want to keep this job? He might be better off working at the Jersey City mayor's office.

He got to his building, but instead of going in, turned back and went into Amsterdam Bank, the coffee shop in the former Amsterdam Bank. It still had the original green marble floor and a mural on one wall that showed Dutch traders meeting the Iroquois, while a troop of beavers watched from a nearby brook with worried expressions. The coffee shop was run by a charity, and most of the employees had cognitive deficits; you often needed to exercise patience, but the coffee was good, and it was for a good cause. Today the girl at the counter was a moonfaced redhead who made the same squinting face again and again but took Ben's order very capably, chatting about the upcoming referendum and what it meant for disabled rights. He wanted to ask if she had a cognitive deficit; it was the kind of thing Kate could have asked without giving offense, but Ben could not. He wished Kate were here. He should have taken Kate to breakfast, instead of storming out like a petulant child.

He took his coffee to the bench out front and was considering calling Kate from a pay phone when Sabine came walking up the street, looking haggard and blank. She was wearing pajamas, but pajamas so expensive they were better than most people's clothes. Over them, a short red puffer coat; Ben recognized the coat because Kate sometimes borrowed it. Now it struck him painfully. He realized his office was only nine blocks south of Sabine's apartment. If he and Kate broke up, he would see Sabine's people all the time in the street. He would see Kate.

Sabine passed Ben without noticing him and went into Amsterdam Bank. Ben watched her through the plate glass while she ordered and the redhead squinted at her. Then Sabine came out and noticed Ben and startled.

"Hi," said Ben. "I was going to say hi before, but you just walked past. I almost called out."

Sabine narrowed her eyes and said without preamble, "Did you hear Martin's having a baby? Garden designer Martin. He's having a fucking baby with a mail-order bride. Not just a mail-order bride. Oksana."

"Huh," said Ben, caught off guard. "I thought he was gay."

"Jesus. Keep up. He still produces semen. He can still engender babies."

"No, you made it sound as if it was—"

"Oh, a mistake? No, totally planned. They did it with a cake-decorating syringe. He's giving her thirty thousand dollars."

Now, despite himself, Ben got swept up. "So he's keeping the baby himself? He'll raise it alone?"

"Yeah. He doesn't even have a boyfriend. He bought a house, though, so that's good. I never thought in my wildest dreams I'd get Martin out of my apartment. But having a baby like that? With Oksana?"

Ben tried to conceive of this, remembering Oksana's duck-like nudity and vacant affect. Oksana was clearly an adult, she ran that organization and made those films, but it did feel weird. It felt a little like abuse. Nonetheless (because Ben and Sabine had a combative relationship; Sabine would always say to Ben's face that he was going to abandon Kate, because men did, and when he retorted, "Sure, we're all cads," Sabine rolled her eyes and said, "We've got a live one here! I like your spunk!") Ben now said, "It doesn't have to be a bad thing. He wants a family. It could be nice."

Sabine snorted. "Fine, Pollyanna, it's beautiful. It's the circle of life when you pay a crazy person to knock herself up with a cake-decorating syringe. That works out great for people."

"It could."

"Dude, no. And I'll tell you another thing. Martin is *not* ready to take care of any baby. His longest relationship was seven weeks. The guy's thirty-eight years old and he gets drunk every night. So he thinks he has a baby and everything falls into place? What gets me is, people have babies and they're thinking what the baby will do for *them*. It's sick. We're supposed to be the good guys. I mean, he's a decent guy, don't get me wrong. I'm not gunning for Martin. He makes gardens for low-cost housing developments, he does a lot of that pro bono stuff. He's awesome. But this thing? Honestly, sometimes I look at the world, and I think it's going to sink under, just, people's personal insanity. I can't . . ." Then she caught her breath and said, "Oh, shit. I don't believe it. I'm starting to cry."

Tears were in fact welling up in her eyes. Ben stiffened. He wanted to say something comforting, he should have been able to—but he had a flashback to Kate's tearful face, her saying *Don't go yet,* and to his horror, tears welled up in *his* eyes. It was Kate and the squinting girl and Martin's baby who would never be happy, and the tears came fast; even if he had wiped them away it would have been too late. Sabine saw and grinned with absolute warmth. "Christ," she said nasally. "Look at us. Well, I *hope* Martin makes it work. I mean, you realize that? I don't *want* it to go wrong."

"I actually had a fight with Kate. I'm not just . . ."

"Ha!" Sabine touched his shoulder. "You were prepped? That's cheating."

"Yeah, we had a really bad fight."

"Aw, don't cry about fighting with Kate. I mean, fighting?" Sabine shook her head, dabbing at her eyes with one mittened hand.

"I was just such an asshole to her."

Sabine smiled over her mitten. "Were you a beast to her? I bet you were a beast."

Ben laughed, sniffling. "I don't know. Kate was being weird about getting a job."

"Oh, I know what you mean. Kate does that. But she'll get a job." Sabine uncapped her coffee and sipped it experimentally. "Shit, how is this still too hot? No, Kate will get a job. You just have to keep after her."

"So you're saying I did the right thing?"

"Whoa, don't put words in my mouth. Goddamn, I still can't believe fucking Martin. Anyway, Kate *gets* jobs, she just has to . . . You have to yank her out of her fairy tale. Don't listen to her bullshit, she's fine with jobs."

"I didn't think you wanted me to be with Kate."

"You thought that? Really? I talk a lot of garbage, honestly. I just want you guys to be happy, but how do you achieve that? I've got no idea."

Ben thought of saying this principle could also be applied to Martin's baby, but he remembered Oksana again and didn't. They both sipped their coffees and sighed. The crying had left a pleasant heaviness in Ben's head that reminded him of childhood.

He was thinking again of calling Kate when Sabine jabbed him with her elbow and said, "Check it out." She nodded across the street, where a wedding party was now spilling out of the revolving doors of the Hotel Ariane. The celebrants were Latino, lustrous and obviously well-heeled. The bride wore traditional snow-white tulle, but the bridesmaids were in hot-pink minidresses and hot-pink boots. A tiny flower girl, also in a hot-pink minidress, hopped down the hotel's steps waving her posy of flowers back and forth as if dispensing benedictions. Dark-suited men filtered out in half steps, somber and subdued, while the girls laughed helplessly at something, gathered against the long black flank of a limousine. At last, the bridegroom came out of the hotel in a white tuxedo. All the girls fell silent and turned to him. That man's life would never be the same, Ben thought.

"Wow," said Sabine. "I fucking love those people. *They* should be having the babies, not us."

It took Ben an hour to get home to Kate. He'd decided not to call, having used his last change to call in sick. Then on the train, he wished he had. What if she wasn't there? The idea of it kept frightening him, the thought of the hours he'd have to wait for her to come home, of another wrong decision.

Then coming out, and the Christmas trees again, different people in the same bright coats. Everything was now infected, an emotional blur. He broke into a run when he saw their apartment building, and went running up the stairs and flinging the door open on that silence.

But Kate was there. She was curled up in bed. She didn't move when he came in.

He caught his step, his heart instantly pounding. It beat in its injury, its terrible injury. He didn't know what to do. Why did she have to still be upset? Sabine had said it would be all right. He couldn't stand to see her in pain. She must have known he couldn't stand it. She was doing this.

But she suddenly stirred and looked back at him, smiling. His anger fled, he could feel it passing dizzyingly. He was full of endorphins. Weak and so grateful.

"Baby," she said. "You're here."

"You're not still angry?"

"No, I was falling asleep."

"Asleep?" He laughed unsteadily.

"I always fall asleep when I'm upset."

He came to sit beside her on the bed. She was wearing one of his old flannel shirts, and the masculine cut of it gave her face by contrast a Madonna-like softness, a glow. He took her hand, and she stroked his knuckles with her fingertips, consciously and tenderly.

"You were right," said Kate. "You were right about everything. When you came home, I was going to tell you that, and then I thought you would forgive me. I had this plan."

"I already forgave you."

"No. You're supposed to say I didn't do anything wrong."

They both laughed mutedly. Ben lay down beside her, and she gave him room on the pillow, so they were smiling at each other at point-blank range.

"Are you okay?" she said. "Where did you go?"

"I was going to work, but then I ran into Sabine. At Amsterdam Bank. She told me Oksana's having a baby."

"I know. I just got off the phone with Martin about a job."

"Really? Martin?"

"I was thinking he could hire me as a gardener. But instead he's going to pay me to paint a mural in the nursery in his new house."

They both looked up at the drawings above them. On that section of the wall, there was a poster-size picture of a sea that was improbably thick with pirate ships, each of them manned with dozens of tiny sailors. The sailors and the boats were in pencil, but the scenery around them was painted in watercolor, faint green and blue and the yellow of sunlight. Around it were a dozen smaller pictures of bears, each meticulously drawn and with a distinct personality. The drawings were odd, warmhearted, pretty. There had always been something comforting about them, but it was the first time Ben had realized how good they were, that they were something rich people would pay to have.

He said, choked up, "You're going to do a great job."

She said, "It's going to be a really happy baby."

10

When it came again, she didn't wake in bed. She woke in the middle of a gesture, in the middle of a facial expression, in the middle of dinner. A dozen other people were seated at the table, in the nonsense clothes of dreams—stout velvet sleeves and lacy ruffs, gilt buttons and little plumed hats. All were gesturing, talking, spearing meat on their knives. That multifarious motion, resuming as she woke, was dizzying. She had the sense of falling into it and continuing to fall as she understood where she was.

It was Surrey, her cousin Andrea Bassano's house, his new-built house of brick. He was there at the head of the table, a man with the weather-beaten, paunchy looks of a horn player and the important manner of a householder who can afford to feed ten guests. The guests today were all Londoners driven from town by fear of plague: Old Lupo the viol player and his hunchbacked granddaughter, Anne; a Portuguese mercer and his teenaged wife; three fiddlers from the London Waits;

and, across from Emilia, two actors of Lord Strange's Men, turned vagrant by the closure of the theaters. All had an air of pleasurable shipwreck. They'd washed up on this quiet, irrelevant shore of the ocean London and were pleased with each other and with their imperiled peace. Pleased with their overcooked meat. An airy hall, open to the rafters; a hearth with a fire. An orange cat stalking in the rushes. Two mullioned windows with flaws in the panes that distorted the view of branches outside, all black from rain and hung with glistening raindrops.

Now Old Lupo was telling a story Emilia had heard a hundred times before: how good King Henry had driven the monks from Charterhouse—and how he had had most of those monks killed for their bad heresy. A fearful thing, said Lupo; may God preserve us from such wrong thoughts. Well, the lodgers who took the monks' rooms in that monastery of Charterhouse were Henry's fiddlers—Lupo himself, and Emilia's father Bassano, with ten other Lupos and Bassanos and Galliardellos, new-brought from Italy and speaking no more English than a Barbary hen. And a scandalous noise they made in the monks' old lodgings with their pipings and blowings and bellowings of outlandish songs, so the neighbors feared them as very devils. And came a day— the occasion being the receipt of their pay—so, on this fortunate day, having drunk some Spanish wine, the Lupos and Bassanos and all their heathenish tribe ventured forth and paraded in the street with their horns. Toot toot! (Lupo sang like a sackbut then, and Andrea laughed and sang the cornetto part, and some others laughed and cried, "Toot, toot!") Then—Lupo went on—the whores and prentices and idle wives came out, and being given wine to share, all followed behind, singing five different songs at once. After that, all in the neighborhood were the fiddlers' good friends. And 'twas well done, for, before that day, the musicians were in hazard of being murdered in their sleep, as diabolical foreigners and outragers of the honest friars' beds.

He told the story in Italian and his granddaughter Anne translated it in a tone of jaded tolerance. In the dream, Emilia knew the story well. She knew it in English and she knew it in Italian; in the dream, she knew Italian, and its lilting cadences soothed her. It was the language of her dead parents. She listened along unthinking and tried to focus on the task she had woken for, the unknown thing that would save the world. But her body was exhausted, still tender from childbirth. She'd been drinking ale since dawn; she couldn't think. It was there, in the shape of the air—or it wasn't. She felt confused and weak.

And, as Lupo told his tale, the two actors tried to catch her eye. She understood, through her dream weariness, that she was the mistress of the Lord Chamberlain, Hunsdon; her favor might determine if a troupe of players would perform at court. Both actors were Williams, both brown haired and wearing the same ill-cut spade beard. The leftward Will was a comical type, with puffy reddened eyelids and a slack, sly grin. The other was masculine and morose; a Will that had seen bad weather. Red Will pulled faces at her, mimicking the pompous glare of Old Lupo. Sad Will only watched her with the frank, tired gaze of a friend.

Old Lupo finished his tale and sat back triumphant. At that moment, the fat orange tomcat leapt onto the table and plaintively miaowed. All the company reached for him; he dodged among the plates to general laughter. Red Will said, "Signor Lupo, the beasts acclaim you, as they did the fiddler Orpheus." Anne said, "Nay, 'twas cat-calling plain. Why, the cat himself hath heard this tale every month since he was a kitten. An old, old story." The cat miaowed again protestingly, and

Emilia said to Lupo, "*Belle parole non pascon i gatti.*" Anne laughed and explained to the company: "'Tis a saying of our noisy people, that we tell each other often and heed little: 'Pretty words will not feed the cat.'"

Then the cat turned and jumped unceremoniously into Emilia's lap. She gathered it instinctively toward her, and everyone was looking at her, grinning.

Sad Will bowed in his chair. "Madam, you are also a Bassano, I think?"

"Ay," said Emilia. "So I was born."

"And are you . . . musical?" He made a shape with his hands that could have been a recorder and pouted his lips toward it suggestively. The company equably laughed.

"My cousin plays many instruments," Andrea Bassano put in, and when this also raised a laugh, added nervously, "And hath played the flute before Her Majesty."

"The flute?" Sad Will turned his airy recorder lengthways. "Why, I would give all I have to hear such a piping."

"An easy promise," Anne said, "as the fellow has nothing."

"Then I would give what I have not," said Sad Will.

"Wit," suggested Anne.

"Nay, you are very hard." Sad Will let his hands fall pitifully. "You put me off my jest."

Everyone laughed again. The cat miaowed peevishly and made them laugh still more. Only Emilia and Sad Will were silent. He was looking at her. Now his hand was on his beard, a long hand with ink-stained fingernails. As she met his eye, there was a shock of unpleasantness. A feeling.

Then it was there in the air. It was her task—or it wasn't. It was like a giddy turning in the world. When she tried to focus on it, it zipped away like a mocking fly. Then Sad Will grinned and it was gone.

She turned from him, annoyed, and said to the cat, "Well, Grimalkin, 'tis a brave man who jests of pipes and nothings, whilst in London our friends are laid into their graves."

It was her tone that affected them, a mean black tone. The company fell quiet and frowned at each other while Sad Will smiled at her.

He said, "If it be a crime that I am merry, I am sorry for it."

"Certes, madam," Red Will put in, "the pestilence is no friend to us. As you see, we must wander abroad to seek our food."

"Ay, we wander very madly and merrily," Sad Will said. "As you see us, we are very Toms o'Bedlam, beggars with no man's love. But if thou wouldst but favor us with a letter to your great friends . . ."

"Ah!" said Anne Lupo. "There it is! Do you hear, my lords, the fellow wants our Emilia to write his begging letters."

"Ay," said Sad Will readily. "If she would write to any great man of her knowledge, 'twould be a blessing to make the world smile."

Emilia said, "I know not why I should be put to such a labor."

"Then I myself will write," Sad Will said easily, "if I may but name thee as my friend. Faith, I will use thy name gently, madam, and dress it in velvet flatteries. It shall go before their eyes as a queen."

Anne said, "But she does not know you, sir."

Sad Will smiled at Emilia, and the shock passed again. "Perhaps she will know me anon."

Now the company relaxed and laughed approval. The cat purred against Emilia's belly. It was warm in the room. Outside, the shiny-wet branches were sparkling in the wind. She took a deep breath (and in the fabric of the dream, she was aware of a static-like interference. It had the tinniness of AM radio, but it wasn't words or music. Wasn't sounds. Instinctively, Emilia shut her eyes, and in that blink, Kate saw a broken city. It was like a burnt Manhattan, its abandoned towers scabbed with dirt and ice. It had no air. No sky. It was a city from a time when all the planet was dead.)

Then she opened her eyes. The vision was gone. All the company was looking at her, bemused. She was here to save mankind.

Then the choice was before her, so clear it was importunate; an open door in a room with nothing in it but one open door. She said (and the words came from a black distance): "Well, you may name me in your letters, sir. We shall see what it may do."

Then she was on her feet with the cat in her arms. She went out the open parlor door, while Andrea called after her solicitously. When she kicked the door shut behind her, the room had fallen into startled silence.

In the parlor, she balked. She was suddenly afraid. The words had come in a black flood of certainty. The moment had opened and closed. She had chosen. But how could that possibly have been the right choice? If she helped some unemployed actor get a patron, how could that do anything to save the world?

Well, it was too late to take back now. Spilt milk.

She opened the door in front of her and came into the workshop where instruments were made, a large, airy room with the peppery scent of sawdust. There were lathes and benches, chisels scattered on rough shelves. Two pallet beds, laid for the guests, looked oafish beside a row of delicate violin tops and shawms. In one corner, an apprentice boy perched on a sawhorse; Emilia's maid Mary and the baby's nurse stood beside a bassinet, which the nurse was rocking gently with one foot. The bassinet's sides were shallow, and Emilia could see the baby's pink face, his fishy mouth that gaped asymmetrically in sleep.

Mary and the nurse made hasty, fumbled curtseys. The apprentice hopped off the sawhorse. The thump woke the infant and he peeped and struggled in his swaddling, jerking like a jumping bean. He still had the wizened appearance of newborns and shockingly clear black eyes. Emilia was terrified by his fragility. Her baby: a thing that couldn't be undone.

Then he squalled, and Emilia's milk let down: a peculiar wash of helplessness, her body obeying a command not hers. There was the soaking of her chest, the warm wet shame of it. She was wearing an old, loose gown that already smelled faintly of mildew. Now of milk. She glanced down before she could stop herself, and the women's faces changed.

Then a clatter outside and the actor, Sad Will, appeared behind her in the doorway.

Their eyes met again. Then the change went through her like a shiver. She knew him. She felt it like setting her bare foot into ice water. He was real. All around him was a dream, but he was real.

Then her heart changed three times. First for him, who alone here was real and must suffer somehow from loneliness. Second for the baby, who was only a figment, who was made by the man's reality into nothing but a baby in a dream. Third for this world that was passing. That was gone. It went black in her eyes, and she felt it in the skin of her palms, an electric jolt as Emilia gasped and was Kate who grasped at air.

* * *

She woke next to Ben, in the half-light of dawn, in their bedroom—which was subtly changed. A pair of blue men's sneakers she'd never seen before were toppled on the floor by the bed. There was a prescription vial on the nightstand for a medication whose name she didn't recognize, although the label said it was hers. Her drawings on the walls that had previously been of bears were now of neat brown horses. Where the curtains had been, there were Venetian blinds; this impressed her the most because the blinds were ugly and plastic. They were something Kate wouldn't have had.

But most things were the same. Her arms looked the same. It was the same room and Ben was the same.

She almost woke Ben to show him the changes. But of course they wouldn't be changes to him. He was a Ben who'd had a different past, a past where Kate had drawn horses not bears, where she would have cheap plastic blinds. Ben would never understand. He would never believe. Only Kate was from Kate's past.

Then she lay for a long time trying to understand. She remembered the feeling of blackness, the static, her voice that felt like power. She had felt the change. It had the brightness of a paper cut. It didn't feel as if it could have been wrong. But she was obviously changing history. That was what it was. And, looked at objectively, Will had guilt-tripped Emilia into doing him a favor and what that made was a New York where Kate had ugly blinds and took some medication, a small degeneration in the world.

Ben woke an hour later and found Kate staring, sitting up in bed. When he asked her if anything was wrong, she said, "What if you had a chance to save the world?"

He said sleepily, "I guess you should do it."

"But what if, in order to save it, you had to run the risk of making it worse?"

"That would be bad. That would be a tough position. So I guess it's just as well you can't save the world."

She laughed but looked a little misunderstood. "I guess."

"What's this about? Did you have a bad dream?"

"I wouldn't say it was bad. I had a dream."

Then he asked her to tell him about the dream, but she only grimaced and shook her head. So he told her the dream he'd had, instead, about a Chinese kingdom where the children were slaves, and he and Kate were children. In the dream, the children had one task. They were painting the white sky blue. It was a blue that had never existed before, a shade of blue so pure it made the children blind, and the blue was heaven.

11

For Ben, the strange phenomena began the day they went to Martin's house in Brooklyn and were quietly amazed by the size of the place, which was Victorian and big enough to be a haunted house; it had a backyard with trees and overgrown grass and a homemade swing; it was a house in which to raise ten children. The interior had already been made pristine by a high-end contractor. Fresh painted, it smelled white. In some places, the paint smell was oddly cavernous; it made the lack of furniture spooky. Then Martin, when he stood close enough, had the stuffy, intimate smell of wine.

Martin talked and talked while he showed them the house; inconsequential chatter, though his voice sometimes had an odd honking tone, the sound of a strained depressiveness. He never mentioned the baby (as Ben kept noticing); instead he talked about his new gardening client, who'd insisted on buying a jacaranda for a climate that would kill it stone dead, and had purchased five ornamental boulders without consulting Martin and today just emailed Martin a photo of a Japanese sand garden with the comment: *Instead of lawn?* "He'll end up living in a gravel pit with a single dead tree in the middle. Fine, if he wants to live in a post-apocalyptic sandbox, more power to him. Except that it'll have *my* name on it. So I have to fight him tooth and nail, he *has* to acquiesce to a beautiful garden . . . And this is the kitchen, though I don't know when I'm going to cook. I might lie naked on the tiles. Come, feel." (Martin crouched down to stroke the tiles, and Ben and Kate crouched down obediently and copied him. The tiles did have a satisfying stony chill.) "I've never had sex on tile," said Martin. "Have you ever had sex on tile?" Then Martin's cell phone rang, and he stood up and transformed into an adult. His posture changed and the expression on his face. He was authoritative and sensible. He was discussing quotes for bamboo. Then he hung up the phone and sighed. "Work is driving me mad. I'd like to just become a Canada goose and fly north. Shall we go see the upstairs?"

For Ben, this all had a sinister feeling, the feeling of a darker time about to begin. He kept thinking he shouldn't have pushed Kate to get a job. How could he protect her here? He tried to catch Kate's eye, but she was cheerful and oblivious, enjoying the house and liking everything Martin said.

This continued through the upstairs rooms, at which Martin gestured carelessly, saying, "Bedroom. Other bedroom. Clearly that's a bathroom." But then he paused outside a door and said, "Now, you have to be nice about this. I wasn't sure I was even going to show you this," and he opened the door to the nursery.

It was the only furnished room, though the furniture had all been gathered in the center of the room to leave space to paint the wall. There was a crib and a double bed (made) and a dresser and two standing lamps that Martin immediately went to switch on, although it was a bright afternoon and he hadn't turned on any lights before. He nodded at the bed. "I'm sleeping there. I started sleeping there last night."

Kate said, "There's really no need to furnish the rest of the house."

"Exactly." Martin smiled, comforted. "I just don't know that I will."

"It needs stuffed animals," Ben said, trying to enter into the spirit of things.

"Yes," said Martin. "I've asked everyone to buy him-her a stuffed animal. So each stuffed animal is someone's good wish? And the room will be full of all these animal blessings."

Kate laughed out of pleasure, a very Katish thing to do, and Martin grinned, though his body was still tense.

"What stuffed animal should *we* get?" said Ben.

"A seal?" Martin said. "I like seals. Little babies are a little like seals."

Kate said, "It'll be amazing to have a real baby. A real live person."

"Shit," said Martin. "I'm terrified. But what if you could make one person happy? That's what I keep thinking. I'd do that, and that would be enough somehow."

"What if?" said Ben, and it came out sour.

Martin and Kate looked at him: Martin with a frightened expression, Kate scowling. Ben said, "Just speaking as a person with terrible parents."

Martin nodded nervously and looked away. "I know. It's fucking impossible. Even if I were perfect—and I'm well aware I'm not—there's the world. There are so many things in this world that can make a little person unhappy. Not to mention killing him."

"I feel as if the world's getting worse," Kate said. "Is it me, or has the world gotten worse?"

"It's worse," said Ben.

There was a minute of silence, then Martin said, "Jackie's making a mobile. But I don't know, I find mobiles creepy? I suppose because they remind me of childhood. I had a terrible childhood too." He looked at Ben. "Do you find them creepy?"

"A little," said Ben, in a deliberately friendly tone. "But I think what's creepy is imagining the mobile alone in the room, still moving. Like it's thinking."

"Like a baby," Kate suggested. "When you think of a baby alone in a room."

"Well, that's okay," said Martin. "Because *my* baby isn't *ever* going to be alone."

Then he switched off the lamps and took them downstairs to open another bottle of wine.

That whole visit was scary (to Ben, not Kate, who said Martin would be a great father, and when Ben cited Sabine saying Martin was an alcoholic, Kate said, "*Sabine* never said that, I don't believe it," and they almost got into a fight on the train) but that wasn't the strange thing. That came later that night.

They'd gone to see the movie *Il Padrone,* which hadn't aged well, or so Ben thought as he torpidly watched, although the scenes of Rome were beautiful and it was somehow comforting to look at so many Italians. So Ben thought, nodding off in his seat: he would like to live in Italy and look at Italians.

Then, as they left the cinema, Kate said, "Is there any way a person could spontaneously learn Italian?"

"I know," Ben said. "I want to learn Italian too. That movie made me want to move to Italy."

"But there isn't any way, is there? Just to learn it spontaneously? Without studying?"

"We could study. Though I think this urge will pass."

"But if you *hadn't* studied," said Kate impatiently— uncharacteristically impatiently. "What would that mean, if you suddenly knew Italian?"

They were on the street by then, and a truck was passing with an overwhelming roar that made Ben feel unsure and windblown. He stopped walking, and Kate turned back to him, her face upset. When the truck had passed, he said, "Hold on, you think you suddenly know Italian?"

"I understood most of the movie. I mean, I wasn't reading the subtitles after a while."

"Well, I guess Italian's similar to French."

"But *you* know French. And *you* didn't understand the movie."

"Well, I guess I'm not as smart as you. What do you want me to say?"

"I thought it might be a thing that happens to people. I thought you might have heard of it."

"Only as a symptom of schizophrenia." When Kate flinched, Ben added hastily, "I know you don't have schizophrenia. I'm sorry."

"I didn't think it was schizophrenia. I thought it was just knowing Italian." Kate shrugged and turned away, and in a car's passing headlights he saw her profile, strained and unhappy. He followed, although he didn't want to follow. The thing was, he didn't believe her. It must be an affectation, at least in part; you couldn't spontaneously learn Italian. At the same time, he was envious because *he* didn't spontaneously know Italian. You could count on Kate to be more magical than you, to have to be more magical. Everything about it got on his nerves.

Now she said, in an odd, strained voice, "I was thinking of getting a flute, but now I'm afraid I'll be able to play it."

"A flute?"

"It's from . . . It was something I dreamed. I thought I might be learning things in my sleep."

"What? You think you learned Italian in your sleep? 'Cause I feel pretty confident that didn't happen."

Abruptly, she put both hands to her face. She was crying. It happened too fast; he couldn't stop being angry. He wanted to comfort her, but violently. He wanted to comfort her by saying, *Would you stop this shit?*

She said, and her voice was frightened, "Maybe you should break up with me."

"Don't break up with me," he said hoarsely. "How did we get to breaking up? Don't say that."

"I don't want to hurt you."

"So don't hurt me. What is this about?"

Then she reached to him, and he took her in his arms. He held her hard; it was a kind of collapse. Her face wet on his neck. He'd shut his eyes, and the adrenaline felt like sex, like he'd never felt love like this. It was awful. It was the relationship he didn't want to have.

She said in his ear, "It'll be all right. Forget I ever said anything. It's all right."

*   *   *

The next weird thing was about José Morales, the golden boy of their political crowd. José was an ex–Navy SEAL, now getting a PhD in public policy at Columbia, two features that were enough, in combination with his affable, regular-guy demeanor, to make him a rising star of the left. In particular, the SEAL thing made him holy; everybody treated him with a certain deference, even though the Guatemalan intervention in which he'd fought had been loudly opposed by those same people and quietly condemned by José himself. Still, he was a Real Man. He'd hazarded his small life. He was bison shaped; his nose had been broken at some point; he had calluses on his knuckles from boxing—but he was just plain nice. Remained polite in the face of anything, of Sabine's worst. He didn't have to prove anything—that was the subtext—but this implied (Ben thought) that the thing you had to prove was a capacity for violence. You got a pass for being a decent human being if you had enough blood on your hands.

Ben had had an embarrassing first meeting with José at a benefit dinner where they were seated together. José had assumed Ben was Latino, as Latino people often did, and was liberally peppering his conversation with Spanish. This annoyed Ben more than it should have, and he said suddenly, rudely, "I don't speak Spanish," which wasn't even true.

José said sympathetically, "Your parents didn't speak Spanish at home?"

"No," Ben answered truthfully.

"Mine didn't either. I picked a little up from *mis abuelos,* but I had to learn the rest on my own as an adult. My parents were that generation: assimilate, assimilate, assimilate. I guess, yours too?"

"My dad isn't Latino," Ben said truthfully. "So . . ."

"It's not that hard to learn."

Then José launched into the story of how he'd learned Spanish, which involved night classes in which he'd struggled, then a breakthrough during a trip to Mexico to visit extended family where José got blackout drunk and delivered a diatribe in Spanish against the US military to a group of relatives who'd finally dissolved in helpless giggles, both because of his terrible Spanish and because they'd wasted so much breath telling José not to join the military, and he'd ignored them so long he'd ended up as a freaking Navy SEAL. "I was like a perfect storm of hypocrisy. But I speak Spanish now," José said, which should have been likable.

But the story's sheer length meant it was now too late for Ben to come clean about not being Latino. This had the result that Ben's ethnicity became a ticking time bomb whenever José was in the room. Ben blamed José for this, because what fucking idiot assumes your ethnicity? How did Ben become the bad guy here?

After that, José seemed to be everywhere; Ben even once looked out his window at work and spotted José below with a group of Hispanic women, all talking and laughing, with picket signs parked across their shoulders that were clearly in Spanish although they weren't legible from this height, and Ben felt an irrational twinge for turning his back on his (nonexistent) Hispanic heritage. It was like something from a meaningless dream. Another sighting that struck Ben with the force of a dream or a premonition was at an inauguration party—not at Sabine's place, but in an uptown club, with deafening music and strangers, so there shouldn't have been any risk of José. In fact, who Ben saw first was Oksana, in her underwear, stridently pregnant, her white-blond hair standing up like a flame. She was talking passionately to a good-looking man who turned out to be José. She was gripping his shirt front with one hand, and her white belly glowed like a light bulb, was weirdly smooth like an ostrich egg. An ostrich light bulb. And they fit together and seemed to mean something, as if they were conspirators meeting in the cover of the crowd. A meaningless dream; a bad, bad dream: so Ben felt, and left the party early.

One night in bed, Ben confided these feelings to Kate—with some trepidation, aware of his own small-mindedness and envy, and conscious of the risk she had a crush on José, as most straight women and gay men did. He was prepared for a kick in the teeth.

He wasn't prepared when Kate said, "José? I don't think I know a José."

It couldn't be true. José was always at Sabine's. Ben and Kate had eaten breakfast with José at least once, which Kate now said she didn't remember, which couldn't be true. You didn't forget José; it wasn't in the range of human responses to forget José.

Ben let that pass, though, and launched into his grievances, assuming Kate would presently remember, or admit she remembered, who José was. However, Kate only looked increasingly puzzled. At last she said, "But why would anyone admire him for being in the army? That can't be a thing."

"Of course it's a thing," said Ben, frustrated. "You've seriously never encountered that?"

"I mean, maybe very old people might. Or conservative people. But people we know?"

"You don't think people on the left will forget everything they claim to believe and get down on their knees for a *soldier*? You really never saw that happen?"

"It doesn't make sense."

"*People* don't make sense."

"But the American army," Kate said stubbornly, "doesn't it just . . . bomb peasants from the air? Or it did, when it even did anything. I just can't see how it's admirable."

"That isn't all soldiers do. It certainly isn't what Navy SEALS do."

Then Ben talked about the Guatemalan intervention, and Kate was nonplussed and didn't seem to understand. She asked if José was in the Guatemalan navy. Ben answered irritably, "No, he was born here. And anyway, he's Mexican, not Guatemalan. And I said he was in the SEALs." Kate said it just seemed weird that America's navy would be in Guatemala, and Ben said, "Well, no kidding." Then he said, to put an end to it, "Anyway, he wasn't bombing people from planes. That's really not a Navy SEAL thing."

"Right," Kate said. "The navy is boats."

Then, when she saw his expression, she laughed, but her laughter seemed anxious, forced. Ben was possessed by the irrational conviction that she *did* know José and had some ulterior motive for hiding it.

Otherwise it was a happy period. He'd finished writing his dissertation, and he and Kate sat up nights discussing whether he should look for a geologist job in Bolivia, Nigeria, some interesting country, and imagining how they would live in those countries and if it would be practical to have a cat there or if they should just get a cat and stay in New York.

And there was a day with Kate (the first day of the blizzard) that exemplified that happiness. He'd bought her a copy of his favorite Dr. Seuss book, *I Had Trouble in Getting to Solla Sollew,* about a creature so beset by troubles it decides to leave its home for the utopian city of Solla Sollew. The creature has a series of misadventures getting there; then when it arrives, it finds that, while Solla Sollew really is a paradise where no one ever suffers, it has *one* problem: a Key-Slapping Slippard that lives in the keyhole of the only door, so no one can get in. Kate was delighted with the book. Improbably, she'd never heard of Dr. Seuss; presumably she'd spent her childhood reading spooky Hungarian children's books. In fact, she talked about the book her mother had mentioned, the book by her mother's old friend Gabor, *The Boy Who Got Lost in a Dream,* and how as a child Kate had tried to escape into dreams, like the hero of the book. But she couldn't; it was like Solla Sollew.

Then Ben talked about his childhood and how his family went to Kolkata every year to visit his mother Swati's family, a huge, excitable, close-knit family who all lived in two adjacent apartment buildings owned by Swati's great-uncle Vikram, and they trooped in and out of each other's apartments all day in a massive, multistory cooking effort; the instant you arrived you were assailed with food and invited to take a bath and pinched, and everyone rudely commented on your size and clothes and teeth. It entranced little Ben; he would fall asleep in his mother's lap to the adults' interminable looping conversations in which they refought the Nepalese War and argued through the films of Majumdar shot by shot and quoted Bengali and American poetry, gesticulating and laughing uproariously and pounding their chests, but by Day Two, Ben's mother would fight with her parents and weepingly accuse her sisters of excluding her and be accused in turn of flirting with their husbands, and on their final visit she lost her temper so badly she shrieked with no words, just squalled inarticulately, hands raised claw-like toward her sisters, then she plunged one hand into a pan of frying luchis and had to be rushed to the hospital. Ben's father went with her, though Swati's family scolded him and told him he should stay with his son. But they didn't comfort Ben. Ben was lost, underfoot in a mob of angry relatives railing in Bengali about his mother, and at last he crept away and fell asleep in a bathtub. The following year, great-uncle Vikram died and Swati sued her family for a share of the apartments and they cut her off. They cut Ben off as if he'd never existed.

Kate pulled Ben down onto the bed then, as if he were crying and needed to be comforted, although he'd told the story in a brusque, cold voice, the voice he always used to talk about his mother. Kate wrapped her arms and legs around him and nuzzled his neck and, slowly, Ben relaxed absolutely; it was as if he were lying underneath a waterfall that coursed through his body and washed it all away. Kate said, "You could cut her off too. I'm giving you permission," and Ben said, muffled as if with sleep, "I only talk to her once a week now. And there's my dad." He shut his eyes and Kate kissed him on the cheek and said, "I just wish I could fix it for you."

Then they had sex twice and read the Dr. Seuss book aloud to each other and recited lines from it while they made spaghetti, and the snow fell all day long, and the city outside became a Solla Sollewish sketch, the buildings softened with snowy mist and topped with oversized white hats, the trees outlined in white, with handfuls of snow uplofted in Seussian abandon.

12

She was the daughter of a courtier, yes, but a low sort of courtier; a Queen's musician. Worse, no Englishman but an Italian. Worse than worse, a Jew by birth. "Jew" was never said in Emilia's presence, but the fact of it appeared in her black hair, black eyes, her ineluctably unwhite face. Never spoken and always there, like unshed tears.

Her father having died when she was small, Emilia was given to the Countess of Kent to be fostered and to work at the interminable needlework gentlewomen did. A boring idyll, a country house. Big rooms that were never warm. The women gathered their chairs at the hearth. Emilia often played her lute while the others sewed and gossiped. Angels were painted on the ceiling above, and the tapestries' softer pictures were hung about: a Juno glared at the bleeding saint on the opposite wall; a hunt frolicked over a painted cloth that billowed in the chimney's draft. There was a chair with one short leg, which

Emilia used to rock unthinking, muttering her Latin declensions as she worked her needle.

There were also real hunts, to the singing of hounds, her heart stooping as the hawk stooped and arrowed from the sky to pluck a fleeing hare. Outdoors; everything one might dream. The fairy-gray clouded sky and the fairy-green misted wood. Her tall horse shying at a sparkling brook. All dreams. What Kate had dreamed; it now awakened and was Emilia's life.

Then the love story, such as it was: Emilia had ridden to court with the countess's household. She'd danced under the eye of Elizabeth, an onyx head among fair heads. She had danced, and the pipers playing were the men of her childhood, her onyx-headed cousins.

Lord Hunsdon was stiff among the dancers. A thing that happened to fatherless girls: old men. But he was still a fine warlike man, and he was Lord Chamberlain and the Queen's own cousin. It didn't matter that he was married, that he had fourteen children grown. There was never any question, and the countess encouraged it. There was no decision to be made.

He kept Emilia richly. She was Hunsdon's whore, but she was Hunsdon's. She wore his jewels and damasked silks. She had the Lord Chamberlain's ear. She was eighteen and a nothing, but every nobleman courted black Emilia. They gave her presents: a silver caul; her little dog, Dinah; a doll dressed to showcase the fashions of France. They whispered to her about their sad ambitions and begged her to bespeak her lord—and she did so happily, feeling her power. Hunsdon laughed and swore to be ruled by her, and it was heady for such a young girl. Heady to be touched, even if the hands were pale and liver spotted, cold. Heady to be shivering, nude, in a curtained bed. To confess to Hunsdon's priest, confess real sins that made the priest hoarse.

And when the Queen was suffering toothache, black Emilia sat at her feet and piped for her, and, at the Queen's bidding, danced to her own piping until her notes went awry for lack of breath. Then Her Majesty laughed, forgot her pain, gave Emilia a gift of velvet sleeves.

When Emilia miscarried her first baby, Hunsdon sent her a doctor at Shoreditch. She lost the second baby at Somerset House, his house. She could watch his barge come and go on the Thames from the window where she bled, seated on heaped linen. But her third baby grew, became a telltale bump, and she was married off to Lanier, Emilia's needy cousin, a piper who expected favors from Hunsdon and grew unpleasant when he was rebuffed. *A strutting meacock fool,* said Hunsdon, *a popinjay.* Well, it was true.

Now Hunsdon needed no mistress more, he was grown too old. He had a dozen bastards of various stamps and five sons from his honest wife; he needed no bastards more—said Hunsdon.

And Emilia wept, brought low. Was lost. A cast-off, big-bellied whore.

Those were the facts of Emilia, which she'd woken knowing. She sat up in bed at Horne, and it was there like the answer to a riddle: Emilia's life. Two months had passed. Sad Will had gone away. She was alone with the precarious world; with the fearful knowledge that she had to save the world.

Well, this time she would go about it logically. Last time she'd let herself be led—by Will, who was real—or she'd decided he was "real."

She'd given what he asked, let him use her name. She had made a small, deliberate change.

But then she'd woken in a skewed, weird twenty-first century, where people talked about "the economy" as if all motivations were forms of greed; where the air was stale with car exhaust—you could hear the cars in bed at night; they were even in Manhattan where it made no sense. Then the war in Guatemala that they called an "intervention," a war that had never existed before Kate dreamed about Sad Will.

Well, now she had Hunsdon in her mind like a sign, like a tool in her hand, like a hammer for a nail. Hunsdon was the greatest man Emilia knew. He had always been the obvious move.

So, the work of getting dressed: a hundred fussy businesses of tying and tugging, of Mary's poking fingers. Walking down the hall to the smells and chills of morning, to the day outside. Still sore from childbirth, she needed a leg up from her man, Arthur, to mount her horse.

And rode for Nonesuch Palace.

So, riding on the frosty overgrown road, the green view interrupted by her horse's ears. Arthur rode ahead of her, humming. There was the treacherous, vertiginous pleasure of the dream, where details were too vivid and emotional: the horse's rocking walk and the damp in the wind, flies veering in with an abrupt big buzz then vanishing into the air. For a while, they were surrounded by a flock of sheep, which followed them, bleating and getting underfoot. Arthur tried to frighten them off with his sword, but the sheep dodged indifferently, unalarmed.

An hour's ride from Horne; no matter. It was still morning when she spotted the turrets of Nonesuch Palace—the loveliest of royal palaces, a Xanadu, an ivory confection with teal and gold decorations on its facade. The clouds appeared to be its clouds, pretty ornaments whose rain and lightning were diversions to watch from its hundred windows. Riding to its gate, you believed in the divinity of princes. It looked like the abode of an effeminate god.

The porter knew her and made no trouble. She left Arthur with the horses at the gate. Then the chilly hallways, the sconces she passed, their candle flames wavering with the breeze she made, their heat a little dangerous by her face. Cold air whispered at her ankles with the movement of her skirts. In some corners, a piss smell lingered. Where people were, it was a war of perfumes and the companionable reek of sweat. Gold chains ornamented her hair, and the pearls at her ears bounced as she went. She was a toy. It was a game. It was Emilia's airy element. So to Hunsdon's door, through everyone she met by the way; a half-dozen circumlocutions and kisses, the old prevaricating dance of court.

At his door. It was done. Hunsdon's man bowed her in. She had time to be aware there was something wrong as Hunsdon rose from his desk.

Then his well-known face, and the hurt of it. He looked at her as a lizard looks up from a wall, as if a wall spontaneously grew a lizard in order to unfeelingly look.

"Mistress Lanier," he said coldly. "I had not thought to see thee here."

"I pray you, sir . . . I would speak with you." Already Emilia was crying.

Then the dream misbehaved. It didn't like Hunsdon. The dream didn't want him, the dream wouldn't have him. It spat him out like a pip. Time skipped and became a strange, intelligent blackness, in which she had knelt and wept into her gloves, their scent of musk and leather stifling, while Hunsdon said something not to the purpose. Promised her money. Whatever men said.

Then she was back in the hallway, alone with her sob-red face. Unnerved. She didn't understand how the scene had rebelled, had fallen out from under her and dumped her here. She supposed it hadn't been Hunsdon she wanted. He was something the dream wouldn't let her do.

She pondered, still weeping lightly, leaning against the chilly wall. It was beautiful to be heartbroken, it was as pleasurable as a thing could be. But pointless. On the wall in front of her, the iron branches and tender flames of a sconce changed subtly and formed the peaks of an apocalyptic city: its broken towers, its airless sky. Where everyone was dead. Static muttered in her head. She could not make a mistake.

Then it cleared: farther down the hallway, a door had opened on a flourish of sunlight. Into the light stepped a youth, white and gold, a celestial apparition—the Earl of Southampton. His face was beardless still, the eyes pale blue and with the lashless look of redheads. His auburn tresses, artfully curled, fell almost to his elbows. He was six feet tall and as lovely as a waterfall, as pretty as a flowering tree. White silk, white velvet, cloth of gold. A gold filigree earring in one ear. Emilia knew him from her days of attendance on the Queen: an uncanny, androgynous youth with the despotic pout of the beautiful, who can never be sufficiently loved.

He noticed her, then he noticed her tears. She turned to him—smiled to him—unembarrassed. This court was a friend to tears. There was never so hospitable a place for tears. She felt her task appear and faced him with the fearful elation of a warrior. The moment opened wide.

"Lady," he said. "Why do you weep?"

She lifted a hand to her tearful face. "My lord, I know not. What is it maidens weep for? Mayhap, for the sailors lost at sea?"

"Nay, madam." He smiled, taking the joke. "I think it is not for sailors."

"Then for mortal time, perhaps? For the springs that will never come again?"

"Yet I think not. Not for time nor spring."

"Then it may be I weep for nothing? 'Tis but a woman's watery nature?"

"Nay. Nor that."

She made a disapproving frown. "Well, to be sure, my lord, it is not for love."

He laughed and came forward impulsively to kiss her—his affection a potent thing, a flourish of light. She was smiling, her tears feeling fresh on her face. He smelled of sweat and roses. She felt it in the palms of her hands, in her loins. It was right. It was Southampton she had wanted all along.

Then he seemed to feel a scruple and turned to look back. In the doorway from which he had come, as if created by the earl's idea, now stood Sad Will.

13

Ben saw Oksana again, and first had feelings about her, the day after the blizzard of 2001. The snow had stopped but the streets weren't cleared. Ben had gone to work on foot because his boss called in a panic, but the trains still weren't running from Queens. Then at lunch Ben went out walking again, infatuated by the streets without traffic, the dumbstruck cold that made his skin feel helpless, the new bright sky in its childhood blue. Ben headed to the park, and on Fifth Avenue, a Car Free NYC gang had built a five-foot snow wall across the street. On its side, they'd pinned a banner saying: 213 KILLED BY CARS IN 2000. A few parka-ed children were balanced on the wall, pretending to be walking on a bridge across a bottomless chasm. The Car Free people were drinking from thermoses while waiting to obstruct the snowplow. Ben recognized a girl he knew and accepted a sip of whisky from her thermos; he didn't like to drink in the daytime, but it was one of those things you had to do to feel you were fully alive.

In the snowy expanse of Fifth Avenue, there were workers on their lunch hour having snowball fights while other people's children tried to intercept the snowballs. Two women from Les Girafes, distinct in giraffe-print hats and scarves, were building igloos for the homeless on the border of Central Park and singing a smutty French version of "The Internationale." Ben could only follow the first few lines: *Stand up, penis of my brother; stand up, prisoner of trousers.* A few homeless men were waiting, not helping but loudly praising the women to each other and calling them Florence Nightingales. Ben sipped the whisky and was briefly high on it, balanced on hope like walking on a bridge across a bottomless chasm; he gazed at the pure white avenue and believed the world could be saved.

It was when he was handing the thermos back that he turned and spotted Oksana. She was on the park side of Fifth Avenue, walking with an involuted shy-girl hunch he'd never noticed in her before, which perhaps she didn't have when she was naked. The clothes she wore were dismal: a threadbare pink ski jacket whose hood was trimmed in dirty white fake fur and which strained and jutted with her pregnancy, shapeless red woolen pants, and grubby once-white tennis shoes. Her platinum hair was neatly combed, but the haircut revealed was aggressively bad—a bad mullet. With clothes on, she looked about fifteen years old.

When she'd said she went naked because of her clothes, Ben had assumed she was messing with Sabine. Now he realized she'd been stating a fact, and that alone changed Oksana in his mind. Also, in the grubby attire, her face shone out and was kitten-like, exquisite. It was suddenly understandable why the yacht man (for instance) was in love with her.

She turned abruptly and walked directly into the knee-deep snow of the park, moving smoothly, glidingly, the snow seeming to part before her like a white Red Sea. It took Ben a moment to realize there must have been a path that wasn't visible from where he stood. He called her name but not loudly enough. He felt too self-conscious to really yell. Nonetheless, when she didn't respond, he was seized by irrational anxiety. *She's walking into the snow,* he thought. *Oksana's walking into the snow to die.*

He knew she wasn't really *walking into the snow.* That wasn't even a thing people did. Still, what he knew of her fell into an ominous pattern: her abortive career as a mail-order bride, Martin using her as a womb for hire, the films she'd made, which were clearly unsuccessful or she wouldn't be hiring out her womb. On the spur of the moment, he decided to follow her. There wasn't any harm, after all, in making sure she was all right.

The path where she'd entered the park was a block away, so Ben decided to cut across. He stepped directly into a snowbank. After a few high-kicking strides, he was sweating and excitement caught in him. It was a good deed, even if it was ridiculous. He could take her to buy a pair of boots; she shouldn't go walking in the snow in sneakers. And there was something in it about all the women in the world Ben should have taken care of—the crazy girls. For him, there had always been women like that: suicidal exes and hapless stalkers and female friends who needed something from him, to talk at 2:00 a.m. or borrow money or be told they were beautiful, and sometimes Ben complied but not always, and sometimes when he didn't, it ended badly. Most of all there were the girls he wouldn't visit in the psych ward, because of his childhood spent at psych wards visiting his crazy mother (his ur-woman, as all mothers were), his mother who'd made little Ben into her confidant and sobbed to him and told him all her suicidal fantasies, then killed herself in the hospital when Ben was thirteen: Mom hanging from a bathrobe belt, undiscovered by the nurse and strangling terribly slowly despite the call button having been pressed, for which Ben's father later unsuccessfully tried to sue the hospital. So it didn't take a genius to put two and two together, to see why Ben had to follow Oksana, who might have been fine, but he had to make sure. It was also why (this came to him out of nowhere) he'd fallen in love with Kate.

Ben was thinking this and watching his footing, and when he looked up again, Oksana had vanished. There must have been a hill she'd descended that Ben couldn't see; the terrain was so uniformly white as to obscure any topography. However, he spotted the path she'd been on, its packed snow showing the spirograph prints of her sneaker soles. He clambered into it and followed, faster now, and almost instantly caught sight of her again—the telltale pink of her coat—at the door of a low drab building. Then its door blinked and winked her out.

Behind the building, its shape confused by trees, was the dull/bright expanse of the skating rink. She'd gone into the skate rental building. She was here to go skating. That was all it was. Ben stood, catching his breath, and watched the rink. He was just making sure.

There were only a few skaters out, in the bright striped puffer coats people wore that year; they looked like bees in fanciful colors and described the heavy, tentative loops bees might make if confined to two dimensions. And, presently, Oksana appeared—a plain pink bee—and shot dramatically through them all, bisecting the rink; then she snagged and fabulously spun on a point, one foot turned aside, the skate blade flashing. She glided away again and picked up speed, sprinting down the ice. Ben's panic came back. He thought: *She's trying to kill the baby. She'll fall and lose the baby, and she'll be free.* She leapt, and Ben's heart leapt. She was going to fall, it was happening now. But she landed, buoyant, like a sailboat skipping on the waves, and skated on. He was a little in love with her at that moment. He wanted to call Kate and tell her about it and say: *I felt a little in love with her.* Kate would say: *Listen, skating isn't everything.*

He turned away then, embarrassed. It had begun to feel like stalking. But he was left with the all-too-familiar feeling of having been infected by insanity, of being drawn into someone else's insanity, although Oksana had done nothing insane. (It was Kate somehow. It was Kate these feelings were about. It was all about Kate.)

He was also left with the image of Oksana, hunched and dirty pink and poor and invincible. It became the image that occurred to his mind when he thought of mental illness. Specifically, it became an emblem of Kate.

Because Kate's anomalies had now spawned enigmas, discrepancies, holes in the fabric of Kate. It wasn't that she was crazy, or not like any crazy girls he'd known before. She didn't weep; she didn't scream. She wasn't hyperemotional. If anything, she was all too sanguine—wore the same clothes for days on end and forgot to brush her hair and was perfectly content. In the daytime, she often went to Sabine's and sat with the mail-order brides for hours, singing along to records and knitting, and she wasn't ever worried about getting older and having no idea what she wanted to be. Once when Ben was furious at his boss, Kate listened to him ranting for a few minutes, then said, "I wish I was angry.

It looks really fun," which was annoying, but it wasn't insane. She was a happy person.

But there was also an incident where Kate told Ben a story about an ex–Green Beret who had climbed the White House fence and broken into the White House and bearded the president and the First Lady in bed, and instead of calling for the Secret Service, the president called downstairs for tea, and they sat drinking tea in the president's bedroom and discussing the treatment of veterans, and the man became the president's personal friend. She couldn't remember which president. It had happened sometime in the nineties.

Of course it hadn't really happened, Ben said. Perhaps it was from a movie?

It absolutely happened, said Kate. It had been on all the news.

But an internet search didn't turn up anything. At which Kate became a little stiff and said, "I don't know how to explain it, but it was real."

Then what was frightening—what made him feel like a child intrepidly lost in the woods—was that he loved her more for that, particularly for that. Could no longer imagine being with a woman who *never* said things like that, a woman who didn't (as Kate did) believe New Delhi was infested by pangolins, and that New Yorkers had a tradition of flying elaborate kites on May Day, and that there was a nation in the Virgin Islands ruled by a "Breadfruit Monarch" descended from the leaders of a slave rebellion. Random nonfacts appeared in her head, and Kate would not exactly admit they were wrong; she tended rather to be sad for Ben, who had to live in a world without pangolin infestations and breadfruit kings. And he liked to keep one foot in Kate's world, even though he didn't really think it was healthy.

Once, when Kate was out at a domestic violence fund-raiser, Ben went to visit Salman and Ágota by himself, and casually mentioned the Green Beret and the pangolins, and asked if they thought Kate believed those things. In asking, he was rationally nervous—they might confess that Kate had a psychiatric history—but he was also absurdly afraid they would say the pangolins were real, and there would turn out to be two realities: an extravagant Persian-Hungarian reality where the amazing people lived, and a gray, time-serving reality for duds like Ben.

But Ágota made her exasperated face, and Salman laughed with paternal pride.

"Kitty!" Ágota said. "She's terrible."

"I love the pangolins," Salman said. "Are we absolutely sure that's wrong?"

Ágota said, "I will tell you, Kitty's *brother* is very sensible. If you call Petey and ask him a practical question—you're renting a car and you want to know whether you should get the insurance—Petey will tell you, 'Yes, you must always get the insurance,' and he has all the facts to tell you. If you call my daughter with such a question, she will say, 'What's insurance?' and you must explain insurance for her, and she is then shocked by insurance and says it is a con and you should please complain to the rental company so they will stop collaborating with this con."

"I wouldn't worry about it," Salman told Ben.

"But does she believe in the pangolins?" Ben said.

"Who knows what Kitty believes?" said Ágota. "I think, yes, she believes in the pangolins. But it is not a firm line."

"Kitty's off conversing with the pixies," said Salman. "How could she be expected to keep track of things like car insurance?"

Ben told them about how Kate believed she had learned Italian in her sleep, convinced that this, at least, would worry them, but they only laughed and countered with an anecdote about when Kate was seven and had woken up convinced she could play the harp, and she made herself so insufferable that they found a store where they could buy a harp, but when Kate saw the harp, she said, "*That's* a harp?" and was crushed and said, "I thought you played a harp like a bicycle."

"Kitty gets mixed up between reality and fantasy," Salman said. "My dad was the exact same way. He used to come back from fishing and tell us all the things the mermaids told him."

"It is not a disease," said Ágota. "If you can't tolerate it, we will understand. It's your life, and we won't hate you. But really it is not a pathology."

A week after that conversation, Kate started painting the nursery wall at Martin's, an event that Ben had been anticipating as a possible antidote to his malaise. Kate would have adult responsibilities for once. Maybe it could turn into a long-term business: Martin had rich friends who might see Kate's mural and want one of their own. Furthermore, money was becoming an issue, because Ben had been made part-time at work. Now, instead of looking for another job, he could use his days off to work on a poetry chapbook and the bills would still get paid.

What Ben hadn't anticipated was that, when he stayed home alone, he would pine for Kate and be both lethargic and restless with bad energy; that he would call Kate twice a day and want to call her five times more; that he would end up calling Sabine to talk about Kate; that Sabine would eventually ask, "Is something wrong? Like, really fucking wrong?" and he would have no answer. There was, but there wasn't. He said, "There's nothing wrong with *me*."

On a day like that, a cold March day, he decided to go surprise Kate at work. He would bring her a tuna melt from Fredo's and maybe they could have furtive nursery sex, although that wasn't necessary, might be inappropriate: he'd leave that up to Kate. He bought the sandwich on a wave of optimism, then on the train he was already self-conscious. How had he become so needy? The sandwich would be cold by the time he got there. She would wonder why he hadn't called first. It was as if he were trying to catch her at something—and what if he did catch Kate with a man? Of course he wouldn't. It was Martin's place and Martin still had decorators coming in, and anyway, Kate wouldn't cheat. Still, the thought of it hurt him. He couldn't stop the scene from playing in his head.

So that was boiling in his mind, recalcitrant and ugly, when he got to Martin's door and rang the doorbell and big male footsteps came and when the door opened, it was José.

Ben went hot in the face. This couldn't be happening. He should have stayed home.

"Ben!" José said, waving him in. José was smiling with apologetic friendliness. He chatted too much as they climbed the stairs, and Ben felt certain he was interrupting something. Maybe Kate had been sleeping with José all along. Now they'd sorted out the problems that had kept them apart. They'd been discussing how to break it to Ben.

Some part of Ben knew this wasn't true. Still he felt it. And why did José have to be here? It was like a conspiracy to make Ben crazy.

At the top of the stairs, the nursery door stood open. There was Kate in her everyday clothes, a sweater and jeans which already had dings of paint here and there. She saw Ben and her posture changed, became resigned—as if Ben were the interloper, the stranger to whom she must be polite. She put her brush down on the drop cloth, then reconsidered and put it in a jar of water.

"I brought you a tuna melt," said Ben.

"Oh." Kate looked at José. "We just called out for pizza. Maybe we should cancel it?"

For a minute, they discussed the logistics of lunch, concluding after a nervous surplus of talk that they could eat both the pizza *and* the tuna melt. Or else leave some for Martin. Not a problem.

"That's so nice of you to bring me a sandwich," Kate said finally, lamely. They all fell silent. They were looking at the mural on the wall.

The nursery furniture had been shoved back to make room for the drop cloth on which Kate knelt. The wall above was a blotched cerulean blue; it was the underpainting for what was going to be a map of a fanciful world with a Cocoa Sea and a Soda Pop Ocean and countries called Centauria and Zoof. Kate had been finishing a border at the bottom: a procession of fairies, mounted on prancing rabbits and cats and frogs and skunks. In the far corner of the room was a collection of a dozen new stuffed animals, all facing the painting so they looked like a rapt cute audience. And the painting—like everything else here—gave Ben a terrible feeling he couldn't explain.

Meanwhile, José gazed at the painting with a kind of faith. It was clear he wanted Ben to admire it—another wrong note, because why should José care? He didn't know Kate, according to Kate. Clearly, Ben should comment on the painting, though you couldn't tell much about the painting yet. But no doubt José had praised it enthusiastically.

Then José turned to Ben and said, "Did you see Oksana's room yet?"

"Oksana's room?" said Ben, and was relieved when his voice sounded perfectly normal.

"Oksana's staying here," said Kate. "Martin's paying her extra to stay and breastfeed the baby the first three months."

Ben must have made a face, because José laughed and said, "Exactly."

Kate said, "I think Martin's scared to be alone with the baby."

"Well, that bodes well," Ben said.

"Right?" said José.

"Maybe we should all move in," said Kate. Then she and José laughed more than it warranted—as if they were laughing at an inside joke.

Ben forced himself to be normal, to grin. "So does it have furniture? Oksana's room?"

"Oh, bro," José said. "Has it got *furniture*? Come on, Kate, we have to show the room to Ben."

Kate got up promptly and went with José. Ben followed them down the hallway despondently, thinking he should make an excuse and leave. Oksana's room was the next one down, and José was smiling strangely as he opened the door. Kate moved aside to let Ben see.

The walls were powder pink, and the curtains were gauzy and pink. The bed had a frilly canopy, embellished with pink satin bows at the corners. The furniture was white and visibly cheap. There was a lamp in the shape of a shepherdess and a lamp in the shape of a swan. On the wall was a large framed photograph of two white kittens looking up from a basket.

José was laughing under his breath. He said, "Kate was saying how it needs a music box with a little ballerina."

"No, it's where the ballerina would live," said Kate. "It's her room inside the music box."

"Martin did this for Oksana?" Ben said.

José lost it completely. He was giggling, breathless. He looked almost hysterical.

Kate said, "Oksana chose everything. We think it's passive aggression."

Ben smiled uncomfortably. He got the joke—that the room was hideous—but didn't know Oksana well enough to find it funny. And again, he got the sense the house was wrong. It was a place where bad things happened.

At that moment, the phone rang in the other room, and they all startled guiltily. Kate went to answer it, and Ben followed after her possessively. José came along, and in that moment, Ben knew what the phone call was going to be. He didn't believe it yet, but he knew. He felt as if José and Kate knew. Like it was obvious.

From there it all went fast, because Ben was right, it was Sabine on the phone, saying Oksana had gone into labor six weeks prematurely. Sabine was demanding Martin and demanding to know how *she* ended up being point man and giving all the hospital details. Then it seemed only natural to pile into José's car and speed off to the hospital. There was a vague impression of racing to the rescue—and what was strange was, the instant they stepped out of the house, Ben's jealousy vanished. He didn't even notice how it went. He was just giving directions as they drove while Kate sat in back and tried different numbers for Martin on José's cell phone. José played Cal-Mex rap in the car and looked inexplicably grim, even angry. When they parked outside the hospital, Ben said to him, "You could go home now," but José just shook his head and got out of the car without answering. In the hospital they got instantly lost. Nothing seemed to be usefully labeled; it was the Dorfmann Pavilion and the Faroukh Building and the Bluebird Pathway and a bewilderment of acronyms. They couldn't find anything, they couldn't find anyone to tell them anything. They roamed the broad corridors, repeatedly ending up at locked security doors and impotently pressing a button for an intercom that didn't respond. They were short of breath from anxiety, walking too fast. Medical staff in color-coded scrubs stormed past, and patients were rolled by on gurneys that rattled deafeningly over invisible bumps in the floor. Some gurneyed patients smiled at them, but the staff didn't seem to see them at all—it was as if Ben and Kate and José were ghosts, and the smiling patients were also ghosts, being hastily removed by living doctors.

At last, they stumbled into the maternity waiting room. Sabine was there, ranting into her cell phone; also Amina, the Nigerian mail-order bride, who was reading an economics textbook, and Raya, the Russian mail-order bride, who was weeping and staring into space (she'd had a miscarriage six months earlier). A large South Asian family was gathered on the other side of the waiting room, talking and laughing in a traffic jam of strollers, all loaded with somnolent toddlers who, in this context, seemed like encouraging examples of successful birth. The strollers were festooned with IT'S A BOY! balloons, and Kate commented, "Those people are really concerned that their sons not be mistaken for daughters," and at first Ben thought she was serious and started to explain, but it turned out to be a joke.

Then a lot of time passed and then more time passed. Occasionally a nurse appeared, and Sabine would rear up to accost her. Then all the others would stand up, too, as if ganging up to intimidate the nurse. The nurse would talk about contractions and dilation; the upshot was, pretty soon but not yet. If it was a nurse they hadn't spoken to before, she would instantly ask if the father was here and look at Ben or José. Then Ben or José would shrink, abashed, and a variety of people would bark, "No, he's not," and when the nurse had gone, Sabine would take out her phone and try Martin again. His cell phone kept going straight to voice mail.

She said to his voice mail, "Get here, Papa, or I'm stealing your baby." She said, "This is your parenting? This is your fresh start?" She said, "I'm going to tear your throat out, Martin. I will feast on your goddamn heart."

And more time passed or dissipated or got lodged and didn't go anywhere. It didn't seem to even *be* time, at least not the same time people had outside. Raya stopped crying and fell asleep. Amina gave up on her textbook and went in search of a cafeteria. Ben fell into a pre-hypnotic state, only disturbed when one of the South Asian women caught his eye and smiled; then, as sometimes happened when he met South Asians, he was visited by the memory of the Indian film festival his father had taken him to the week after his mother's death in a misconceived attempt to compensate Ben for the loss of his Indian parent. The lead actress in the movie had resembled Swati (the kind of unhappy coincidence that inevitably befell Ben's father) and the Swati look-alike was beaten by her husband, then raped, then blamed for her rape and ostracized, then finally hanged herself from a tree, and Ben wept from only one eye through the movie, freakishly, inexplicably, as if only one hemisphere of his brain had really loved his mother.

And time passed, longer and longer. Amina returned with sweet potato chips. Sabine called friends of Martin's and sent them to hunt for him in his favorite bars. Kate was drawing babies in her checkbook, while José watched over her shoulder apprehensively, as if concerned she might introduce a deformity and hex the approaching birth.

To Ben, it was increasingly unclear why they were there. *Someone* had to be there, and maybe you'd expect the mail-order brides to be there for Oksana, but not Ben, Kate, or José—or even Sabine, who'd never seemed to like Oksana. He had a melancholic sense of waiting for nothing, superfluous and unwanted. He was there because he had nothing better to do. He needed a real job. He was twenty-eight, he had to move on with his life. To reassure himself, he looked at Kate—who might represent moving on with his life—and was instantly comforted by her serenity, her look of gleaming health. He and Raya and Sabine were slouching, lopsided, looked like broken machinery, and Amina hunched condor-fashion over her book, but Kate was effortlessly upright like a beautiful horse. José was, too, Ben couldn't help noticing, but that was military training, it wasn't the same. Still, the likeness was annoying. Ben decided to take Kate home. He'd had enough.

But at that moment, a nurse appeared and headed straight for Sabine with a look of happy purpose. The passing time stopped neatly on a dime. They all stood up, feeling totally different.

"Miss Takova has given birth to a healthy boy," the nurse said to Sabine; then she faltered and said to Ben, "Are you the father?"

Sabine said, "Hold up. The baby's two months premature. That's not a problem?"

"No," said the nurse, confused. "The baby isn't premature. Unless . . . You *are* here for Oksana Takova, right?"

"Oops," said Kate, and made a face at José.

José said, his voice cracking weakly, "It's for certain that he isn't premature?"

Then a shock went through them all, a pricking of the hairs on the backs of their necks. (So Ben felt and almost laughed as he realized. Amina's mouth was open in wonder, while Raya grimaced and looked more Russian than ever, hard-bitten and undeceived. Kate was gazing at José commiseratingly—José who was visibly sweating, exposed—and it suddenly all made sense.)

Sabine turned to José and said, "You've got to be shitting me. It's *your* baby?"

The nurse said, "Should I give you guys five minutes?"

"No," Sabine said. "The *father's* going to see his baby."

José said, "I don't know if Oksana wants to see me."

But he went with the smirking nurse obediently, looking as if he'd been apprehended and was being taken into custody by the nurse. Kate touched Ben's shoulder and said, "I couldn't tell you. José made me promise," and it all made sense. *Of course* José had confided in Kate, because everyone did, even strangers did. *Of course* it was José's baby. Ben even had room to care about the baby, to be perversely relieved that the baby was José's—not the offspring of a legal contract and a cake-decorating syringe, but an outlaw baby, a love child, the natural expression of mischievous Eros. And in the grip of that high, Ben suddenly decided he wanted to marry Kate.

14

It began with the memory of a long afternoon with Southampton; a day of tippling and banter, a scene with a few spare noblemen sitting on the floor. Sad Will stood like a sadly observant hawk at Southampton's gold-embroidered elbow. Two servants were taking down the tapestries from the walls of Southampton's chamber, preparing for his departure from court. Sweet wine from Spain and gossip from France; the sun in the windows dimmed, sorrowed prettily as the day declined, until the candles' light was mirrored in the glass. Their dabbling flames were like guesses at a feeling, the hearth's fire like the feeling itself. It was a beautiful pastime she had missed; hours that had stepped light-footed on Emilia's memory and passed on.

They were ahorse in the night. It was two days later, and Southampton had invited her to his country house, Cowdray. They were having a sudden friendship, because they were lonesome and so young, and neither had a thing in the world to do. So, the night with its moon and hooting owls, odd rustles in the trees that might have been brigands but weren't, again and again. From a burnt-out cottage they passed rose a frail excitable twinkling of bats.

Some of the men rode ahead, some behind. Southampton rode beside her, as if courting her, although he wasn't courting her. He was complaining, as the beautiful do: of the girl he was expected to marry, who was no maid, who had lain with two men of his certain knowledge; ay, and he had known her from a child, she was a serpent of luxury. He complained of the court, a stew of slow-headed ruffians who thought it a great jest to piss in the fireplace; blockheads all, whose most manlike work was feigning to be the old Queen's lovers. Nay, their most manlike work was sleep, where they might dream they were men. Nay, it was playing at flapdragon.

He took a hand from his reins to mimic the flapdragoner's hasty gesture of snatching a raisin from a burning cup of brandy. Emilia laughed and said, "Indeed, we are prodigal of our time, that we spend it in such flapdragons and flatteries. But, good my lord, is not all life beneath the heavens an idleness? For, as the prophet saith, all is vanity: *Vanitas vanitatum et omnia vanitas.*"

"Yet we need not be idle-witted. We may pray; we may become wiser by study."

"But wisdom is also vanity. 'Tis a nonsense that passeth and is no more. So the prophet writes: *There shall be no remembrance of the wise, nor of the fool forever: what now is, shall all be forgotten.*"

Then the earl agreed with her, grew heated and glad, and complained of his studies at the Inns of Court, and the scholars there who, every night, turned a dozen hogsheads of wine to piss and a dozen fresh country maids to whores. "But there must be something in the world yet pure, must there not be one thing pure?"

"Well-a-day. If there be a pure thing, 'tis not a man."

Then Southampton swore she was a spleenish wench—but his voice was luxurious, friendly. And he sighed and said again, "Yet is there no thing pure?"

They rode in silence a while then. Emilia kept expecting to be prompted to her task; but the dream was tender, it gave her time, and the pleasure unfolded and grew like a real sky. Sad Will rode behind. Her doing: he'd written a letter to the Earl of Southampton and used her name, as she'd said he might. Everything fit. Felt right. Felt real: the rocking, meditative carriage of her horse, the night clouds and the half-seen blowing of the grass. They passed a yeoman's cottage, black and asleep, with the scent of wood smoke still lingering about it. Its warm life lingered in the air, its breath in her breath. She was on the right track at last—she felt it—riding secretly, directly, to save the world. She would make the world perfect—so she felt—and the wild night meadows of its youth acquiesced. She was a candle in the night, a bright seed of heaven.

But then what was strange was that nothing happened. Nothing felt important and she didn't wake up. It went on just like life. They rode another hour and stopped for the night at the house of a gentleman Southampton knew. They were given cold meat. All talked of the plague. It didn't matter that Emilia felt stymied, aimless; that she felt the point slipping away. It went on. She was given a bedchamber to herself and paced there, trying to perceive her task. She stood in the middle of the room and shut her eyes. The floor trembled gently as servants passed. Her body was sore and tired from riding. The thigh that was turned to the hearth was hot; the other thigh was cold. Nothing more.

She tried to think of mistakes she could have made. Perhaps the task was nothing to do with Southampton; perhaps it was back at Nonesuch Palace. She wondered if she ought to flee into the night, if she could have missed the moment, being tipsy and aroused. She was afraid to fall asleep; she might wake in New York, and she wouldn't have accomplished anything. Then the world might end—here she looked into the fireplace, expecting to see the blasted city. It was a homely little fire, haunted only by smoke. Nothing more. It was just real.

At last she did sleep, giving up, assuming she would wake with Ben—and was woken by a drunken man pounding on her door. There were other voices dissuading him. He said, "God's death! It is a whore, hold me not." The other voices rose, and the drunk cried out, "Wilt thou cut my throat?" in a shrill, disbelieving voice that made the others burst out laughing. It all died away amidst thumping and grunts; the other men had dragged him away. Then from the hall came Southampton's soft thrilled voice: "I hope thou wert not affrighted, madam."

She went to the door in bare feet, the dry rushes catching between her toes. She put her palm to the door. She could feel him there. There was the moonlit window, the embers of the fire. The room was cold and real.

She said nothing. There was no one she knew in this world.

And she might live a lifetime here, and die, and never see Ben or her parents again. Perhaps this was the only world. Perhaps Kate was the dream.

His footsteps went away. She went to bed again and curled up ter-rified. Fell asleep again and woke in the same low chamber, with the fire burnt out and the chamber pot beginning to stink, still lost in the dream.

Another day. They rode out as the sun rose. It was raining and the earl rode ahead. Everyone was silent, plagued by rain. She kept praying to wake, or for the dream to skip and reveal itself as a dream. It didn't. The rain went on, until it seemed impossible there was so much rain in the sky. She was tired and her hips hurt more and more. Woods and meadows and sheep. She wanted Ben. How did anyone bear the time?

But then Sad Will began to sing, his voice a smooth baritone that sounded from his chest: a well-trained actor's voice. The song was "Tom o'Bedlam" that everyone knew. One by one, they began to sing along. Emilia sang, it was a pleasure and she licked the rain from her lips. Took deep wet breaths. She improvised a harmony as Kate never could; her voice was sweet and powerful as Kate's never was. She closed her eyes and let her hood fall back, let the rain stream down her face and sang:

With a host of furious fancies
Whereof I am commander
With a burning spear and a horse of air
To the wilderness I wander

When they finished, Will started to sing it again. Then they saw it for a joke; they laughed and sang with him; they sang of their mad-ness and the mad wild road. They were singing it a third time when the roofs of Cowdray were spied. Then they all kicked up their horses and shouted. The horses wouldn't gallop, but managed a heavy-footed, mud-spitting canter and that was enough. The rain blowing in her eyes, the relief; this would be it, she thought. Now her task must appear. She could do it in an instant and wake in New York. She would reach out and there would be Ben.

Nothing happened. They rode through the gates and nothing. There was the business of giving the horses to grooms, the stilted ceremonial of any such house. The stewards and sewers and ushers must bow and be greeted, the guests be taken to view the features of the house—the Great Chamber with its nautical paintings, Buck Hall with its eleven stags carved in oak, the knot gardens and the Neptune fountain. Then Emilia was shown to a chamber. A fire was built in its hearth. She was brought a clean smock and a basin of water. She endured every dullness of Emilia's life, and sang under her breath:

By a knight of ghosts and shadows
I summoned am to tourney
Ten leagues beyond the wide world's end
Methinks it is no journey

And she was led to supper in the Great Hall, where all the household was noisily arrayed, a hundred people at ten long tables; and seated at the corner of the lowest table, disappointingly far from the Earl of Southampton, across from a plump gentlewoman and beside Sad Will.

Will greeted Emilia, then was silent. The gentlewoman talked and talked. Her name was Mistress Bewley; she was the widow of a steward, living now by the kindness of my Lord of Southampton. Dishes were set and passed, and Mistress Bewley talked very merrily, nodding so her face joined into her double chin, then rose distinct again.

Emilia sat next to Will. He was real: like sitting beside a deep well. For the first time, she wondered what it meant that he was *real*. Surely everything was real here, or nothing was. But when she tried to focus on it, the difference vanished. He was nothing. An unemployed actor. Just a man.

Meanwhile, Mistress Bewley was speaking of the slowness of a country place, so dull the birds fell drowsing from their perches and dropped into the mouth of the yawning fox. "Why, even the plague neglecteth us here; it hath spied us from the road and scorned our dullness." Mistress Bewley herself passed the time in the making of masks, which she sold to gentle ladies through a glover of the town. Masks were never more in fashion—as Emilia must know—for preserving of the skin from weather. The fairest skins of the court were kept white by their aid; without a mask's protection, no lady would hunt. Here she looked hintingly at Emilia; it was clear she was hoping for a sale.

"I fear no mask will serve me," said Emilia. "I was tawny in my mother's womb. I might lie in a dungeon a year and walk forth again as brown as bread."

"Then a mask may hide thy brownness," Mistress Bewley said. "It is more sure than paint."

The gentleman beside Mistress Bewley—a man with an extravagantly lacy ruff and cuffs that made him look as if he were frothing over—objected that masks inclined ladies to vice. "For a lady dons a mask when she will meet a gentleman in secrecy. This wearing of masks is no Christian matter."

"True, a harlot may wear a mask," said Mistress Bewley, "but she also wears shoes. She sups on meat. Shall we now blame the shoes and the honest beef for her ill-doing?"

"But a mask she wears only for the business of harlotry," the gentleman said.

"Am I then a harlot?" said Mistress Bewley. "'Tis well. I am grateful to be instructed."

The gentleman smiled primly. "I said not that. But these disorders cannot be winked at." He looked at Emilia, implicitly singling her out as an example of a harlot. Will saw it and laughed softly. Familiarly—as if he had teased her about her harlotry many a time. She suddenly suspected him of being the impediment, the thing that was preventing her from seeing her task. But when she looked at him again, he was nothing again. Just a man.

Emilia said in a deliberately courteous voice, "I fear me the gentleman is right. Nor is it only ladies that will mask for evil purpose. For in Venice, there are boys that wear a mask they call the *gnagna*. It hath the face of a cat, and such a mask is the sign of a masculine whore. The gnagna boys go garbed as ladies and lead gentlemen into unnatural vice—as, I am told, do the boy actors of London."

In her peripheral vision, Will was smiling, but unpleasantly.

"*Gnagna*," the frothy gentleman repeated. "It hath the very sound of popish naughtiness. An ill-sounding word for a worse thing."

"Boys?" said Mistress Bewley. "I sell no masks to boys. I am a plain English harlot, as the gentleman saith. I sell *nothing* to boys."

Then the men all around laughed at the pun—*nothing* was slang for *pussy*—while Mistress Bewley made a face of great innocence, and put a fresh forkful of meat in her mouth.

"But you had not done with your tale, I think?" Will said to Emilia.

She felt his voice like a familiar touch, and frowned. She said without looking at Will, "How it went on . . . the lady whores of Venice conceived a great hatred for the gnagna boys, as being their rivals for the pockets of gentlemen. So the whores took their grievance to the bishop of Venice. By his judgment, the lady whores now be allowed to lean from their windows bare-breasted, that gentlemen might know them for women, and not be tricked into lying with boys."

She finished her speech breathless. The men laughed again and Mistress Bewley praised the bishop of Venice for a merry priest. Will said, "A very Solomon. God send that our boy actors of London be so wisely served."

There the conversation halted. Mistress Bewley excused herself and went to fetch her masks. The frothy gentleman finished his meat and gazed dully at his empty plate. People all around were sitting back from their tables; the supper was coming to a close.

Then Will said in Emilia's ear, "I fear I have offended you, madam."

She stiffened. "Offended me? I know not how."

"Nor I. Yet I am sorry for it."

"And if you should offend me, it were no great matter. I am no one to you, sir. It can be no matter."

He was about to object, when a stir went through the room. Southampton had risen from his table on the dais, and other gentlemen hurried to attend him. The frothy gentleman stood up with a foolish smile and began to pull on his gloves.

When she turned back to Will, she found him watching her. She ended up looking at Will's hand, still loosely holding his knife—a long hand, marked by ink, the pads of the fingers visibly callused. He must play the viol, as many actors did.

She rose from the table. Will rose, too, and bowed very slightly to her. He turned out to be a tall man, which she hadn't noticed before, which made her feel wrong-footed. He walked beside her as they left the hall, and was telling her about the plays he'd written, plays "infant-like and green," but which had won an approval beyond their worth. He was now like any man talking to a woman: a little too prolix, a little too loud, a little too aware of the impression he made. But it was also a joke; within it was intelligence, a tune half-heard in the wind. He was smarter than Emilia was. She was afraid.

And they followed the tide of the crowd up a broad stone staircase and into the gallery, where a long array of windows showed the rain still falling outside, all the world cat-gray. At the far end of the gallery, a viol consort were arranging their chairs. The musicians were Frenchmen and Italians, all known to Emilia; the men of her youth.

That was when she thought of Will's name and was instantly convinced it was the key. As it came to her, the air changed. Her palms tingled. Will was telling the woeful tale of Lord Strange's Men, embattled by the worthies of the City of London, and now unhoused by plague. She interrupted him, saying: "All I know of you is *Will*. It seems not name enough for such a well-approved man."

He balked, then bowed. "I am William Shakespeare. I repent me that I have no better news." Then he paused. It was the pause of an author who hopes his auditor will recognize his name.

She didn't. Kate didn't and Emilia didn't. And yet it was as if she did recall it. It gave her a vertiginous déjà vu. For a moment, she was even sure she would wake; she knew the shibboleth and she would be freed.

She wasn't. People went on chattering around her. Some women now wore Mistress Bewley's masks; among the crowd were faces of green and scarlet velvet, embellished and embroidered. On some, the eyes were occluded with lace. Emilia was sweating now, afraid. She had to wake up, but he was real. He had brown eyes. He was masculine and tired.

She looked away to where the viol consort were preparing to play. One of the fiddlers was watching her—a Bassano cousin who had once put his hand up her skirt on a flight of stairs. Catching her eye, he licked his lips. She flinched.

"Madam?" Will said. "Is aught the matter?"

She said, "Yon fiddler is a countryman of mine. A base fellow."

Will followed her eye. "Your countryman—so, a base fellow of Surrey?"

"Nay, an Italian. And a Jew."

At this, a superstitious qualm appeared in Will's face. Of course—she knew belatedly—she couldn't be a Jew. It was a thing you couldn't say about yourself. It was a gaffe Emilia couldn't have made.

But something had shifted. She pursued it, saying, "My father was a Jew of Venice. 'Tis true: I am of that hated race."

He said cautiously, "Much evil is spoken of Jews. But men will speak villainously of anything strange. I am sure they say much that is false."

"All true," she said (and the room grew vague; the words flew ready from her mouth like a curse). "There is no devilish thing, but 'twas invented by Jews. Witchcraft is our proper religion. We get our wealth by usury and our children by fornication. Why, 'tis by our villainy that the plague came into the world."

She turned from him again; she was almost done. Couples had joined now, preparing to dance. The nasty Lupo had his bow poised, his violin tucked underneath his chin. Another fiddler nodded and all the bows struck. The music struck up. Lupo's face seized and disappeared in concentration, like biting down hard on an idea.

People jigged and hopped in a distant light. All waning, and she said as the room fell away, "Jews are devilish spirits; we abide by night in a fiery realm. There can be no friendship between our peoples. We live in your nightmares, and you are but our dreams."

Then she seized and disappeared. The world went black. She stretched out her hand and felt a sheet, Ben's arm, the caressing breeze from a ceiling fan. But Will's voice pursued her with the slow, tired cadence of a man who has seen through a frivolous evasion: "I had not known it. And do the Jews dance?"

15

Then they all lived at Martin's house. All of them who'd been at the hospital went, because the baby went there, because his things were there. Then somebody always had to be with the baby. It was tricky to coordinate if people didn't live in the house.

Kate stayed there, so Ben stayed there. José stayed, and slept in Oksana's ballerina room, where Oksana came and went, never seeming to notice José, although Ben assumed they must have sex. Even Sabine stayed on and off; she felt responsible for everyone's disasters, so she had a bed delivered and it became her second home. The ground floor was all mail-order brides, and they made a lot of noise and had fights and sobbing episodes but somehow made the place feel cheerful.

The only one who didn't live at Martin's was Martin. When finally contacted by phone and informed he had a baby not genetically his, he had said in a bruised small voice, "Oh, God, does that serve me right for not adopting? I'm tempted to say it serves me right," then went and checked himself into a rehab. An ex-boyfriend dropped by to pick up his clothes and told them Martin had experienced a mental collapse.

"I'll mental collapse *him*," said Sabine, but no one did anything to Martin. They lived in the house.

The baby's name was a sticking point initially. Oksana had named him Qued Nodian McDaniels, McDaniels being Martin's last name and Qued Nodian a name from a series of dreams Martin had, in which he was introduced to men with ridiculous names—Merguidd Wink and Pluribus Fudge and Qued Nodian—and woke up laughing. He'd talked about the dreams a lot when he was thinking of baby names, though he'd decided to name the baby Ryan.

However, Oksana was obsessed with Qued Nodian, because (she said) she had dreamed about him too. She'd decided he was real and asked everyone if they had ever met Qued Nodian, and even once approached a man on the street to ask if he was Qued Nodian. She said Qued Nodian was her fate. She never did find him, so (as she commented in her unearthly, toneless voice) she had made him in her body. And she said the name would give the baby power. She said, "I think he will be grateful he has not a name like every person."

This outraged Sabine, who insisted on calling the baby Ryan and enunciated *Ryan* domineeringly and stared people down, so in her presence they called him Ryan. But he seemed like a Qued, very pensive and Zen, with lily-white skin and coal-black eyes; a changeling from the Pluribus Fudge universe or from a sci-fi movie about uncanny children born to unsuspecting small-town couples. Not cute but pretty, even when he was a newborn. He gazed beatifically at nothing, then (as his eyesight developed) at everything, squirming restlessly as if he couldn't wait to get out of this irrelevant body. Kate said he was preparing to turn into a butterfly. Sabine said he was planning to invade Poland. Ben said he was the sort of baby you would see from the window of an airplane, crawling insouciantly on a cloud. José said Qued was like all other babies and hadn't they ever known a baby? But it was clear he did it from a knee-jerk humility, hoping to be contradicted.

Oksana was the mother, of course, but she exerted no rights. As soon as she was on her feet, she left and spent her days making a film about the Union of Unreasonable Workers; she often slept in their squatted office in Bed-Stuy and didn't come home for days. When she appeared, José followed her around with Qued in his arms and tried to reason with her. She said she was a monster. She said she was depressed. She said childbirth was monstrous, all people were monsters, and she didn't have the will to pretend. When she left, José would get hives and have to lie in a bath of cold water; even the mail-order brides considered Oksana's behavior beyond the pale because they loved José, as all girls did. Sabine said they had to keep Oksana away from "Ryan" before she turned him into a troll, because Oksana was a troll, *she was of the troll race.* Ben said keeping Oksana away would be surpassingly easy, but Sabine said, "I know José, he gets what he wants, it's that Navy SEAL shit." Kate said Oksana was a nut that perhaps even Navy SEALs couldn't crack, and Comfort, the Liberian mail-order bride, said, "Not Navy SEALs, not God, can make that woman love her own baby, oh."

So Qued was an orphan; so they stayed. For days, for months, for whatever it was. Just baby time, like living at the bottom of the sea. The night sea: Qued woke the whole house with piercing, choking screams; then everyone convened at his cradle, sitting on the nursery floor in the dark. Someone warmed the formula and someone made chamomile tea. Brought wine. They took turns walking with Qued, who nursed or continued to scream, or nursed then screamed. They told stories about other babies. About being babies, and mistakes their parents had made. Kate's map of Centauria and Zoof loomed above them, shadowy in the dark; the tenebrous fairies rode along the baseboard. They fell asleep on the floor. They fell asleep at the kitchen table. An alarm rang, and José stomped back and forth among them and showered and dressed, annoying like a fly that had got into the room. Then he went out to work, a relief. Ben dangled his keys in front of Qued so Qued could grab a key with an infantile satisfaction that focused his body. Qued peeped, and Ben said, "Key. Key. Key," while Kate was warming up more formula. Or a mail-order bride walked back and forth with Qued in her arms and sang in a mail-order bride language, while other mail-order brides made eggs and Ben and Kate slept on the sofa and dreamed about Qued.

Kate or Ben went out and came back. José came back and went out. People came, people left. It was as if they never left. That spring (to them all) was a baby-scented ritual: a basin where Qued screamed as he was washed; heaps of laundry being carried down to the basement, past the dark racks of Martin's wine cellar to the dank alcove where the washer/dryer was; the looping scene of the diaper bin lid springing open and your hand casting in the heavy warm diaper; the thermometer for the formula, another baby wipe, Qued waking up, Qued sleeping.

Toward evening, Sabine appeared, full of the world. She was a breath of fresh air, though all she did was complain. Sometimes she leaned over Qued and complained to him in baby talk. The immigration bill her congressman had sponsored was dying in committee; a rival, evil congressman had introduced a rival "guest worker" bill that was legalized slavery. She'd campaigned for this president, and now he was all about "balancing the budget." The left wing was nothing but doe-eyed idiots raising funds to raise awareness, and all the money went to their own salaries. The best lacked all conviction, and the worst were full of passionate intensity, and the best weren't even that good. The best took marching orders from the worst. You couldn't get anything done, and Sabine was thinking of taking that job at the investment bank, because what was the point? She felt like King fucking Canute.

Qued squeaked in her arms and Sabine said, "Aw, that's cute. He thinks it's a joke. No, he wants me to join the investment bank and leave all my money to him. I'm onto you, kiddo. I see right through you."

And Sabine calmed down because, baby. It was spring already (somehow), and they went out back and put burgers on the grill. They were happy all night because babies like happiness. Bea, the Filipina mail-order bride, taught them all to tango because she was taking a tango class; José came home again and played the guitar. They were a family. Or something like a family: when the door closed, it kept something in. It made them feel their fragility. Sabine's complaints made them feel their fragility, as if this house were the last outpost of civilization in a land overrun by barbarians, and perhaps that was what all families were, or felt like. All good families.

And Kate would sing to Qued (a spooky Icelandic lullaby they'd learned from a transient mail-order bride):

Sleep, sleep, you black-eyed pig
Fall into a deep pit of ghosts . . .

And they were up all night in a deep pit of ghosts where they'd forgotten how to sleep or to abandon anyone and loved this creature who was born among them, who gave them something to be.

Meanwhile (in the parallel world outside of Martin's house) Ben was laid off from his job. When he thought of it, he pictured a cow's skull in a trackless desert: the economy. He was living on his savings and applying for everything: jobs he wasn't qualified for and didn't want, jobs in Vietnam and jobs in Cleveland, jobs involving moral compromises that made him despise himself for applying.

On nights before job interviews, he stayed alone at the apartment in Queens to sleep, although he didn't like being there alone. He would end up staring out the window with the television on behind him, wishing he still smoked. Then he wouldn't sleep. Couldn't sleep without Kate. After the interview, for a few days he would feel as if he already had that job and be accordingly elated or filled with self-loathing. A Schrödinger's life, he didn't know what he was. Then he didn't get the job, and he was nothing.

Kate had another mural gig, a picture of a teddy bears' picnic for Sabine's cardiologist's baby. Ben would visit her at the cardiologist's house and they would listen to NPR while she worked, then go back to Martin's together and look after Qued together and sleep together. When Kate wasn't there, Ben felt unpleasantly exhilarated, freed from some necessary stricture, as if he'd been ineptly launched into space. He needed Kate's weight or her wild long hair or the prescient movements of her hand when she drew. She went through the world so easily, like a dandelion seed floating on the wind.

In the throes of that need, he asked her to marry him. It was a morning when José had taken Qued to the park and the mail-order brides were sleeping in. Ben and Kate were planting marigolds in Martin's backyard, and Ben just said it, and he added that he couldn't buy a ring right now, but he'd get a job soon and then he would. Kate said she didn't like rings anyway. "They make me feel like I have something on my hand." Ben laughed and stood up as if everything was settled, and they went straight out to get a marriage license without even changing their clothes.

It was there, at the courthouse—where you had to take a ticket and wait for your number to be called, so it was like a very beautiful DMV; marble floors and polished oak, but at the end of the day, you were waiting with a ticket in your hand—Kate mentioned the dream again.

It began with her asking, "Have you heard of a poet called William Shakespeare?"

Ben was startled from a reverie about getting married and it took him a moment to focus. Then he said, "I don't think so. Should I have?"

"You haven't? A sixteenth-century poet?"

"I might have, but I don't remember. Why?"

"I dream about him."

"Oh."

His *oh* was a bleak and critical note, but Kate just smiled. She said, "He keeps reappearing in my dreams. It feels as if he must be important, but I looked him up, and he just dies without doing much of anything."

Ben forced a smile. "Are we sure this was a real poet?"

Kate was sure. He had certainly existed. He'd written some plays that weren't extant and a long poem called *Venus and Adonis*. They had a copy of the poem at the New York Public Library, but when Kate requested it, it turned out to be missing. She supposed other copies must exist somewhere. Anyway, he'd died young. There was a record of his burial in London in 1593, when he was thirty years old. And what was odd was, 1593 was the year Kate always dreamed about. "Anyhow, I keep dreaming about this poet, and I can't figure out what it means."

"I have a favorite sixteenth-century poem."

Kate balked, then said, "Okay," and made a listening face.

"It's Thomas Wyatt." Ben recited:

They flee from me that sometime did me seek
With naked foot, stalking in my chamber.
I have seen them gentle, tame, and meek,
That now are wild and do not remember
That sometime they put themself in danger
To take bread at my hand . . .

He stopped because he couldn't tell if Kate was listening. She looked harsh, distant. Her eyes were black black—insect black, like the eyes of a sapient and beautiful wasp.

"Kate?"

She said, in a suppressed, sad voice, "When I have a dream now, I'm afraid I'll wake up and you won't be there."

"I'll be there."

"I don't mean I'm afraid you'll leave."

"Then what do you mean?"

"I don't know. It's just a feeling."

"Kate, are you sure you want to get married?"

She said, "Yes," but in a way that didn't satisfy Ben. He realized they weren't really going to get married. They would get the license, but then it would just sit in a drawer. Nobody would mention it again.

He thought this but refused to believe it. He said, "I really want to marry *you*."

Then their number was called. They went to the window and provided ID and filled out forms, behaving very cheerfully and naturally. And they walked away with the license, relieved, and Kate said dazedly, "*That's* good, anyway."

The next week—and somehow this felt like a shocking, unforeseeable blow—Ben got a job. It was at Exxon, in the public relations department, so something that you couldn't do and be a good person. But he couldn't turn it down. It was reliable money. It was structure and people depending on you. Even though he didn't want to *do* the job, he wanted it like wanting to breathe.

When he told Kate, he was braced for opposition. But Kate just said, "What's Exxon?" and then she seemed bewildered by his answer. She objected that oil was a thing of the past, because you couldn't burn oil because of global warming. Ben said he thought oil still had a few good years left in it, and Kate said no, but then became unsure and said, "People still use oil?"

"You may have noticed these things called cars."

"Cars still run on oil?"

"Are you serious?"

"But you'll be contributing to that? You'll be contributing to keeping oil going?"

"I'll also be contributing to rent."

And she said she guessed it wasn't really Ben's fault, and he said, "That's how I plan to sleep at night," and by then they were laughing and Ben was relieved. The job had taken on a sort of pink unreality. Kate forgave him, and that was all that mattered. He could live with the jeers from Sabine.

But he couldn't help noticing it was strange. And in the following days there were more strange things, or specifically lacunae in Kate's memory. Kate was startled to hear England still had a queen. She claimed not to know what "plastic" was, and when Ben showed her a plastic spoon, she said, "Oh—you mean celluloid." She thought the Louisiana Purchase hadn't taken place until the 1930s and that was why Americans still spoke French, and when Ben said they mostly didn't speak French, and for instance he didn't, Kate said, "You did when I met you," and then got upset and remote and refused to explain.

On May Day, they were on Sabine's rooftop, waiting for the fireworks to begin, and Sabine was complaining in her usual way, and she mentioned President Gore. Kate said, "Wait, Gore's *president*?" But when she saw Ben's and Sabine's reaction, she pretended she'd only been expressing a feeling that Gore was ridiculous in that role. Sabine said, "We campaigned for Gore. *You* campaigned for Gore." Kate looked surprised and even faintly resistant but said, "Well, I know I campaigned for Gore."

She hadn't known. Ben could have sworn. But afterward, he couldn't exactly believe it. Of course Kate knew who the president was, it was an Alzheimer's symptom if you didn't know that. And Kate wasn't doddering. Her parents weren't worried. It had to be a misunderstanding.

Nonetheless, it left him with a terrible doubt, a fear that inhabited every scene. He would argue against it in his head at work while he edited press releases and endured pep talks about "Exxon culture." At Martin's, he compulsively cleaned up after everyone. He couldn't let anything go. He started to run five miles each morning, a practice Kate called fascist, and Ben was weirdly comforted to be called fascist, as if it meant he could exercise control; if he was willing to be evil, he could have control.

Meanwhile, May turned into June and became oppressive, listless, mephitic. Martin had never installed air-conditioning, and Sabine wouldn't pay for it because of the environment, and everyone else was broke. They took Qued to the park, to the zoo, but they were groggy and sweaty and irritable. They had fights about nothing; about ten dollars. And one night, when the humidity had turned into a bank of sinister gray-black clouds, and the air was charged with a steamy malignity, Ben and Kate went out to a poetry reading.

They had gone with the glee of being free for the night, but the reading was immediately galling. It was in a slick, loftlike hipster bookstore, and the poet was a rich girl who wrote confessional poetry about her anorexia, the poetry mediocre and the poet suspiciously not that thin. There were a hundred people there—more than Ben had ever seen at a poetry reading—all spindly hipsters who cheered indiscriminately after every poem. In the Q and A, they revealed themselves to be the poet's college friends; they addressed her as "Sammy" and referred to things that had happened in their Indonesian shadow puppetry seminar. The event had been catered by a Williamsburg taco stand, and after the reading, the hipsters chatted knowledgeably about the swordfish tacos, not the poems. As Kate said in the line for tacos, it made you feel like life was a great big sham, a form of Indonesian shadow puppetry gone wrong. But she said it good-naturedly (as Kate would); she didn't mind humanity's vacuousness, while Ben felt hateful, despairing, and vulnerable among the cheerful hipsters, who reminded him of the bullies at his middle school who'd called him Pocahontas and Tarzan and cheered him on the soccer field with Indian war whoops—they couldn't even light on an appropriate racial slur. Of course, the hipsters weren't really like the bullies—but no, they were alike somehow. They were alike in how they made Ben feel.

In this mood, he had to find an argument that made his reaction reasonable. He started by commenting sourly that everyone here, apart from Ben and Kate, was white. Kate said, "You're right. That's weird," and added that of course it wasn't weird that it wasn't full of Persians, but this was an Afro-American neighborhood, and yet there seemed to be exactly zero Afro-Americans there.

"Afro-Americans?" Ben said.

"What?"

"It's just a kind of outmoded term."

"Oh, well," Kate said fatalistically. "*Celluloid*. I know not your words, Earthman."

Then Ben went on a detour of accounting for the absence of African Americans, going all the way back to the slave trade, with the strong implication that the hipsters were complicit in the transatlantic slave trade, while Kate frowned and looked unnerved, as if she might be hearing about the slave trade for the first time.

"Anyway," Ben said in conclusion, "that's one thing, but what really gets me is the poems. Not just that they have no artfulness or wit, it's how they fetishize mental illness. They're treating mental illness as something profound, when really it's ugly and meaningless. It's all that post-Plath wallow. I find that bullshit hard to take because of my mother."

Kate nodded; she was along for the ride. She was good about things like that. She seemed to be marshaling supportive arguments as she turned to discard the paper basket from her taco.

But when she turned back, what she said was, "Have you talked to your mother lately?"

He felt as if someone had poured ice water down his back. He wanted to just walk away. He couldn't do this.

He said in a tenuously calm voice, "Kate. You don't remember that my mother is dead?"

She winced, then thought very carefully about it, her black eyes cowed and serious. "I'm sorry. Somehow I thought she was alive."

"No, seriously. How could you forget that?"

"I didn't forget it."

"You didn't?"

"I really thought you said she was alive."

Ben said, "We're going home right now and you have to see a doctor tomorrow." His voice cracked. He stepped back from Kate. She was petrified and tearful immediately. Ben turned and Kate came after him, Ben walking stiff legged, blind, through the crowd. All the people continued talking and laughing, they were having their normal evenings. Now they didn't seem like hipsters; they were people trying to have a good time like normal people. Ben felt an unbearable nostalgia for them. He wanted to run from her. His whole body wanted it.

Out in the street, the sky was black and thick with rain clouds, the hot wind pulled crazily at their clothes. It felt like a storm already, though the air was dry. Ben's mind raced, insisting it wasn't that serious. Her parents weren't worried. Kate walked by his side, she was smaller than him. He couldn't look at her, but he wanted to hold her. He wanted to make her be okay.

As they came under a restaurant's storefront awning, there was a crash of thunder. The sky flickered. They instinctively stopped beneath the awning, braced against a downpour. But the rain didn't come.

And Ben remembered Oksana at the skating rink: Oksana dusty pink and hunched and poor and invincible, skating out and bisecting the rink, so quick it was as if the other skaters were frozen to the ice, as if they weren't people but clumps of dirt. Because crazy people weren't weaker than you—he'd often thought this about his mother—they were stronger. They outlasted you, even when they died. They would tread you underfoot without noticing.

"I love you," Kate said. "Ben? I'm sorry. I don't know what's happening to me."

He couldn't say anything. The sky gleamed balefully, black and gray. The wind fell still.

Then they stepped out from under the awning and the rain came.

16

She was asleep in the dream, but she was at Cowdray. She slept and wouldn't wake; she was afraid to wake. Something bad happened here. It was a thing that couldn't happen.

But one night she woke and the foreboding was gone. She was warm in bed; the bed curtains were open. Mary was asleep on a pallet on the floor. Emilia paused to remember how Mary had come, to remember the ordinary days that had passed, the hours of walking in the gallery while rain beat on the windows, of sitting at needlework. She'd finished a cushion of Irish stitchwork with a picture of a lion lying down with a lamb. They had talked of the plague, of the wars in France. Emilia had played on a virginal that had fallen out of tune, so that Southampton complained at the off notes and fidgeted; at last he had risen to hold forth tragically about the misfortune that it was to be alive.

Now the still night. There was a night robe on the bed, a long linen shift with fur-lined sleeves; she pulled it on and crept to the

143

door. *On naked foot, stalking in my chamber* haunted past her mind; she stopped with her hand on the latch, her throat tight and dry. There and then, she almost cried about Ben. (They'd run home from the poetry reading in the rain, but they hadn't been laughing. The rain had soaked and weighed down her clothes and she'd fallen behind. He didn't look back.)

She opened the door and took a deep breath. At the end of the blind-dark hall, the moonlit entrance to the gallery hung like a picture. She stepped into the colder rushes outside and walked to the light with a feeling like climbing effortlessly out of a well. Then the gallery was silent, its windows silent. Outside, a vista of neat knot gardens: a quincunx of little trees and flowers, then a flower-shaped pattern of hedges with pale rocky pathways woven through. In one of the squares, deer grazed, their movements uncannily delicate, tentative, as if they had that instant come to life. Above, the stars were a child's stars, big and friendly and simple.

And down the broad stairs. Each step had been made by a person with a chisel; each step had been shaped by hand. It was a small world here, you could live in it. Safe. A world where everyone slept at night, and the sounds outside were frogs and owls. There was nothing but God above.

And perhaps she was meant to be riding forth to perform some heroic feat. In stories, there was always a tyrant to be slain, a war to be prevented—an obvious move. But this was reality, occluded and delicate. She felt her way, she groped among instincts—and Emilia was human, with an animal heart; she was a thing that couldn't concentrate when it was thirsty. She wanted to know what to do, but she didn't. She knew she was going to Will.

These past days, he'd waited for her in every company. She'd dressed for him; she'd woven ribbons in her hair. He'd looked up as she entered the room, and something physical occurred that no man saw. Between them was also the conspiracy of all poor scholars and performers and companions, living on a lord's munificence, on the insubstantial goodness of the great. They were the children of the house, or the pets, and if they crept from their masters' feet at night, what they did in their ramblings was illicit only because it was so insignificant. Nothing so small should care for itself; must every insect raise its banner and make war against every other insect?

But their eyes met and she hurt with knowledge. He was real. It was the hope of the world.

He was sitting on the floor by the drawing room hearth. The room was moonlight and he was firelight, changeable and red. The chimneypiece was painted with grotesques: a rabbit pulled an imp's long nose; a little dog bit a manticore's tail; a mermaid matter-of-factly doused a flaming salamander with a bucket. They all seemed to move in the firelight, so he looked to be surrounded by his curious thoughts. He'd been watching the fire and, hearing her step, looked up into the darkness blind.

She said, "It is I, the fair Israelite."

At first he blinked, mistrustful; he was trying to see her in the dark. Then he knew her and smiled. He reached back for a cup he'd set by the fire. She came forward to take it from his hand: spiced wine. She settled on the floor beside him, arranging her robe around her knees. He was a plain-looking man with big-knuckled hands. Just a man. She thought: *They put themself in danger to take bread at my hand.*

"Lady Israel," he said. "Why so late waking? Art thou called to the Jewish Sabbath?"

She answered lightly, "Nay, I wake not. I lie asleep, and thou art my dream. As I have told thee, in no other wise may Jew and Christian meet."

"I am thy dream—but mayest thou not instead be mine?"

"I can answer for no other man's dreams. But that I am asleep, I can well swear."

"Well, if I am thy dream, what I do now is not my doing. It is only the making of thy dream."

"So it follows."

They passed a precarious moment then. She could see his intensity, but not his thought. Her mind ranged through superstitious guesses, while her body expected his hands.

But at last he said, with the same brisk lightness, "Well, I have passed this time in writing, so thy dream must answer for my poor verse."

She smiled. She wouldn't show her disappointment. "But thou hast no paper. I have dreamed thee an absurdity. Or dost thou write in ash?"

"No, I am the son of an unlettered father. I can write in my fancy and read the air."

"And what dost thou write?"

"What may be a play, if it go well. I have only a few fair lines."

"Fair lines and few," she said politely. "'Twould be a shame, then, didst thou not speak them."

He paused. She could see he was thinking; perhaps he was editing his new-made lines. In that pause, she was Kate, who didn't see why he mattered. It was pleasant by the fire and the spiced wine was

pleasant—but ultimately just a waste of time. Like the ride to Cowdray, like all these days. He was nothing, after all: a minor poet. Just
a man.

Then he collected himself and said, "It is a scene of the sad king
Richard. He receiveth ill tidings of his wars, such that he must despair
of his throne. His officers bespeak him courage, but the king is stubborn
in desponding. Now he speaks:

For God's sake, let us sit upon the ground
and tell sad stories of the death of kings;
how some have been deposed, some slain in war,
some haunted by the ghosts they have deposed,
some poison'd by their wives: all murder'd.
For, within the hollow crown that rounds
the temples of a king, keeps Death his court . . .

He spoke the lines with the rich and mournful timbre of a tragic
actor. It went on a little while, and coursed and grew and left a hole
when he fell silent. Then Emilia was chilled. Wrong-footed. It was as if
she had heard the words before, in a time of great happiness that was
now lost. It was fey, it was familiar. It was like nothing else.

But she said with forced calmness, "Marry, a sad prince indeed. It
is my Lord Southampton to the life."

Will laughed. "Nay, malign him not. It is myself."

She laughed in return; there was a spark. She stretched her hand
to the fire and his eye followed. Her body expected his hands.

"Well," she said, "thy verses are wondrous fair; 'tis as if sugared
raindrops fell into my mouth. But thou makest a goodly heap of dead

princes. Her Majesty will like that not. Nor will her officers smile at such a hecatomb."

He frowned. He seemed ready to explain why she was wrong. But he said, "No matter. 'Twas writ on air and will be gone when the next wind goes."

"'Tis like the psalm: 'The wind goeth over it, and it is gone, and the place thereof shall know it no more.'"

But when she smiled at him, he'd shrunk from her—retracted like a snail. There was a chill. The sexual spark was gone. And Emilia remembered his death—the fact printed baldly in a book, *A Companion to Tudor Literature,* which Kate had read at the New York Public Library: *Buried at St. Leonard's Shoreditch, London, September 1593.* Kate had read it and been spooked and titillated. Kate who was still like a child.

As she thought it, he said in a soft, cold voice, "There was a man of my company that lately died, of eating over-much pickled herring."

"Herring?" She laughed from nerves. "What man?"

"He was called Rob Greene. A wit of the taverns, a writer of pamphlets, an unthrift maker of plays. Even as he lay a-dying, he delivered his confession not to a priest, but to a printer, and made of it a pamphlet to sell for sixpence. I know the book well, for he railed on me in it. He named me upstart crow and thief. He was one who could not speak, but he railed."

Will had pinched up a few rushes from the floor. Now he tossed them into the fire. They writhed and became a bright scribble and shrank to ash.

"'Twas a toad-like, sulphurous wretch," he went on, "and a whoremaster and a drunkard. 'Tis said, 'The fox fareth best when he be most cursed,' and Rob Greene was a fortunate fox; he never lived a week that he was not cursed seven times by all who knew him. 'Twould seem, he was little enough to mourn.

"Yet in the market, I have lately seen some pages from Greene's six-penny confession, where they were used as a paper to cover mustard pots. On the crowns of the pots stood the words: *Black is the remembrance . . . black as death.* And I wept for pity, that any man's life should become such a mustard-paper. It hath troubled me, these days."

She said, "Thou art much taken with thoughts of death."

He looked at her then. He was real and hostile. He had pinched up more rushes; now he crushed them in his fingers. His hand closed into a fist.

He said, "I would be remembered, madam. Perhaps thou canst say how I will be remembered?"

"How thou wilt be remembered?"

"Make not thy puzzling faces. Thou knowest."

She said, and her voice was hoarse, "I cannot tell what ails thee, sir."

"Canst thou not? Then I must give thee another story for thy book of secrets. Know, then, that I was once as thou art. I have been such a Jew, whose sleep was waking. I have walked in the skin of a stranger and conversed with the dead. I have lived another life in the dark."

Then all shifted and appeared in a different pattern. They were a deep well, apart from all the world, and she knew. He had chosen and pursued her because they were the same. He was real to her because they were the same. He had once traveled in his dreams to a different time; he had lived another life in sleep. There were others like her. Of course there were. How had she ever thought there would not be?

And she would have spoken honestly then—made certain what he meant, made him say where in time he went—but his body was tense and hostile. And she didn't want to be a madwoman here. She was a madwoman there, and she wanted to be safe somewhere. If she told him of his future, she had no good news. He was only a man, as fallible as all men were. He was nothing to trust.

He watched her think all this, and when she looked away without answering him, he sighed. He said, "We are agreed I am thy dream. Now I shall tell you a dream of mine, that thou mayest know me for thine own. For I trust thou hast seen this vision. Methinks, 'tis a goblin all our dark folk see.

"So, as I slept, I saw a dead city, a city such as never has been in the world. 'Twas wondrous high; the brows of its roofs touched the misty clouds. Its walls were wrought of coals and ice, and its earth was unnatural stone, where no beast lived. In that place were no forests, no healthful meadows. No birds; all the vasty air was dead. The dirty beetles had perished, and their paper armor drifted in the streets. 'Twas a kingdom of naught, of winds and silence."

She was looking at the fire, and saw it there. It was the same evil city she'd seen before, its towers aglitter with dirt and ice. It was seething in her head. It was a noise that wasn't noise, as if a wind blew mutteringly, vilely, in her head.

He said, "But this dream is thine also, madam. Is this dream not thine?"

Emilia shuddered, and the vision was gone. She was looking into Will's eyes, though she couldn't see his eyes in this light. She couldn't tell what was real.

"My lord," she said, "are we then met for the saving of the world?"

She touched his hand but he didn't respond. His hand was stiff. It trembled.

"Speak not of the world," he said. "It is a crow to pick mine eyes."

"A crow?"

"Nay, tell me what thou knowest of me. Tell me what thou knowest or be damned."

Then the dream flickered. The fire grew huge, ringed by its grotesques. She was gripping his hand while the fire tried to blow her away. Will talked somewhere; he was raging while Emilia was afraid and couldn't breathe. The fire was cold and pleasant like a bed. He would die in four months, and she hadn't tried to help. She had made the wrong choice, missed the obvious move. She deserved his hate. She was a fool.

When the dream came back, he was gentle. He stroked her palm; he let her lie in his bosom. She lay there, weak, and watched the fire grow dim. And he sang in a low voice, lost in the tall room, sang "Tom o'Bedlam" that was (she thought) the voice of his outraged heart:

From the hag and hungry goblin
That into rags would rend ye
The spirit that stands by the naked man
In the Book of Moons defend ye

And when the song was done, she said, "What I know . . . Go not to London in this year. For if thou goest to London, thou shalt die."

She woke next to Ben. It was hot and gray; a sallow half-light spread from the curtainless window. She didn't know where she was. She didn't recognize the room. For a while, she lay and breathed and supposed that all the world she had known was gone.

Gradually, it came back to her: Martin's house and Qued and the slow hot summer. The curtains were gone, but everything else was the same. She crept out of bed, leaving Ben asleep, and went to the bathroom and looked in the mirror. She was Kate. She was the same. She put her hand to the mirror and the glass was normal. The shower curtain with the dolphin pattern was the same. The air she breathed was air. The same.

Then she went to the window and saw the street.

17

She went to a psychiatrist. She went to a neurologist. She got three different scans. She spent a night in a sleep clinic with electrodes pasted to her face with gauze, and when Ben visited her there, she was peaceful and Kate-like, pleased by the oddities of medical science. She said, "Does it look like they're stealing my brain?"

"It doesn't really look like the electrodes do anything."

"No," she said. "It looks like an experiment done by an eight-year-old. I want to wear them home."

Then she insisted he take her picture, even though it made him feel like a ghoul.

The neurologist couldn't find anything. Kate didn't have seizures. Kate didn't have tumors. She hadn't had a stroke. Kate said innocently, "That's *good*, right?" and she and the neurologist laughed with relief while Ben continued to worry.

The psychiatrist saw Kate five times before she would venture a diagnosis. There was a sense of the psychiatrist dragging her feet and wanting Kate to manifest some unequivocally damning symptom. Finally, at a conference with Ben and Kate, she listed Kate's symptoms and said (her voice hypnotically calm while her eyes were pained and frantic) that the strong probability was schizophrenia, although there were atypical aspects and she knew the word was frightening. However, many patients had full lives. And there were still many things that weren't known about the brain.

She wrote Kate two prescriptions, and Ben and Kate went to the pharmacy together, a couple on an outing like any happy couple on a nice summer day. They would never go out like this to buy clothes for their baby. They would never shop for wedding rings. Ben was sick, somnambulistic, while he joked and acted like nothing had changed. Kate acted like nothing had changed, her black eyes deep and soft with fear.

And she was kind, as no one else exactly was. She was generous and gallant in the face of it. He loved her. He couldn't make do with anyone else.

But he didn't want to be his father. To have the years pass and all the optimism go, and the love, and then the madwoman went and died anyway. He couldn't walk into that prison of his own free will.

"Pills!" said Kate, at home with the vials of pills. She shook them to make a maracas sound.

Ben said, "Are you okay?"

"I'm okay. But I don't know if I really ought to take these pills."

He caught his breath. He said, "Kate, listen . . ."

*　*　*

But she wouldn't listen, so Ben called Ágota. Then he called Salman, then Ágota again. He called Sabine. He told the story from beginning to end, four times, until he was choking on the story and he hated himself. He so didn't want it to be true. Why did he have to tell it that way, like it was true?

Then a long period in which he met people for drinks behind Kate's back to talk about Kate. The world was a stress miasma; the people were faces in that miasma. He told people Kate would take the pills and it would all go away; or it would turn out to be nothing, it was all a mistake. Kate was such a happy person. And wasn't schizophrenia a catch-all diagnosis for anything the doctors didn't understand? It wasn't schizophrenia, he said, but his mind said, *It is schizophrenia, it's fucking schizophrenia. You don't get better from that.*

She took the pills but nothing changed. Days passed, and she was only more forthcoming with absurdities. She now explained that her dreams about the sixteenth century affected her waking life. She would wake to find the world was changed, as if her dreams were actual visits to the past, and the things she did there altered history. There, she'd met another time traveler, a man who was a minor Elizabethan playwright. They both had visions of a future apocalypse: a burnt, empty city in a world that was dead. She'd been trying to avert that doom, but now she was certain she was making things worse. She hoped the poet could change this picture, but she didn't really see what he would do. He would write a world-changing play? It seemed like grasping at straws.

Ben asked if she seriously believed all that. Kate said no—but still puzzled over it as if it were a matter of life and death. And she still talked about the world she had lost, the world with the Breadfruit

Monarch and the pangolins, a world where the president was (Kate now confessed) not Gore but a woman named Chen.

Of course, Chen was better than Gore. Everything was better in Kate's lost world. The real world harrowed and shocked her, and Kate now openly remarked on its badness. She was scandalized by all the advertising (which was strictly regulated in her world) and surprised that people didn't "just rise up." How could there be so many homeless people when everyone else had money to burn, when they were going out to restaurants and buying new clothes? Why did policemen all have guns? If people could vote, why would anyone vote to give policemen guns? She had woken one morning and naively gone to the window and seen the street and found it lined by stores with dirty plastic signs that were bullyingly ugly, and above the stores were five stories of apartments—as Kate would learn that day, every city street was overshadowed now by walls of apartments, because there were seven billion people in the world, and all the billions kept breeding more people as the world died around them and it made no sense. Ben reacted defensively; he was of this world that wasn't good enough for Kate. He bought new clothes. He liked some ads. He worked in public relations for ExxonMobil. He had always wanted children, ideally three. He had wanted children with *Kate*.

One bad night, he mentioned nuclear weapons, and Kate said, "Wait, they *make* nuclear weapons?" and Ben said, "Uh-huh," and Kate said she knew about them as a theory, but why would you make them when you knew you couldn't use them? So Ben explained Hiroshima and Nagasaki, and Kate got a terrible expression and said, "And they kept on making them?" Ben said, "Kate, you know all this," but she needed him to tell her how many there were. Ben said he didn't know, and she said, "How can you not know? Are there ten? Are there a thousand?"

He pointed up to indicate there were more, and Kate freaked out and paced the floor all night and he only got three hours' sleep.

She was often unhappy. It wasn't like Kate. The medication made her slow and stunned. She stared. Her eyes lost their keen profundity. She rapidly put on weight and would touch her newly amorphous belly with a tentative worry. She cried sometimes and didn't want to say why. She didn't want to see her parents. She wanted to go to sleep at nine.

Most days, she sat around knitting or drawing. She acquired a guitar somewhere and would sit strumming sad, antiquated tunes she said she'd learned in her dreams. She hand-embroidered her clothes with birds and flowering trees and leaping deer; the embroidery was competent and pretty, but tended to make the clothes lose their shape. In them, she looked unpleasantly eccentric, like a member of a cult that required its followers to wear embroidered clothes.

One week, her brother, Petey, came to visit, or was dispatched to visit by Salman and Ágota. He was surprisingly short, compact, and baby faced; he looked too young to be in college, although he was actually twenty-two. The first night he was there, Kate talked about her dreams, and Petey interrupted her unhappily, saying, "If talking about this stuff helps, you should feel free to talk about it anytime"—his way of saying he couldn't stand to hear about it, that her sickness terrified him. After that, Kate stuck to Petey subjects—his college courses, the bike he was building, his Dungeons and Dragons character—and, possibly for that reason, seemed better. She started to laugh at jokes again, to comb her hair, to eat dessert. One night, she and Petey started speaking in Hungarian accents, saying lugubrious Hungarian things like: "I hope your year has not been *too* dismal" and "Well, it is marvelous that we are at least not dead," and they conversed for an hour in these personas, making each other laugh so hard Petey curled up on the floor and kicked his feet. But then Petey left. It was back to square one.

Another thing that comforted Kate was Qued, but her attachment to the baby was too intense; Ben suspected her of wanting to raise Qued according to the precepts of her imaginary world. It also meant Kate was often with José while Ben was out at work. She was always talking about José: what José had said, what José had done. She taught José one of her weird dream songs (about a man escaped from Bedlam, who roamed the streets begging) and they sang it as a lullaby together although it never put Qued to sleep. One day, she and José took Qued to the park and rented a canoe and rowed around the lake and both came home with sunburns, and Kate seemed happy for a change, much happier than Ben could make her. When Ben asked what they talked about, Kate said she couldn't remember and looked defensive in a panicky way, as if Ben were threatening the one safe thing in her life.

Ben couldn't quite believe they were sleeping together. He didn't like José, but it was partly because José was so morally serious; he made Ben feel meretricious by comparison. José knew all the local homeless people by name; he had a favorite Catholic philosopher; he wrote long letters to his mother in Denver because she didn't like to talk on the phone. José wouldn't sleep with someone else's girlfriend. He wouldn't take advantage of the mentally ill. Still, as a friendship, it felt implausible. It was like things Kate had told Ben in the early months, anomalous things that turned out to be symptoms.

One day, Ben went with Kate to meet a mural client, a friend of Sabine's who wanted a trompe l'oeil grotto painted in her bathroom. To Ben's dismay, Kate announced up front that she had a mental illness and embarked on a description of her alternate world. Luckily, the woman (a veterinarian who was enormously fat and carried it in a no-nonsense way that made her immediately likable) was fascinated by Kate's delusion. She made Kate sit while she opened a bottle of wine. The vet's husband took Ben to see his vintage gun collection, to "let the ladies talk," and Ben eavesdropped on Kate's conversation while the husband handed him various rifles. It progressed exactly as Ben would expect, up until Kate said the worst thing was loneliness. Nobody else remembered Kate's world—she was alone with her grief for losing that world—but she didn't belong in this world, either.

"Is there anyone you can talk to about it?" the vet asked sympathetically.

There was a long pause then. Ben's hands tightened on the Enfield rifle he was holding.

Kate said, "Sometimes I talk to my friend José."

The flip side of that scene was a time Ben had lunch with Sabine at Amsterdam Bank, the lounge bar in the former Amsterdam Bank. It would have felt different (Ben thought afterward) if it had happened anywhere else. Even in the daytime, the place was deafening: club music and the people's voices blaring over it, glasses and the screech of the espresso machine. The waitresses were all models and wore a uniform of short shorts and gold bikini tops. It was exploitative and crass, a Weimar atmosphere, the feeling of an orgy taking place as an asteroid approached that would obliterate Earth.

That day they weren't talking about Kate but about Sabine's job at Credit Suisse and the bank bros there who threw screaming tantrums or bragged about prostitutes they'd fucked or hatched plots against each other, in the course of which they literally hissed like Kaa from *The Jungle Book*. Kindergarten bullshit, said Sabine; she didn't know why she didn't just quit. Why couldn't she be like her cousin Eddie, the kaleidoscope heir, who didn't feel like he had to do anything? Who flew to Capri and back or bought houses in Maine, that was all he did.

"You could do something else," said Ben.

"I already do something else." Sabine picked up her drink, put it down. "Look, they gave me three olives in this fucking martini. It's a meal. I should give this to the poor."

Then she talked about her political work, but by now she was forgetting to project her voice, and Ben couldn't hear. He drifted off and thought about Sabine's anorexia—whenever she mentioned food, it was impossible not to think about her anorexia, once so extreme it had given her a heart attack; she'd had to be shocked back to life by EMTs on her kitchen floor. The one time he'd been to Sabine's apartment—a twelve-room penthouse where Sabine lived alone, and which belonged to her uncle who was currently away, as Sabine said, "raping Africa"— Ben had said, "Apartments this size scare me." Sabine had said, "Well, it's haunted. I died here." (But Sabine had gotten better, so Kate might too.)

At this point, Sabine stopped talking and made a face of unpleasant surprise. A shape loomed behind Ben—Oksana, who had crept up under cover of the noise and the golden, giraffe-like waitresses. She wore a faded bikini top and terry cloth gym shorts; it looked like a spoof of the waitress costume, although it was just what she often wore. On her bare midriff, you could see the nacreous pattern of her stretch marks, and on her arms a miscellany of self-harm scars and ballpoint-ink tattoos.

Without preamble, Oksana announced it was her thirtieth birthday, and she'd decided to honor it by charging any man who wanted sex with her a thousand dollars. Fucking only; she wasn't doing any other sex, because the fuck was the real, it was the animal act. This wasn't prostitution. She had done prostitution, and so she knew. "The money is for the meaning when I am now a mother. I think it's maybe not enough, one thousand, but I try this first and see." By now, she was speaking directly to Ben.

"So it's a performance thing?" asked Ben uncomfortably.

"I don't know," said Oksana. "I don't care what is performance."

"I mean, it's a kind of art," said Ben.

"It can be art, if someone wants."

"She wants to fuck you, Ben," said Sabine. "That's all it is. This is just her fucked-up idea of flirting." Sabine said to Oksana, "Ben has a girlfriend. A girlfriend with *mental health issues*. Don't be a cunt right here in front of me."

"I maybe want to fuck Ben, okay," said Oksana. "But it's not why I told about my birthday. And if I fuck him, it's not another person's business. He's not a child."

"I don't even have a thousand dollars," said Ben, then realized belatedly it was the wrong thing to say.

Sabine shook her head disgustedly. "I think we're done here. Are we done here, Ben?"

And he went home to Kate. And on the night he went for drinks with the ExxonMobil people, and Alicia—his beautiful, sane co-worker—stroked Ben's arm, pretending to be checking the texture of his absolutely ordinary shirt, Ben went home to Kate. He went home every night, though every night he balked at the door and didn't want to go in. He would ache on the doorstep with some inexpressible thing. He would want to call his Dad, even knowing that his Dad couldn't help; his Dad had fallen at this same hurdle. And he went in to Kate, even though seeing Kate didn't solve the problem of agonizingly missing Kate.

She would say, "I do like some things here. I like *you*," and it wouldn't be enough.

He would say, "I like you, too," and it wouldn't sound true.

Ben would shut down. Would not be able to talk to her. His mind would run back and forth, insisting that he had to leave her, but he couldn't bear to leave her, but he had to leave her soon. When they made love, he couldn't shake the idea that it was sexual abuse, that Kate was mentally incompetent. Some days, she was pain incarnate. She would suffer all day and he would try to cheer her up and fail, and he felt like an irrelevant gnat.

The marriage license sat in a drawer. Ben never mentioned it and Kate never mentioned it. In his low moments, Ben wondered if she even remembered they'd meant to get married.

The last day began with inexplicable grace. They were at the apartment in Queens and woke in the morning to intense strange birdsong. They sleepily went to the window, where they saw a new neighbor moving in and carrying birdcages, four at a time. Already there were two dozen cages in a cluster underneath the sycamore in the courtyard. Presumably he'd brought the birds there first so they wouldn't have to wait in a car in the heat. Because of the inexplicable grace, Ben and Kate didn't hesitate but threw on clothes and went out to meet the neighbor, who turned out to be not just a bird fancier but an ornithologist, and he explained the jealous nature of cockatoos and the fragile constitutions of finches and told them how he'd taught his canaries to sing by playing them tapes of more accomplished canaries, though this had the unintended effect that his parrots and mynah and even some parakeets began to sing along, so now his home was a cacophony of bad canary imitations. He'd given up the records, he'd sold the canaries, but the other birds still taught it to each other. "I'm beginning to be afraid," he said, "it will spread to all the birds in the world." At that point, the macaw in the cage at his feet said, "Christ! Do something, Jack!" and the ornithologist excused himself and went back to toting birds.

From then on, the day was under the sign of magic. It was Saturday; they had the whole day free, and the temperature was already ninety-five degrees. You took a step and you were instantly bathed in sweat, loose limbed, and dazed. Somehow this freed them. They went out to breakfast and got chocolate cake; there was a sybaritic happiness that just made sense.

Leaving the diner, they ran into their neighbor Paola, who was walking her Great Dane and crying. She said she had to pick her mother up from the hospital but now she'd locked herself out of her apartment, and she didn't have time to get a locksmith, but she couldn't bring the dog into the hospital either. So Ben and Kate took charge of the dog—an irresponsible, dragon-like, piebald beast named Butch—and walked to the river and bought Butch ice cream, all the while sweating torrentially, until Butch lay down on the sidewalk and sprawled and lolled and refused to budge. They tugged. They cajoled. Threw sticks. Nothing doing. At last, Kate sat on the ground beside Butch and explained that at home they had air-conditioning, and Butch nodded—actually nodded—and got to his feet and walked sensibly home.

(In all this time, Kate hadn't said anything about her world or the dream. Ben started to think the pills were working. They'd taken their time but now they'd worked. It could all still be all right.)

At the apartment, Butch stretched out on the floor and filled the living room from end to end. Ben and Kate stood in the doorway and laughed at the dog until tears came to their eyes. Then they sat around the edges of the dog and watched a video—*Terminator 2*—which turned out to be about a woman who was locked in a mental ward because a time traveler had come to warn her about an impending apocalypse. It was just close enough: Ben and Kate laughed helplessly, they laughed until their stomachs hurt. It was a joke no one else in the world would understand.

But as they watched the movie, they gradually sobered. They sobered until it was a kind of malaise. And when it was over, they watched all the credits, afraid of whatever the next thing was. At last, there was nothing left and Ben turned the television off and Kate said, "Listen, if you need to break up with me, I get it. I know about your mother. I'm not going to blame you. Do you need to break up?"

And Ben said, "Yes."

18

And asleep into a dark that was thoughtless May, prolific of stars and clear sweet nights and airs that tasted starry. Awake to a bright, brave night, a night to stalk from bed on naked foot and go—

(you had fallen asleep in tears, you had cried yourself to sleep like a child)

(that someone in the night could forgive you; there could still be one thing pure; you had cried yourself to sleep like a child).

He expected her.

He waited in the garden with the dark world redolent of grass and lavender and rosemary. He took her hand and as they crept into the orchard a moth flew ahead of them and vanished in the moonlight. The trees wheeled in the wind overhead. They didn't say anything. Will spread his cloak on the ground.

His hands were callused like workmen's hands, like the hands of Emilia's violin-playing cousins. They rasped on her thigh; they were strange on her cunt. She clung to him. The stars stood absolutely still in the sky.

When it was over, she thought of Ben and wept in a fit of sentiment. Will made nothing of it; a thing women did. He stroked her absently and said, "Thou art as the tender leaves of spring; as dew thereon. As the infant morning, thou art fresh and bright. Thou art all new things in the world."

It meant nothing, perhaps. It was a species of courtesy. Maybe he was sketching a poem and it wouldn't come right.

She said, "Well, thou know'st it is false."

(But neither of them mentioned the dreams. They were there being lovers like any real lovers, and the woods and the spring; it was enough for the time.)

Another night the same. And another night. A night when she sent Mary away so she and Will could sleep together in Emilia's bed. Toward dawn, they crept down the stairs to the buttery and drank milk from a jug. They kissed with milky mouths. And the orchard again, and the scratches on her thighs. Already it was brazen and everyone knew. Her head was full of the scent of midnight flowers, like the ghosts of daytime flowers; her skin raw and aware, her body's blood still full of the touch of his hands.

One night she gave him a token, a scented handkerchief embroidered with silk moths. One night he was jealous and came to her door; then Mary (who hated him for being no noble lord, who had wanted it to be Southampton) called out savagely, "Begone, we want none of thine indecencies here." One night they fucked in the orchard while the rain turned into a downpour; they came back bedraggled and stumbled on the frothy gentleman—the scholar Florio—reading in an office, surrounded by a fairy circle of leaning candles.

"Hunting my lord's game by night?" said Florio to Will, with a smirk at Emilia.

"Nay, we have taken the beggar's bath," said Will, "in the tears of the moon. So our thoughts are made clean of such impure fancies."

At which Florio laughed uneasily, and resented Will thereafter.

Another rainy night they sat at the drawing room fire. The silver-haired cat stalked back and forth, pausing curiously to sniff Emilia's toes. Then she wistfully talked of her makeshift husband, her cousin Alfonso Lanier, and said she hoped she might be brought to love him, that she might yet make a wife. Will swore she would not. He said he would put the feeble husband in a play, which Emilia might watch and be healed of her strange ambition.

"He is no hero for a play," said Emilia. "He is but a poor piper and no ill-omened king."

"Nay," said Will. "'Twould be a comedy. And a comedy must have its cuckold; else how shall our rakes be made to laugh?"

"If they laugh or no, let it be without me."

"Nay, madam, but say how thy husband offends thee. I'll trim my lines to fit."

"And how doth thy wife offend thee?" (For Emilia knew Will had a wife, a dull Ann, who waited at home and brewed beer and grew fat, and Will brooked no jokes on his Ann.)

But now he said, "Why, she offendeth me even as the cruel and hard-beaked bird offendeth the tender worm. It is a comedy we write: If a man have a wife, she must be a shrew. So, madam?"

"And if he offend me not?"

"Then he is no husband, nor no man. Give me but one bough on which to sling a jest, and I shall see the beggar hanged."

Then he pestered her—relentless, merry, irresponsible—until she surrendered and said, "He offendeth me in spending of my money and pawning of my jewels that I had before we wed."

"Ah!" he said. Then he looked into the fire and frowned. Emilia sighed impatiently and held out her hand to the cat—but Will had already turned back. "'Tis done. We begin with a knave and a wench who speak scurvily together of thy husband. 'Tis a common contrivance and plays well.

"So, Sir Lackpenny speaks: *God's bread! This Lanier is a sort of cattle that cannot wear his horns in peace, but must shake them at every penny; if he hath not his daily fodder in gold, he kicks the barn to shivers.*

"Mistress Slackpurse answers: *Nay, 'tis a worshipful ox, that will be fed on angels and crosses; the mildest that ever ate coins from a woman's hand.*"

Emilia said, "Now thou makest me to repent mine honesty. My husband is a good youth and took me when no man else would have me. He spends from my purse—well, there's no marvel. He married my purse and not my person. His plunders please me not, but he hath not earned my mocks."

"And yet the scene plays well."

"Nay, can you not write an honest play, wherein a poor man is not scorned for doing what every poor man would?"

"Thou speak'st wisely, fair mistress," Will said, "but it maketh but a dull-going play. Thou makest a play for booing, for hurling of pippins at actors' heads. I have a play, and thou hast no play."

"Thy play is stale. 'Tis a hard-mouthed jade. Thou sell'st a wine that hath been in a thousand mouths."

"And 'twas applauded by all these mouths. Were I to give thy play to the players, they would send for Tom Nashe straight, to write it over with a cuckold and a shrew."

She scoffed and said she knew no Nashe; then he led her to a pantry and they fucked against the wall. The night was close and soft. The pounding of the rain in the windows was an unsteady heartbeat. She felt every blink of her eyes as pleasure, as a tragedy. Every breath was real.

They didn't mention the dreams. He didn't, and she didn't know why. She didn't; she felt that if they talked about the dreams, she might wake up, and she couldn't face that again—to be a crazy lady, bloated from meds; to walk on eggshells and understand nothing. It was that or the starry orchards and wine and the cat creeping by to inspect them in the firelight, its fur damp from dew and scented with the garden's rosemary; the long soft days. There was really no decision to be made.

But then another night he came to her bedchamber not in jealousy but in fear. He had dreamed of the city beyond the world's end, its broken towers in their cloaks of dirty ice, its ash and silence. She went with him, and they crept through the slumbering house. Then he spoke of the city—a harmless apparition that touched him not, yet he feared it as a fornicating priest feared hell. There death itself had perished, and yet drab eternity must go on. It could never be done with being.

Then he spoke of his time as a "sleeping Jew," when he'd lived another life in dreams. He was seventeen then, a green boy like any—but each night in sleep, he rode with conquering Alexander to his wars. It was the antique east, Macedonian Greece. He had worn a bronze cuirass, curiously formed in the likeness of a man's bare chest.

He had fought with a spear, and once thrust the spear into a man's open mouth; then in dying the man's jaws clenched and wrenched the weapon from his hand, and so in the melee the spear was lost. At Persepolis, where it rained unluckily on their battle, Will's horse had gone mired in bloody water; it came forth with four socks of blood and went queerly lame thereafter.

The dream was greater than a dream. It was a greater life than life. And in waking, Will doted and doubted his memory. He forgot the very names of the places about him. He forgot the day before and the name of the queen. He woke to find that England's church had put the pope out of doors, and the saints had different names. The bears had all been hunted from the forest, and the fringey storks were gone from the air. His father had become a swine-drunk bankrupt; his mother a greensick scold. How it seemed to him, he had dreamed a thousand evil changes on the world.

"So I was famed for my madness," he said. "But God be thanked, that hath now passed."

They had stopped in the gallery, before the tall windows. In the garden, a wind was blowing; the grasses flattened and sprang up again as if stroked by an invisible hand. They watched and felt the feelings of their kind, as if they read the starry page of night and found written there: *The wind goeth over it, and it is gone.*

She said, "And hadst thou a friend like me in Greece? Was there any there who dreamed?"

"Ay, the prince Alexander. He dreamed of Troy. There he had lived as the lady Cassandra, who warned of the city's fall, but none would hear." Then Will fell silent; a disconnected moment.

She thought he was marshaling his memories, but when he spoke again, he said, "And in the time of thy waking, hast thou such a friend?"

"Yes," she said and fell silent alike.

At last, he touched her arm. She sighed and said, "But thou dream'st of Greece no more?"

"No more. These ten years I am free."

"Free," she repeated. "And how wert thou freed?"

He laughed. "Ask me not. For here I have no other friend. I would keep thee here and be not alone."

Then he led her to the garden, to the shadow of the woods, and they fucked to the courteous hootings of owls; when she opened her eyes, a fox stood silhouetted on the starlit lawn. And the world was forgotten. She was fucking, she was real. They walked back barefoot through the damp grass, and she was shining with fear, with knowledge, with the blackness beyond the world's end.

By that time, their trysts were the gossip of the house. People smirked and relished the topsy-turvy: Emilia should have been Southampton's mistress; her being here otherwise made no sense. There were other lovers at Cowdray, but theirs was the chaos that inspirited the place; theirs was the May and the name of debauchery. If the household had a Dionysian air, it was theirs.

They were Southampton's. When Will wrote sonnets, they extolled Southampton's beauty, not Emilia's. She played her lute at Southampton's feet; she sewed Southampton a shirt of lawn. In the long spring days, they were figures in Southampton's idyll and only thought to please their youthful lord, so glorious and pure, like an animated jewel. The nights were sneaking infidelities, therefore, or else the days were lies. Or the other way around; it was never really clear. And the confusion spread to everyone there.

All the company soon was restless, sleepless, troubled by lascivious dreams. The scholar Florio began an affair with a laundress but pined for Lady Danvers, who became infatuated with the Earl of Rutland, who made cow eyes at the teenaged Lady Montague, who naively doted on her tosspot husband. Even the cat conceived an unrequited passion for Sir Harry Danvers. The maidservants all were in love with Southampton, in a rapt unhoping way, like a tribe of poets in love with the moon; one would have a fit of tears, then it spread to another and another, until all the house heaved with love's calamity. Mary, infected by the spirit of uproar, announced to Emilia that, when she was grown, she wanted to become a great lady's fool; she would ride a caparisoned cow and fall from a tree limb into a barrel, like Her Majesty's fool, Lucretia the Tumbler. Minor disorders broke out everywhere. A gentleman usher beat his wife, and she ran into the night and tore her hair. Stockings were found in the Neptune fountain. The horses neighed and kicked in their stalls.

Last of all, Southampton fell. It began with a letter from one of his friends that mentioned "your man Shakspear" and spoke of the very great fashion his poem *Venus and Adonis* was in at the Inns of Court: "No carouse can be drunk without a verse therefrom." Southampton called for a copy of the poem—which, like all Will wrote, was dedicated to him—and read it through one rainy day. He saw himself in the figure of the pure Adonis and confirmed with Will it was so; then he must ask everyone if he were truly held to be so virtuous. He read Adonis's lines out loud and laughed and insisted that everyone marvel at the wit and honeyed poetry.

The next day, Will wore the earl's livery badge, a jewel of a hawk in enamel and gold, which he continually, absently, hid with his hand. He ate at Southampton's table; he was given a suit of the earl's old clothes. He spent an hour closeted with Southampton in his rooms, while all the house around grew restive. The housemaids squabbled. Viscount Montague drank. The Earl of Rutland said that if the theaters must close, the players should be shut up in them, lest they spread infection through the countryside. Sir Harry Danvers said every theater was a stew, and the players were panders who grew rich from the whores that plied the crowd; then he absented himself to play billiards and chase away the cat with his cue. Even Lady Montague said it was queer so rough a man should be so favored; poesy was a fine thing, she knew, a great thing. Still, it was queer.

When Will and Southampton at last emerged, Southampton walked glidingly and seemed dazed. His eye kept returning to Emilia—and at supper, he spoke of the loves of poets and shepherds, their free and graceful loves. He wondered that lords should be so chaste while men and maids played wanton. Will spoke not at all. He had an air of thinking and thinking and ever coming back to the same bleak point.

That night, Mistress Bewley presented the company with a mask of Vice, horned, warped, and black, which she awarded to Montague for his drunken lechery. Montague neglectfully tossed it at Danvers, who instantly threw it in the fire. Southampton leapt and snatched the mask from the flames. He raised it, smoldering and smoking, then hastily dropped it and stamped it out.

"'Tis like a painted cloth," Mistress Bewley said, "of Virtue's triumph over Sin. My lord hath trampled Vice beneath his heel."

And when Emilia crept to the wood that night, it was Southampton waiting under the trees, his auburn tresses dull, diminished, by the overcast moon. He wore Will's cloak. He was grim, he was hesitant; she knew then, with an outraged, humiliated certainty, he was gay. She must fuck him so he didn't have to know he was gay. Will had sent him with the cloak because Will wasn't gay; and a man couldn't give his body that way, from generosity or pity, to appease a great lord. He couldn't be a man and a whore.

So Emilia did what a whore must do, like a fool that rides a caparisoned cow and leaps into a barrel for her lady's entertainment. She lay down, and the occasional stars seemed tangled or strangled among the groping boughs. An owl cried and she hated the owl. She wanted the owl to free her. She helped Southampton with her hand, and the moist, warm skin of his penis was a horror, even though it wasn't anything. Skin. He shut his eyes, and his face was a study of loathing. She shut her eyes. It didn't have to be real.

And in her mind, "Tom o' Bedlam" muttered, singing its refrain:

While I do sing, any food, any feeding
Feeding, drink, or clothing
Come, dame or maid, be not afraid
Poor Tom will injure nothing

When it was done, he left her without a word. She rose from the dirt alone. She walked back through the empty gardens, where the cat hunted silently, creeping under hedges and furling its tail. There was a chill, light rain, and she took off her cloak to feel it on her arms as she walked to the house. She was alone like a cat, like an owl, as if she walked, unobserved, out of her human life.

The next day, waking to it. An hour when she wept into the sheet, the sheet translucent and dim across her face, Mary's sleeping weight against her arm. Then at breakfast, Southampton appeared at her side and was suddenly a teenaged boy, unsexually pretty, at sea. He led her to the Great Hall and handed her a perfumed sonnet, written in the prickly workaday hand of a man who did much writing—Will's hand. It read:

> *In the old age blacke was not counted faire,*
> *Or if it were it bore not beautie's name:*
> *But now is blacke beauties successive heire . . .*

And she could see how Southampton must have woken Will in the night to talk about his exploit, needing a man to tell him it was right, that it was what men did. Will laughing in the necessary way and hunting out a pen and suggesting the poem. She forced herself to scan the page, feeling hot and faraway. The whole of it was a backhanded compliment, a teasing dig at her blackamoor looks. Will had known she would know who had written it. It was a wink behind Southampton's back.

And she remembered a time at her cousin's house at Horne, when she had played the virginal and Will sang a pitiful ballad about a maid, dishonored beneath a tree, who had hanged herself from that tree's limbs and thereafter the tree flowered all winter long. He sang it with such falsetto wails and grimaces he made all the company roar with laughter.

Watching her, Southampton was afraid. He was a child.

She said, "I am sorry, my lord. I like it not. It praises brownness, but is itself a painted poem. It hath not your accustomed purity."

The earl blushed. She turned by instinct and he took her arm. They walked back together, the rain trembling at the windows, the light gray and secretive. As they came to the stairs, he paused and said, "Yet I do love thee. That was not false. And if thou wilt have it, I would keep thee well."

And she went back to her chamber, where Mary waited jubilant—knowing about Southampton as servants know all hidden things. From triumph, Mary showed her new fool's tricks: turning somersaults in the rushes on the floor, chewing rushes like an ass. Then she sat obediently at Emilia's feet to have the wisps of hay picked out of her hair. Emilia said, "I would not part with thee, imp. Of all foolish things, I would not lose thee."

Mary said drowsily, "Why, how should we be parted?"

"Shalt thou not be a great lady's fool and go away?"

"Nay, I would be your fool and your maidservant both. So you will need no other girl."

Then Mary leaned back against Emilia's knees and shut her eyes. Emilia plucked more straws from her hair, and for a while Mary chattered about the unknown language God spoke to Adam in the garden, wondering if it were a tongue the beasts knew, so Adam might chide the wolf when it would not peaceably lie with the lamb. "*Blotona lona*," Mary said, guessing its sounds. "Which meaneth: Bite him not, wolf."

Emilia smiled at the crown of her head and petted her until Mary began to drowse. Then Emilia gazed into the fire and saw the flickering shape of the terrible city, its sky that flowed with dull aurorae, its ashes and dust that floated like breath. It was familiar and closer than before. It was a place. It was a day that would be. At the same time, she was cozy in the room, Mary dozing against her knees, the rain companionably bleak on the window. So went an hour of Emilia's last day; she stroked Mary's head and thought of giving her a jewel or a gown for a keepsake. But a servant fetched Emilia to the gallery before Mary woke, and so the whim was lost.

All that day it rained and darkened until it seemed a rain of shadows. The company gathered in the rain-lit gallery and played at fortune-telling with a volume of Virgil. All the same faces: fair Rutland and hatchet-faced Danvers; Montague, red and drunk and neglecting his diminutive, moonfaced wife; Florio who'd shaved his beard and had a look of tender, bald surprise; Will Shakespeare. And the Earl of Southampton, as pretty as a dragonfly, who now avoided Emilia's eye, who was absorbed by Will.

Will stood at Southampton's elbow. He avoided Emilia's eye. She was alone.

And it fell into a pattern, black and white. From the time she'd first met Will, she had been the tool of Master Shakespeare's greatness. She had helped him win Southampton's favor. She had warned him from his early death. She had puzzled and planned, but at the end of the day, Will had needed and she had done. Now she'd given her body like a worthless thing, so that Will might comfortably keep his patron. Will had needed and she had done.

And still the world burned. She looked at him and hated him and wished him in hell. He would not look at her.

The cover of the volume of Virgil was embroidered with South-ampton's arms. To find your fortune, you opened the book at random. The verse on which your finger landed told your future. They all knew Virgil well, and cheated by angling for a flattering passage; the gentlemen fished heroic feats for themselves and the ladies noble loves. Emilia fished, too, but her finger mistook. She opened to the fall of Troy.

She read the Latin with calm self-deprecation, then translated: "I saw all Ilium sink in flames, and Troy uprooted from its base."

The others smiled with a suppressed, pleased malice. There was something unstable in the air.

Emilia said, "Well, my lords, this undoes all. It seems the country must fall in flames whilst you perform your happy destinies. Belike, they shall be sooty triumphs."

"Nay, thy verse standeth not for us," said Danvers tetchily. "Each chooseth for himself."

Southampton said politely, "Mayhap, it presages that the Spanish will now sack London."

"The flames may stand for love," said Lady Montague. "Love is a woman's calamity."

Emilia looked back at the page of Virgil—and the neat lines of words changed subtly. Blurred. They became a familiar broken skyline, a cinder skyline with no sky. And the static in her head. It was a noise that wasn't noise. For a moment she was in the blackened city, with the husks of dead beetles that had gathered in drifts, with the ice and eternal time. The world's end.

When the room came back, no time had passed, but she was saying in a harsh, frail voice, "Nay, I know it. It tells of the end of days."

Will flinched and the others frowned. Danvers said coldly, "It does not."

"May it not?" said Lady Montague fearfully.

"It does," said Emilia (and her voice rang hollow), "for is it not foretold in scripture: 'Lo, there was a great earthquake, and the sun was as black as sackcloth of hair, and the moon like blood. And the stars of heaven fell unto the earth, and heaven departed away, as a scroll when it is rolled.'" She added, "I have seen it in dreams. As I know, another here has seen it also." She looked frankly at Will. His face was white.

"Yet it does not," said Danvers.

"Madam," said Florio. "I pray you will spare us these anabaptistical heresies of the murder of creation. 'Tis a poor recreation for a wet day."

Lady Montague said, "But Mistress Lanier speaks truly. For England is now much troubled with plague. In Revelation, doth God not send a pestilence?"

"'Tis not the first plague in England," said Florio. "'To be sure, it is a grievous thing, but no prodigy."

"And we are well here, far from the city's infectious airs," said Rutland. "If there be a plague, we scarcely know."

"Nay, but here we are plagued by a walking infection that pursueth us to our very beds," said Danvers.

An uncomfortable silence fell. Some glanced surreptitiously at Emilia.

Rutland said helpfully, "He means the cat."

All the company laughed, already very far away. Will was watching Emilia, he was white. The windows seethed and moved with rainlight. Everything unpleasantly alive. A deep well. And she said straight to Will, with an edge of hysteria, "Yet there shall be such a city, and its people destroyed. There shall be Sodom, and all that lives must burn."

Will turned abruptly and strode from the room. The others startled and straightened, like trees shocked upright by a gust of wind. Southampton rose abruptly and went out after Will—and the world wheeled. It seemed that a breeze wafted Southampton out and flung the door shut. It blew out the light and the scene rolled up like a scroll. It dropped, like a great heart skipping a beat

She and Will were ahorse in a chill gray morning. Alone: and for the first time, Emilia didn't know where she was. The weeds growing in the road looked unnaturally green beneath the lightless sky. Small grasshoppers sprang from beneath the hooves of the horses, flew up in a pattern like splashing. She knew they had left Cowdray, but she didn't know why.

And it skidded through a time without any detail: the grasshoppers splashing and the green in the road, something happening just out of sight. They'd stopped. It was a wood. Will led her as Emilia was accustomed to be led. It was the cloak and the shapes of twigs underneath, their angles beneath her back. She drifted in and out and made the cries women make.

And stopped. It was real: his sweat on her sweat, the trembling cold where her leg was bare. He shifted his weight from her and left her bright, bare cunt in the air. He sighed and he was talking, as any lover might. He was telling her about his life.

He said, in the days of his youthful dreaming, he had thought his dreams might deliver mankind. But he dreamed and woke, and all things flowed perversely and lost their sense and beauty. There was no thing that was not made worse. If a woman baked a pie and put it up for the night, Will could dream it bad by morning. His own memories were made false; his learning turned to a vaporous madness. "'Tis said that a bat, if he be struck by a leaf, will lose all his remembrance. So it was for me; life melted in a sleep. My very dreams passed in a sleep at last, and Alexander appeared to me no more.

"All that lasted were the creatures of mine own mind, the fools and shrews and sad kings of my fancy. What I had written on air was more lasting than stone, than men and their kingdoms, than men's gods. And I swear, it is of a more fearful greatness than all the red spears of the Grecian host, and I more great than Alexander for its making.

"So, madam, I would that my plays might prosper. Thou wilt say it matters not; we will all be ash. But they are all I have seen to love."

Emilia tried to think. It was an effort like swimming against the tide of the world. Then Will's eyes met hers, and she grasped it. She said, "And had Alexander such a wish?"

"Belike," said Will. "For he saw the ashes of Troy, and of the world. Yet he would conquer Asia as a child will play. He reached for his greatness like a toy."

"And used thee for his greatness?"

Will's mouth narrowed. "Ay, he made the little matter serve the great. He was no Antony, that would lose a realm for love."

"Yet the realm must burn. The world must burn."

Then it seemed Will made an effort but said nothing.

"Prithee," she said, and her breath came short. "If we may by any means prevent this evil—"

But Will had turned away. He was straightening his clothes. And he said he now remembered Alexander but poorly. Indeed, he wondered if any man remembered all he claimed, of dreams or waking. "One who seeks to remember, 'tis as if a man sailed upon the sea and commanded it to be still."

"And the wind goeth over it," she said hollowly. "The place thereof shall know it no more."

"Art thou well, my lady? Shall we ride on?"

"Nay, but tell me whither we go. My memory plays me false. It is as thou sayest; it is water."

He told her and she listened and stared like a silent bird. She was trying to breathe. She was afraid. She saw the horses tethered, their brown glowing silhouettes, broken and crossed by the lightless silhouettes of branches. Against the white sun. A black blink of the eyes.

They were riding again, in a white light like a blank page. Surrey, that was where they were going. Horne, Surrey. They'd excused themselves from Cowdray by telling Southampton she wanted her baby. They were going to her cousin Andrea Bassano—Will a friend of the cousin, a companion for the road. She remembered it now, and it made plain sense.

But for a moment she felt she, too, was a dream; that it was Will who had dreamed this world from air. He had sung their journey and told their days. He had written her out of bed and down the stairs in the soft black nights. She had no world. She was free to be a fool. This was nothing but a soap bubble Will had blown. He would burst it with his fingers and she would be free.

But no, he knew nothing. He was nothing: just a man.

It grew dark. She couldn't breathe. They rode faster and faster. "Tom o'Bedlam" played, faster and faster, in her head. The night drew in and they were galloping. The clouds raced overhead, blue and black.

And the neat brick manor showed now on the hill, its muddy yard spread before its door. The horses trotted. It was ordinary now. They stopped in the yard. The swing and fall of dismounting, it was flying in all directions. It held.

Then her cousin Andrea and the greetings that passed in a glare, in a bloom of noise. She walked through the house, her boots thudding, squeaking, past where she'd first seen Will, where he'd appeared in his body and broken her life. Her baby was crying. The clucking of the nurse was like a metronome in its wavering scream. Will wasn't behind her. It was almost gone. Emilia opened the workshop door.

There were the sinuous, sinister shapes of half-made shawms and viols, the chisels on shelves and the dull, dumb light. The painted bassinet was there, the nurse perched on a sawhorse beside it.

Emilia came forward and the baby was a dream. It wiggled unnaturally, batting its false flat arms. The world went black.

Kate woke in a high, exposed place. A wind was blowing with a stench of burning, uncanny and vertiginous beneath the blue sky. It was New York. Sabine's rooftop. She knew it by its shape. She tried to sit up and met a heavy resistance, at once unfamiliar and well-known. Her belly woke, taut and twitching and enormous. Her back twinged. She was pregnant.

On the horizon, there was a bloom of smoke that dwarfed the city beneath. It was beautiful, cat-gray smoke, but the air had a penetrating stink like a mattress fire. A dull pall covered the whole southern sky. The central plume seemed to loom at her precipitously, although she stared and stared and it remained at the same airy distance.

But it wasn't the apocalyptic city. It lived. There was still the mutter of traffic below. All the buildings she saw were whole. She hadn't failed—or if she had failed, she wasn't living in the failed world yet.

It took her some time to get to her feet. Going down the stairs, she had to lean on the banister; the baby was kicking and her back was in a cramp. The top floor of the apartment was silent and untenanted: the beds stripped to the mattresses, the windows bare. Kate caught the faint jabber of a television set. She followed it to the floor below.

In the living room she found Sabine and Ben and Martin and Martin's ex-boyfriend, James. They were all hunched forward toward the TV. On the screen, there was a scene of wreckage and smoke and a reporter talking rapidly, intently. Then it cut to an image of a skyscraper, steely, gray, and anonymous; a little airplane ran into its flank with a puff of fire.

There was a war going on in this world, Kate guessed, a war in which airplanes were used as weapons. The skyscraper seemed to be a major development, but she couldn't tell how long the war had gone on. She didn't know if she should already know about the skyscraper. She couldn't guess what a normal person would say.

At last she said, "I just woke up. Has anything important happened?"

19

Ben had arrived at work that morning knowing nothing. It was Midtown and the towers hadn't fallen yet. When he got out of the train, the sky was blue. He came into the office and found everyone gathered round a television set, their backs tense, and a man saying nervously, "We ought to get out of here. We're sitting ducks here."

First, Ben thought something had happened to ExxonMobil. Then people noticed him and manically explained, talking over each other, contradicting each other. On the television, planes flew into the towers, again and again, from different angles. Tiny figures leapt and dropped from windows. Ben's body understood and was high on fear, sweating and needing to punch something, while his mind kept insisting it couldn't really be as serious as it seemed. Someone else straggled in late and, as Ben joined in the manic explanations, behind his back, the news reports changed. The Pentagon had been attacked. After that, he was afraid to look away from the TV.

Then it seemed to go on a long time, with all of them stalled, in a static hysteria, pacing to the window where they couldn't see anything, jabbering and hushing each other and jabbering. A few people kept trying to make phone calls, again and again, until their repetitive poking at their phones looked like an OCD ritual. Some people were holding hands, and it made Ben feel left out, although he'd only been working there a couple of months. He joined a group that was trying to guess who the attackers were. One man said a Palestinian group had claimed responsibility. Another said they'd *disclaimed* responsibility. Ben's head of PR said in an overbearing tone that Osama bin Laden's people had bombed the World Trade Center before. A marketing woman said, "Lightning strikes twice?" and laughed shrilly, covering her mouth. Ben said, trying to participate: "I think they're called al Qaeda," and everyone looked at him, then looked away. There was an awkward pause in which Ben was aware of looking vaguely Middle Eastern; it was the qualm he always had, approaching airport security. He added, "I don't know if I'm pronouncing it right."

At that moment, on the TV, the South Tower fell. They all took a step back and covered their faces. The tower crumbled silently and turned into a giant pillar of smoke, while the anchorman incongruously calmly stated that there had been a horrific explosion. They swore and hushed each other and swore; one man threw his cell phone into a wall. Then a subtle odd chill: in the office's Thirty-Fourth Street windows, the sky had blurred and dimmed, although the windows on Madison showed the same blue day. Ben felt sick but weirdly relieved, thinking, *Now the other tower has to fall, and that's it.*

After that, people began to disperse. Ben left with the second wave and couldn't help noticing he was left out when people hugged each other. Well, he was new there. He hadn't made friends yet. He didn't have to take it personally.

But it was one of the reasons, when he found himself alone in the strange bright street, he ran uptown to Kate.

He hadn't seen Kate in the weeks since the breakup. The psychiatrist had said to give Kate space, and she was staying with Sabine, she was being looked after. He'd had no real excuse. But now the rules were suspended. You were clearly going to run to your emotional center. Even if it shouldn't be your emotional center, you would have to run to it, and you couldn't be judged. He'd only been to Sabine's place twice, but the address was unforgettable: 86 East Eighty-Sixth, the penthouse floor. It felt effortless like something he'd already done.

So, his satchel in his arms and the simple athletic problem of running that way, the liberating feeling of running for a reason, dodging people and cars and it felt superhuman. Once, a cluster of women broke up and gaped at Ben as he passed, thinking (Ben imagined) he was a terrorist fleeing from the scene of the crime, that the satchel in his arms was a bomb. Then he was filled with a glorious hatred of everyone, and an exalted love. Ben was one of them, American, and running on a rescue mission and still the fools wanted to hunt him down. And Kate was Iranian—half-Iranian—she could fall under suspicion too. He was transported by endorphins and the awe of the day to a mythic lunacy: he would save her, they would swim across the Hudson to safety (and any petty shit like schizophrenia forgotten) and he imagined them standing on the river's far shore, looking back to see New York City falling in a sky-eating tumult of smoke and flame and Ben holding sobbing Kate and saying, "It's all right, baby. I've got you."

So he ran through the streets while sirens cut into the sky from all directions, and he ran from the sirens and he just ran. Sometimes he couldn't bear it. He felt sick; he remembered the little people falling from the towers, and he wanted to collapse in a doorway. But it wasn't that far. He was in good shape. Sooner than he even wanted to, he got to Eighty-Sixth Street. Then it was two short blocks from the park. He sprinted through the last intersection. Brakes screeched, and Ben laughed breathlessly, high on it, not even looking back at the furious horns.

Then he saw Sabine's building and slowed down gratefully, happy for the first time in weeks, and was coming up the steps when it struck him like an anvil that Sabine worked at the World Trade Center. He tripped on the step, he almost fell. His head went funny. He wheeled back as if he could see downtown and spot Sabine in the wreckage and know.

Then it all cleared like cold clear water: Sabine didn't work in one of the towers. Credit Suisse was in a short, uninteresting building: 5 World Trade. It would have been evacuated, certainly evacuated, and she must be safe.

Still he couldn't calm himself. He kept seeing the South Tower falling and Sabine dropping, crushed, in that gargantuan calamity. He saw the little people leaping out of the windows. He saw himself running from the scene of the crime.

But he walked into the foyer, and there was Sabine. She was standing by the elevators with a tall man Ben didn't know. They were both wearing business suits, coated head to toe in dust and detritus, in a way Ben had only seen in movies where the heroes fly a biplane through a chicken coop and then through a construction site and then the plane crashes and they stagger from the wreckage with every form of excrescence clinging to them. They were talking to the doorman, who was wringing his hands and offering help in—Ben realized with a rush of foolish gratitude—an Indian accent.

Sabine noticed Ben and said, "No way. You're fucking kidding me. Ben?"

Ben walked up, light-headed, and explained why he was there, and Sabine said, "Yeah, yeah. Kate's upstairs." Then Sabine and the man in the business suit (a Credit Suisse guy named Ian who was British and stared at Ben in a glassy, hilarious way that was probably shock) explained how they'd been evacuated from their office as soon as the first plane hit, but then they stood rubbernecking in the street like assholes until the whole fucking tower fell down on their heads. Then they were running with shit pinging off their faces and the air just white, and they clambered underneath cars and ran again and clambered underneath other cars. They couldn't fucking breathe. A van was crushed right next to them. They thought they were going to die.

"So we've learned a valuable lesson," said Ian, and he and Sabine laughed until tears came to their eyes. Ben grinned along with them, thinking: *Shock.*

When they'd calmed down, he said, "You weren't injured?"

"Fuck, yeah, I was injured." Sabine held up her fist, which was patterned all over with blood.

"She cut her palm open diving under a car," said Ian. "It was probably just broken glass. But it's a hideous gash."

"We got a ride uptown in an ice-cream truck," Sabine said. "The guy dropped us at Mount Sinai, but my cut hand wasn't a real big priority today. I'm going to call the veterinarian."

The doorman said, "You must put alcohol on it. You do not want septicemia."

"Thanks, Mom," said Sabine.

Then the elevator opened. Sabine and Ian and Ben got in, and when the door closed and it shifted upward, Ian cringed back against the elevator wall and grimaced and shut his eyes.

Sabine said to Ben, "Ian's all fucked up. He had friends in the towers, on the upper floors. We're pretty sure they're dead."

Ian said with his eyes still shut, "Sabine's being my family today. Which is very fucking much appreciated."

"Anyway," Sabine said, "tall buildings."

"Never mind," Ian said. "You have to get right back up on the horse."

Ben leaned against the elevator wall as if in sympathy. Then, as if in sympathy, he was afraid. The elevator seemed to vibrate more than it should. He was adrenal and sweaty. He was conscious that he smelled, though he guessed Sabine and Ian smelled, too, and it wasn't important today.

The elevator opened. They all stumbled out. Sabine unlocked the door, and Ian pushed in past her, saying, "Going to take a shower." Sabine went straight to the landline phone. Ben wandered haplessly down the hall toward the sound of a television set. At first he couldn't figure out where the noise was coming from; he opened a door and found a coat closet compactly stuffed with coats. Then the next door was the living room: Martin and Martin's ex-boyfriend, James, were there on the living room couch in pajamas. They were watching the news and crying.

Ben said, "Hey. Are you okay?"

Martin got up without saying anything, came immediately to Ben, and hugged him. Even though Ben didn't like hugging men, he felt a flood of relief, as if he'd been welcomed back into the fold. He hugged Martin back; he felt as if he could have cried. Over Martin's shoulder, he watched the TV, which was reporting that a fourth plane had crashed in a field in Pennsylvania. Ben had a fleeting fantasy in which he was a hijacker convincing the other hijackers to land the plane safely and give themselves up. He was stuck in it until it concluded successfully; then he sighed and detached himself from Martin without any conscious intention. Martin looked back at the TV and said, "We can't stop watching. It's so fucking awful."

"Are you staying here?" Ben said.

James said, "Martin's staying here to make the transition from rehab. I'm not staying here."

"James came over to make sure I don't drink." Martin laughed. "I think that's what the whole country is most concerned with today."

"Nevertheless," said James.

Sabine came in and said, "The vet's coming over in an hour and bringing pet sedatives, if anyone wants pet sedatives." Then she said to Martin, "Not you."

"Oh, I know," said Martin with a martyred air.

They all turned back to the TV. There was an update on the whereabouts of President Bush, and Ben compulsively listened even though he didn't care about Bush. Then the now familiar clip of a plane flying directly, undramatically into a tower, the outsize explosion of orange flame. Ben found himself watching intently as if some crucial clue might be revealed that only he would notice. He was staring that way, in a pinpoint daze, when Kate's voice said behind him, "I just woke up. Has anything important happened?"

Ben whirled around. Kate was squinting at them with her provisional face, the face she always had now when she woke up. In the weeks since he'd seen her, she'd gone from pleasantly rounded to awkwardly pregnant. Her face was puffy, her hair unwashed. She wasn't looking at Ben.

So he stared at her while James and Martin explained, talking over each other and getting choked up. Kate's eyes became more complex, more fraught. She had begun to scowl and bite her lip when Sabine said, "Kate, just don't."

Kate flinched and looked guiltily at Sabine. Her eyes immediately filled with tears.

"I mean it," Sabine said. "Don't get started. This is nothing to do with you."

Kate shook her head and hastily wiped her eyes. She was trembling.

"I'm serious," Sabine said. "I don't have the energy, so please just believe me: *you* didn't do this."

Then Ben got it. He said, "Kate, how could you have done this? How could terrorists be your fault?"

"Oh, you know." Kate made an indeterminate gesture.

"Because you fell asleep?" Ben said. "Because you had a dream?"

"It's okay," Kate said. "I know I'm being crazy."

Martin said in a studiedly calm tone, "Just don't focus on it. Label it as a mad thought and try to distract yourself."

Kate said, "I should call my parents. They're downtown, they could be—"

"No," said Sabine. "We're *not* doing the parents thing. Kate, do you see what's happened today? Do you see how this isn't about you?"

"I'll talk to her," Ben said to Sabine.

"Talk to me about what?" Kate's voice cracked. "Are my parents dead?"

James flinched, and Martin put a hand on James's shoulder.

"They're not dead," Ben said hastily. "It's fine."

Sabine said to Ben, "Tell her in the other room. I don't want Ian walking in. He's got enough to deal with today. It's just a bad fucking time."

The other room turned out to be a library, complete with rolling ladder and Chesterfield armchairs and green-shaded lamps; the sort of library (Ben thought) where you expected to find Captain Nemo. He'd had to tell Kate about her parents before, and he'd tried different ways of telling her, but there was no good way. This time he just said plainly, "Do you remember that your parents split up?"

"No, I don't remember that." Kate took a deep sharp breath. "When did that happen?"

"A long time ago. When you were two. And your mother isn't downtown. She lives in Ohio, so you don't have to worry."

"Ohio." Kate laughed. "I can't imagine her in Ohio. And my father?"

"We don't know where your father is now. The last time your mother heard from him, he was living in Berlin. But Kate, you don't know him. You shouldn't imagine the person you remember is your father. That's what the psychiatrist said."

She was nodding as if to reassure him she was absorbing this. "And my brother? Petey?"

"You don't have a brother." Then Ben added inanely, "It's okay."

Kate stopped nodding and turned away. She went to an African drum in the corner and laid her hand on its skin. "I don't see how this could happen. I'm not saying you're lying."

"It didn't happen, exactly. All that's happening is that your memory isn't reliable."

She said in a strained voice, "But you met my parents. We went to their apartment together."

"I know you have a memory of me meeting them. I'm sorry, it's not real."

"No, you used to go and see them without me." She flinched and laughed shortly. "Oh, I see. That's just a memory of mine. It's as if we're coming from different pasts. In your past, you never met my parents."

"Try not to think in terms of different pasts. This is just something your brain does when you're asleep. It manufactures false memories. It's as if you haven't fully woken from a dream, and the dream people still feel real."

"My father is not a dream person."

"Okay. But the psychiatrist thinks—"

"Ben. Could you give me a minute?"

"Sure."

Kate spread her hand on the skin of the drum, as if she were drawing strength from it. She stared at nothing. Ben assumed she was processing the loss of her father (whom she'd never really known) and her brother (who had never existed). The other times this had happened, Ben had felt it, as he might if she'd lost a real father and brother he'd never met. This time, it was hard to engage. He kept wanting to go back and check the TV. Something might have happened, and he was stuck here, talking Kate through her delusions again. Of course Kate mattered, but in this context, it felt Sisyphean and trivial. He didn't know what he'd expected when he'd come here.

At last, she said, still staring at the drum, "Can I check something with you?"

"Of course."

"I'm sorry, I know I should know this. But is this yours?"

At first he thought she meant the drum; but she turned to him and touched her pregnant belly.

Ben smiled. "No. It isn't mine. It's Martin's."

"Martin's!" Kate laughed breathlessly. "He's paying me?"

"He wanted to pay you, but you said no."

"I did? Did he know I was crazy?"

"No. We didn't know you were sick then."

"He should have known I was crazy when I didn't take the money."

Ben laughed, but now Kate didn't laugh. She took her hand off her belly and placed it by the other hand on the drum. The pregnancy had spoiled her posture, once so weightless it had seemed a kind of physical candor, and now Ben realized she was using the drum to lean.

"He'd still pay you if you asked," said Ben. "He feels responsible. The doctors say the hormones might have triggered the illness."

"The insanity, you mean," Kate said. "Poor Martin. He always has a crazy woman having his child. Do you think he'll abandon it?"

"The baby? Of course he won't abandon it. He's buying a house."

Kate laughed and shook her head, still looking at the drum. "A house."

"It isn't just the house. He quit drinking. He takes it very seriously."

"Well, it's nice I did that for Martin, but I'd rather it was yours. Though I guess . . . we've broken up?"

"Yes." Then he added, though he didn't believe it, and he hated himself for his cowardice, "It could be temporary."

"Oh, shit. Because I'm going to get better?"

She looked back at him then, her black eyes incandescent with pain. He couldn't stand it. He went to her and took her in his arms. Her belly made the hug an awkward shape; he had to hunch to embrace her properly. She leaned on him and didn't cry but went quiescent in a manner that suggested tears.

And out of nowhere, Ben was weak with love. His body was euphoric and he wanted to kiss her. It was an energy that filled him and insisted he could save her. He felt powerful; he felt he was a wonderful person; he would do whatever it took. It was wrong and Ben was afraid of it. He tried to think about what was going on on TV.

Then Kate detached herself subtly. She said, "Could I get a minute alone?"

"Sure."

He let her go too quickly; it was clear he wanted to get away from her. But Kate had turned obliviously back to the drum. She laid her hand back on its skin.

When he got back to the living room, Sabine was on the couch with Martin and James, staring vacantly at the TV. She had showered and now wore a cashmere bathrobe, tailored for a man; Kate had an identical bathrobe, which Ben now realized must have come from Sabine. With her wet hair, Sabine looked scrawny and ill. She held her injured fist, now closed on a washcloth, stiffly at her chest. Ben could still hear a shower, and he almost told Sabine she'd left it running. But of course there was more than one bathroom here. The shower still running was Ian's; he presumably was stuck in the flow of water, still scrubbing at what might be his own friends' remains.

On the television, Bush was making a speech. Ben wondered if Kate knew Bush was president. He tried to imagine seeing Bush as president for the first time, but his mind drifted off. He imagined being in a tower when the plane hit. He imagined being in the plane.

Then Sabine said, in a constrained, nice voice, "Ben, could you take Kate tonight?"

"Take Kate? How?"

Martin said, "We were thinking she could stay with you, just while Ian's here."

"We're broken up," said Ben automatically.

"Ian needs a safe place," said Sabine. "If Kate's here, it's all going to be about Kate."

"We love Kate," Martin said. "But if you could take her for just one day."

"Ian doesn't know a lot of people in New York, and half of them died today," said Sabine.

Ben said, before he could stop himself, "Sabine, I thought you hated the people at Credit Suisse. I mean, I never heard of this Ian."

"You're kidding me," Sabine said. "*That's* the issue? I talk shit about people, that's important today?"

At that moment, Ian walked in. He was wearing a bathrobe identical to Sabine's, looking similarly wet and afflicted. He said, "Am I being discussed?"

Sabine looked at Ben and grimaced in annoyance.

Ben said, "It's not about you. Sabine wants me to take my girlfriend home with me. But we just broke up."

"She creates too much drama," said Sabine. "And Ben came here to see her, so I don't see the problem."

"I was certain I heard my name," said Ian.

"Look, you need some peace and quiet," said Sabine. "You're a human and you need some peace and quiet."

"Oh, great," said Ian. "It's a psychiatric conference. You're determining my course of treatment."

Sabine said, "Trust me, you are not the psychiatric case here."

"You're really not," said Martin.

Then Sabine and Martin explained Kate's madness: how Kate thought she could travel in time, and walked around with a face like Munch's *The Scream,* apologizing for the state of the world, which she thought she should have fixed in the sixteenth century. She thought she had a brother and a father, so every morning, she had to be told she didn't, and every fucking time she was devastated. They'd tried pretending she did have a father and brother, but she always tried to call her father on the phone; she was unusually close to her nonexistent father. Kate was also just a really shitty roommate; she would never buy stuff like toilet paper, and when challenged on the toilet paper issue, she would claim she *had* bought toilet paper, but she'd traveled in her sleep to a different timeline in which she hadn't bought toilet paper. Then she would cry. And it obviously wasn't about the toilet paper, but still there had to be a bottom line.

At the end, Ian shrugged and said, "Half my family's mad. My uncle just had to be rescued from a tree by the fire department."

"No, Sabine's right," said Martin. "It doesn't sound that dreadful, but it's really distressing. We have to keep an eye on her at all times. And, if we hadn't mentioned, she's eight months pregnant."

"My uncle thinks angels talk to him," said Ian. "But he has to get up in a tree to hear it. Then he won't come down, and he gets dehydrated and faints. He's sixty."

Kate came in then and everyone turned to her with false smiles. She held up a copy of *King Lear.* "Does anyone know this writer?"

Sabine said in a weary voice. "Yes, Kate, we know who Shakespeare is."

"So he's very well known?" said Kate.

"Kate, we do this all the time," said Sabine. "You ask us if we know who Shakespeare is, and then we have to explain Shakespeare. Could we please not do that today?"

Kate was silent for a moment. Ben was thinking how to ask her to come home with him and struggling with the petulant feeling that it was unfair. Even though Sabine was more traumatized today, Ben was more traumatized by Kate specifically. But he'd come here, of course. He'd walked right into the trap.

Kate nodded at the television set. "I was thinking I might be able to fix this."

"Oh, Kate," said Martin.

"What's this now?" said Ian. "Does she think she's God now?"

"It's the time travel thing," Sabine said. "Kate thinks she'll go into the past and prevent this horrible dystopia from becoming a reality. Then we'll all live in Kate's world, where everyone lives rent-free and there's fucking world peace."

"To be fair," said Martin, "the world does feel a tad dystopian today."

"Don't encourage it," Sabine said. "Last time it ended with her trying to jump out a window so she couldn't make the world any worse. And today I would let her fucking do it. I don't have the strength."

"I wasn't thinking of killing myself," said Kate. "I was thinking of killing him." She held up the book.

"King Lear?" said Ian.

Sabine said, "She means Shakespeare. She thinks she's Shakespeare's girlfriend."

James laughed, then covered his mouth and muttered, "Sorry."

"It's okay to laugh," said Kate. "It was just so weird when I saw all his books. In my world, he never wrote all this. And then I thought—I know this is a crazy person thing—I thought his writing must have ruined things somehow, so maybe he *should* die young. And if I think about it, most of what I've done in the dreams is making sure he lives and becomes successful. So I had this idea we'd have a vote about killing him, and then it wouldn't all be my decision. I'm sorry if I've said all this before."

Before Sabine could answer, Ian said, "Well, what is your other world like? We might not want to live in it."

"I don't know," said Kate. But then she thought and answered, "People talked to each other in the street."

"Sounds dreadful," Ian said. "Put me down as a no."

"No," said Kate, "It was good, because everyone knew everyone else in the neighborhood. If you were broke, someone would always help you out. You could find a spare room if you had nowhere to stay."

"*My* spare room," said Sabine. "I mean, what if you're an asshole? Do I still have to have you living with me?"

"You have assholes living with you *now*," said Martin.

They started to actually discuss whether Kate's world was worth killing Shakespeare for. The absurdity was a welcome distraction, though Ben kept thinking it was bad for Kate. At least the issue of Ben taking Kate away was shelved, since Ian seemed to like having Kate there; Ian even took it upon himself to explain Shakespeare to her, and expanded on the subject of Shakespeare's greatness while Kate looked bemused and faintly resistant. At last she said, "He wasn't very good to me," and Ian said, "No man is a hero to his valet."

Then Kate told a story from her world, about the election of President Chen, the first Green president, and how there was an impromptu parade up Broadway, and the mayor was in it in a crazy red ball gown, sitting in an armchair on a makeshift float her staff were pulling with ropes, and people would get up on the float and dance with her; a friend of Sabine's was in the band that followed it—a woman who didn't exist in this world, or perhaps had not been able to escape from Afghanistan, the country of her birth that was, in Kate's world, best known as a place where apples were grown, a place that the horn player, Safya, only left because she'd fallen in love.

Kate's eyes were matter-of-fact, remembering; it was Sabine who got emotional, white-faced, so upset it wasn't clear if she was angry or sad. Kate noticed and said, "I know this is crazy. Sorry, I know you don't think this is real."

Martin said, "You do have a sweet imagination, Katie."

Sabine said, "Fine, kill Shakespeare. Do it. But can we please not talk about utopia today?"

After that, the conversation drifted back to the attacks, and they started to debate whether there would be a war. Ian said there'd better be a war, and belligerently talked about an eye for an eye, and the only language these people understood. The others gently demurred, until Sabine said they didn't have to be so nice, because Ian wasn't just bereaved, he was a neocon. Then they argued for real, which Ian seemed to appreciate; he cheerfully sneered about bleeding-heart liberals and said, "Tell me one place that isn't a make-believe world where all that Kumbaya crap works. And don't say Sweden or I'll take a shit right here on the floor." Then he launched into a rant about left-wing hypocrisy and how the really charitable people were conservatives, and talked about the month he'd spent in a trailer-trash region of Idaho, doing an internship for a rural entrepreneurship trust, and in that town—all redneck Republicans—there were two soup kitchens and everyone tithed ten percent of their income to charity, and if someone had an Alzheimer's grandma, she lived in the trailer with the rest of the family and their seven rescue dogs, until Sabine couldn't stand it and said, "You *hated* those people."

Everyone laughed, and Ian said, grinning, "They did talk rather a lot about Jesus. And thought I was gay because I had an English accent."

"Oh, how awful for you," James said.

"You hated them," Sabine said. "You called them troglodytes and said they shouldn't have the vote."

"They *were* troglodytes," said Ian. "And they voted for Bush, so I think it's very fair-minded of me to say they shouldn't have the vote."

Kate asked who Bush was, and everyone groaned. Ben took Kate's hand and whispered the answer in her ear, and she leaned against his shoulder and cried a little bit. For a while Ben and Kate were whispering about Bush and Gore and her imaginary brother and father, while the others peaceably argued and watched TV and argued.

At last, Sabine turned off the TV and opened some twenty-year-old Scotch her uncle had been given by Mobutu, so Sabine got to talk about Mobutu's atrocities; it put the destruction of the towers in perspective. The veterinarian arrived and gave Sabine five stitches. The veterinarian's husband had come with her and brought a wheelie suitcase of vintage guns, "in case it all kicks off." They all, except Martin, took pet sedatives. They all, including Martin, sat with guns on their laps and inspected the bullets with a certain sad prurience but, after some discussion, didn't load the guns. They talked about Martin's baby, sometimes directly addressing Kate's stomach. They turned the TV back on, but there was no real news; they scoffed and turned it off. Then, frustrated by their helplessness, they went out to donate blood, and the line was two blocks long and they were woozy from Scotch and pet sedatives, so Sabine called a caterer and ordered sandwiches for everyone in the donation line. Then the whole line was turned away: too much. So they went and walked around the reservoir in Central Park, all breathing self-consciously, commenting on the possibly imaginary taste of smoke, and they felt consumptive and tragic as the sun went down and the buildings lit up above the trees in pale bright colors, like a coral reef glowing with bioluminescence or an alien city on a long-dead planet where humans couldn't breathe the air.

20

It recommenced in Southampton's barge, a slender ornament of teal and gold, which rocked on the water and trailed perfume: a fit conveyance to the land of dreams. The handles of the oars themselves were prettily painted. The oarsmen's doublets matched the boat. Southampton sat on a velvet chair with rose petals strewn about his feet. At the bow of the boat, a recorder consort perched on a bench and played a watery, delicate tune to the beat of the splashing oars. Laden boats came and went from the water stairs of the nobles' houses on the northern shore.

Emilia's husband, Lanier, sat among the pipers. Above his recorder, his brown eyes followed Southampton's hand as it stroked Emilia's hair—Master Lanier a good-looking man, but unremarkable: the sort of man whose pretty looks are noticed and forgotten; who marries a nobleman's whore for her fortune and spends it in a year on horses and shoes. Not only a cuckold, but (Emilia now knew) a pander to his own wife. A pleasant laughing fellow, but without her infidelities, no lord would want him; it would be a poor life.

So the recorder consort had been hired by the intercession of Emilia—that was his pander's pay—and so Southampton was free to familiarly lay a hand on her bare shoulder, while she rested her chin on his knee and indulged a facile melancholy; she gazed at the dappling spoons of light on the water and thought of weeping black tears from her black eyes. There was the dagger at her waist, a whore's trinket with an ornamental hilt that could nonetheless kill. She should know what she meant to do, but she didn't. She knew she was going to Will.

Many years had passed here since she last woke. Ten years—a gap that felt punitive, ominous, a part of the things that had now gone wrong. Emilia was heavier and older; Southampton a grown, broad-chested man with a beard. It took her time to remember and to know how it was—that they were now old friends in the manner of friends who were once unsatisfactory lovers; that she'd been his mistress, then the confidante who covered for his trysts with men. She had lain with him in a chaste, sleepy nudity and told him tales of a later, better time, where the lion lieth down with the lion, where men may love if God so made them. When Southampton slept, she had crept from his side. She had cried at the window, writing letters, and the day dawned as she fell heavily asleep. A strange affair, a heady error of the young; a force that was spent and had become a peaceful medium for outings on the river. For trips like this, to the theater at Southwark.

With them today were three redheaded teenage girls who clutched each other and laughed when the barge rocked, nudging against the water stairs. They were the daughters of Harry Percy, being taken to their first London play. They held hands in a line as they climbed the bank and picked their way through the Southwark mud; they wrinkled their noses at the smell from the bear pits. It was still half a dream, Emilia still woozy as she followed their skirts up the theater's stairs.

They took their seats on the stage itself, among the fashionable theater lovers and poseurs. A box keeper fetched the multifarious baskets of their picnic and was given a coin. The littlest Percy sat on the floor among the rushes; she hated a stool above all things, she said, while her sisters rolled their eyes. The theater was new and painted every bright color; red and green and blue and gold; its wooden pillars had been painted to resemble marble. Whatever wasn't painted was carved, and every flat surface was filled with the biblical pictures one saw in inns: Daniel flanked by grinning lions, Susannah interrupted at her bath, Dives tormented by long-snouted demons. It was open to the sky above. Then the noisy sea of heads, in the galleries and the pit below, all shoving and shouting to be heard over others' shouts. Peddlers elbowed through the crowd, selling apples and hazelnuts and plaster souvenirs; they were followed by the peppershot crackling of nutcrackers.

Southampton began to tell the Percy girls about Will Shakespeare, whose tragedy would be played that day. He said in his youth Master Shakespeare been stricken by a curious madness. He'd fancied himself a Grecian warrior of the host of Alexander, and persisted in his folly many years, so his family despaired. In his madness, he fell into brawling and lechery; he got an old wife by lying with a gentleman's daughter in a fit of antic lust.

"Fie!" said the eldest Percy in feigned amazement. "Do men do so?"

Then the Percy girls giggled and leaned on each other. Southampton said, with a glance at Emilia, "'Twas even said, he had lain with boys."

At this, the girls hushed and made serious faces. They frowned at the stage with new respect, as harboring men who lay with boys.

"Yet he had not," Emilia said. "Rumor often miscarries so; then the truth disappoints us with its dullness."

Southampton touched her sleeve and said playfully, "Some portion of his madness remained when the man was with us at Cowdray; Mistress Lanier might attest to his strange lusts there."

"Well, 'twas a strange season," said Emilia. "Cows mewed and cats laid eggs. Great lords took actors for their friends."

Southampton laughed and looked again like a boy. He asked if Emilia recalled when the men at Cowdray donned masks with the faces of cats and caught Harry Danvers and tossed him in a blanket. That was Will Shakespeare's notion, though he had kept aloof from the doing of it, fearing Danvers's resentment.

"Well, that was no madness," Emilia said. "Harry Danvers hath spitted more men than he hath ever wished a good morrow."

"But 'twas strange," said Southampton equably. "It made a scene of feline demons, see you."

"Harry Danvers having a very great hatred of cats," Emilia explained to the Percy girls.

Southampton then turned paternally to the girls and assured them Master Shakespeare was well restored and his lunatic capers forgot. Not two men in London knew of them. "Thus madness may pass and sin be cleansed and a man be again made whole."

Then trumpets played, heralding the entrance of Prologue. All the audience stilled and hushed. Their thousand faces turned and were presented to the stage like outstretched posies.

The Percy girls were still whispering, huddled together, as Will stepped onto the stage. He wore a suit of Southampton's old clothes, which Southampton had once worn at Cowdray. On his chest was Southampton's old livery badge, the jewel of a hawk in enamel and gold. His hair had receded and his brow was lined, but in every other way he was the same.

He bowed to the audience and said:

Two households, both alike in dignity,
In fair Verona, where we lay our scene,
From ancient grudge break to new mutiny
Where civil blood makes civil hands unclean.

Then the play was strange, a pretty nothing of elaborate sex jokes in which the characters bloodily died. The house laughed itself breathless, then gravely wept. It was, she supposed, like life.

Meanwhile, Emilia's mind strayed and tried to understand. There was a thing she must remember, but it flashed in her mind like a fish and vanished like a fish in a river's murk. Will was there—the same—and her desire for him, which flashed and vanished like a wise bright fish. At last, she found a memory that fit. That hurt. It was the night Harry Danvers had fled to the Continent. A party had gathered at Southampton's London house to drink to Harry's fortunes in exile. Because it was Southampton's house, among the carousers were actors of Will's company, including the reigning "boy," still costumed as a fairy queen. The boy was getting old to be playing women and filled out his bodice with a broad-ribbed manly shape. He was beardless, with long beribboned red hair, and he wore a gilt tiara and had painted his lips but was unapologetically a man in a dress. A male queen, then, who listened to the chatter with a green-eyed, contemptuous stare and scratched his chin with an ostrich fan.

Southampton came behind him and touched his nape. The male queen flinched and spoke to Southampton in a low, harsh voice. From only that, Emilia knew they were lovers. And Southampton stood blushing as the male queen gracefully rose and walked away.

But the boy had only gone upstairs to a bedchamber; Southampton followed to be further insulted. And she'd gone up to another bedchamber, where Will was already lying in bed, half-asleep and annoyed with waiting. He had helped her untie the knots of her clothes. She had stood in the rushes, nude and shivering. And she'd asked, in an idle voice, as if she'd never asked before, "How wert thou freed from thy madness of dreams?"

He said drowsily that he had been given a token that would free him from the changes of the world. It was a gift of Alexander of Macedon. 'Twas a humble thing of bronze, a kind of sword. So went his dreaming life.

Will had closed his fist, remembering. Emilia crossed his knuckles with her finger and he wrestled her down. That was all she remembered.

And the play wound to its funereal end. Will stood above the other actors' splayed bodies and intoned:

Go hence, to have more talk of these sad things;
Some shall be pardon'd, and some punished:
For never was a story of more woe
Than this of Juliet and her Romeo.

He bowed. It was done. All the audience roared. They pounded on the railings and screamed the actors' names. The dead actors came to life and bowed or curtsied in the rain of noise. Then a little knot of men in the pit started booing, throwing nutshells at the stage; others seized them and it turned into a fight that made waves throughout the sea of heads. It was loud enough to frighten the Percy girls to their feet.

"'Tis always thus," said Southampton deflatingly, and herded the Percy girls back to the stairs. They went noisily, shoving and flapping their fans and accusing each other of having been afraid. Southampton yawned painfully and followed. Emilia made her excuses and stayed.

Then the time in which the theater slowly emptied and became a great gaudy roofless barn. The sun had declined and all the place was in shadow. The last stragglers kicked through rushes and nutshells, looking for fallen coins. Mice emerged and started nosing for apple cores. The noise was all gone. She heard birds overhead.

And Will came back onto the stage. It was his habit (as Emilia knew) to return while the play was fresh, to pace and write in air. Today, of course, he knew she was there.

She rose to meet him, and they both were impatient while she courteously praised the play and remarked on the years that had passed since they last met. Then she said, "But thou knowest I am come for no play, however it be well made. I am come to speak of dreams."

His eyes became evasive and cold. He looked past her and nodded at someone in the wings.

"Dreams," she insisted. "And a sickness of dreams."

His eyes returned to her coldly. "I know naught of thy dreams and Jewish riddles. They are pastimes for a lord, who hath time for every idleness."

"Nay, thou hast told me of thy dreams."

"I told thee, madam? I remember it not."

Then she thought of grabbing his sleeve but didn't. They were frowning at each other as another actor passed behind Will, raised the trapdoor in the stage, and climbed down without giving them a glance. They were still frowning silently when he came back up with a little black dog in his arms and walked off into the wings, bouncing the dog in his arms and whistling. Her hand had gone to her waist, where she wore the little dagger. It was jeweled and slight, an unthreatening bauble, but it still had a working blade.

She said quietly, "Dost not remember thy dreams? Thy horse that went in blood, thy cuirass? Alexander?"

He flinched at the name but said, "So thou hast come for . . . Well, I know not. Must I dream thee a horse? A cuirass, that thou feel not the stings of love?"

"Thou know'st of what I speak. When I wake, 'twill be in a world disfigured. It is made so by mine own dreams."

"So thou art mad."

"I am mad as thou wert mad. I would know how I may heal my madness, sir."

"Purge thyself with hellebore," he said, "and wear an agate."

Her hand clenched on the hilt of the dagger. "As I stand before thee, I dream. Thou know'st it. Thou hast spoken of a token that thou hadst from Alexander."

"Indeed?" His voice was glib, but his face was tense and miserly. "Then thou art come far for small cheer. For, as to the token, I have it no more."

She drew the dagger. "Wilt thou give me my answer, or must I seek thy life?"

Then he threw back his head and laughed. All his body changed and was suddenly easy, as if she'd released him from a physical weight. And easily he bent to the floor, plucked up a nutshell, and offered it to her on his palm.

She frowned, still clutching the dagger. "Dost thou mock me?"

"How? 'Tis thy token. Hadst thou thought to have a coin?"

She lowered the blade. But when she reached to take the nutshell, he threw it away, and as she startled, he seized her other arm and wrenched the dagger from her hand.

For a moment they were grappling, Emilia still looking after the nutshell. He caught her against him so she cried out. Then she tore herself free and took a step toward the nutshell—but of course it was nothing. A decoy. She stood foolishly with nothing in her hands.

"Fear not," he said. "Thou shalt have thy token. But I will be paid for it before thou be free. So: tell me but one thing of the place of thy waking."

"'Tis not a place," she said, hoarse. "As thou knowest, it is a time."

"Ay. And in that time, are there theaters?"

She laughed unkindly. "Thou wouldst know, do men remember thee there?"

He was silent. But still he waited on her answer, his fist on the dagger tense and white.

"Well, be of good cheer," she said. "Thou art remembered. For four hundred years and more, men will go to theaters and applaud thy works. They will repeat thy name as a shibboleth; every good household will keep thy books. And then, as thou knowest, the world will burn and all be forgot in the general pyre. Is it all thou wished'st?"

His jaw was set, but tears grew in his eyes. "Ay. I thank thee, madam."

Then she wanted to hate him, but her own eyes softened. At that moment, the sun broke through the clouds, and the air became lucid, empty, strange. It was as if only she and he were real, and stood alone in a tempest of shopworn semblances.

He said softly, "I was once as thou art. I came to my madness with great vaunting, as a hero that would deliver the world. And yet the world burned. And thus was Alexander once the lady Cassandra, who tore her hair and wailed truth—and yet Troy fell. Yet all the world burned. And there may be a thousand other such wights, who dream the green world out of shape. Yet the world will burn as the sun will rise.

"I am a fool, and my greatness is the mumbling of fools; a paper greatness that will burn and be naught. But there is no greatness else. Thou shalt know it. There is no greatness else."

For a moment, she was dizzied. "Well, thou hast got thy greatness, sir. 'Tis well."

He laughed and raised the dagger. "And the wind goeth over it, and it is gone, and the place thereof shall know it no more."

Then he turned the dagger in his hand and held it out to her by the blade. "Here is thy token, if thou wouldst be free. 'Twill burn in the throat, but it is quickly done."

She understood in an instant. She took the dagger. He was watching her with his customary weariness: a weed-brown man; a morose, plain man. The stage makeup he wore was scored through on the brow with runnels of sweat. Behind him were the painted heavens of the stage, their yellow-tentacled sun, their bright blue cloth. She loved him as she might have loved a difficult brother. She drew a last clean breath.

And it was still her dream, her Albion, where recorders played to the splashing of oars, where she'd hunted with a hawk in lime-green woods, where she'd galloped through a meadow on a black-maned horse and a fairy-tale palace had appeared on the horizon, where she'd lived half her life. And it had been a greater life than life.

But she knew.

She touched the blade's point to the apex of her throat. She shifted the hilt to hold it with both hands. Well, it was only a dream. She would wake in bed.

Will said, "Be not afeared, my love. 'Tis but a sting, to spur thee home."

She braced and drove the blade into her throat. The blow jolted in her skull, a numbing agony. Will stepped back as she swayed. She snatched at hot blood that struck her hand like a breeze. Her hand went numb. The dagger clattered, far away. There was a teetering moment, a refusal to believe. Then she fell hard, like being kicked hard here and there. On her back, and the searing. The last thing the painted heavens. Blue cloth, and beside it real sky that was gray and translucent as if it might be soft to the touch. She blinked her eyes. The painted heavens and the gray heavens. Still alive.

Then she was watching the scene from above, like a bat, like a beetle that clung to the painted heavens. She saw Emilia kicking as she struggled to breathe. Will suddenly crouched and pressed his hand to the wound. He pressed his sleeve against the wound and cried for help—a coward after all, who was panicked by blood, who could tell his lover to kill herself but could not watch her die. And still she hadn't died. She was choked, she was in agony. Pounding footsteps came that she felt in her flesh as an intimate vibration—and Kate lost her grip. She couldn't bear it. She was gone.

(Then a time where she was nothing. She was no one in the world.)

(And she woke into a dream about Kate's own life, in a timeline Kate had never visited before. In the dream, she was sitting with Ben in a bus. It was a chartered bus, going to a protest in Washington, a protest against the war. In the dream, she didn't know what war it was. She only knew it was a terrible, unjust war, and they were bombing helpless people from the air.

But the Kate in the dream was happy. She was sitting with Ben and it could all still be all right. And the people on the bus were happy; they were singing "No Pasarán" in gringo accents, pressing their protest signs to the windows, very happy because they believed in themselves. They thought they could make it all all right. Kate laughed, understanding, and sang until the song was over somehow and time had passed.

Then in the dream, she was telling Ben about the dream of the apocalyptic city. She said, "It's like the movie *Terminator 2*. Like the worst version of the Skynet future, a planet of machines where all the people are dead. But in my dream, the machines didn't kill the people. We killed each other in a nuclear war. And the machines don't inherit Earth. They rust and fall apart. Then Earth becomes completely uninhabitable. It doesn't even have bacteria. It has no life."

"So not very similar."

"Well, it's an apocalypse."

"And does anybody send a robot assassin back in time to prevent the apocalypse?"

"I wish," said Kate. "That would be great. But what happens is, they send me.")

21

Ben brought Oksana because there wasn't anyone else. José was in Afghanistan and Martin was in London. Kate's mother wasn't coming until she took Kate back to Ohio at the end of the month. Sabine was busy wining and dining donors and making calls for the Soros people; since the war began, she'd had no time. He was the only one there when Kate gave birth, and since then, it was only Ben.

Even the hospital was trying to get rid of her. She'd gone into labor in the psychiatric ward, and the maternity ward hadn't wanted to take her. They'd said they didn't have security for mothers who "might grow agitated and harm themselves." That was one fight. Then, when the baby was born, the psychiatric people didn't want her back. They'd said they weren't set up to accommodate the mothers of newborn babies. Meanwhile, her insurer had cut her off. Ben had to take a day off work and go to different offices and shout at people, and even so, he ended up paying for a week of her hospital stay up front.

Kate was a money suck, a time suck, an energy suck. As Sabine put it, she was human quicksand. Ben blamed other people for neglecting her but knew his own loyalty was perverse. They'd only been together a year. She'd cheated on him. At the end, she'd been unhinged and cried all day and didn't think Ben was real. Still, he kept rehearsing every childish illusion: that their sex had been supernaturally good and their first months together his one real happiness; that she was kind, funny, magical, as no one else was; that if he tried hard enough, he could save her life.

So he went to the hospital three times a week. Every time, he swore it was going to be different and every time it was the same. When he arrived, Kate attempted to be cheerful and normal, but her eyes were plaintive and she couldn't understand. She wanted Ben to take her home, or at least to be solicitous, to show her love. But Ben couldn't show her love, because he couldn't take her home. So instead, he found himself asking questions designed to expose her as insane, to prove to himself he wasn't a monster for leaving her in that place. Kate tried to guess the right answers. It was torture for her. That made it torture for Ben, and how that manifested was anger.

At last, Ben always broke his promise to himself and asked her why she'd fucked José. Then Kate was amazed and said she didn't remember that. She was shocked when he said the baby was José's. Once she'd said thoughtfully, "That's so weird." Then Ben would lose his mind and berate her for the months she'd let him think the baby was Martin's; she'd let him think she'd done this altruistic thing, when really she'd been fucking José. Kate would cower and sob. The baby would wake up and shriek inconsolably. Ben was exposed as a monster after all. It happened every time.

And then, every night now, he slept with Alicia—Alicia whom he still called, behind her back, "the ExxonMobil person," even though saying it gave him a thrill of shame. And she wasn't just an Exxon-Mobil person; she was secretly addicted to romance novels and had been a semipro skier in college and still went skiing in places where she had to be helicoptered in, where she was sponsored and the money went to multiple sclerosis. She spoke Japanese but couldn't speak it on demand without blushing and covering her face. She was smart, even if she never really made jokes and she had no political opinions. She was kind. She deserved to be loved.

Ben couldn't love Alicia. He was doing things purely because they weren't other things, the things he couldn't face. He was spinning his wheels and hurting people—despicable. He knew it but he couldn't stop doing it. He couldn't sleep alone.

Oksana met him at the street door to psychiatric, where the junkies were already lined up waiting for the methadone clinic to open. Ben had to dislodge a junkie from the doorway to clear their path to the security desk. Ben paid the visitor's fee for them both, and—because Oksana insisted—for another man who didn't have the money and said he was desperate to see his son. Oksana was wearing only jeans and a bra; the security guard wouldn't let them in until Ben gave her his jacket to wear, and then Oksana made a fuss about having her picture taken for the visitor's badge. Ben talked her down, but by then the guard was angry and insisted on patting them down.

Inside the hospital, no one cared. There was no one there. No nurses, and the patients on that level were all locked in. There was occasional, directionless moaning. Half the lights were out. The smells were urine and bleach and pesticide. The floor was always wet from being washed, and the cheap gloss paint looked perpetually damp; in the semidarkness, everything glistened and swam.

They came up a pitch-dark flight of steps and had to buzz to be let into the open wards. Here, patients in the corridors stared and shuffled, and Asperger's Andy announced who Ben was in a deafening, seal's-bark voice. The walls were covered in advertising posters for candy, fast food, cigarettes—anything a mental patient might crave and ask to have bought for them by guilt-stricken relatives. Even the hospital pajamas had a NyQuil logo with a picture of a sleeping kitten. From open doors came the chatter of the therapeutic radio that played all day and couldn't be shut off; once Ben had brought Kate earplugs, but they were confiscated and Ben was told officiously that Stanford had done a study where the therapeutic radio worked. Still, he couldn't forgive the radio; its cloying inspirational jabber embodied his feeling that this wasn't a place that cured sick people but a dungeon where hapless people were imprisoned and methodically driven insane.

They found Kate in the cafeteria, drinking a vending-machine coffee from a paper cup. No one else was there; the cafeteria didn't serve food at that hour, and the more functional patients were all in the TV room. There was a faucet dripping in the kitchen and a sluggish water bug inspecting a spill in the corner by the vending machine. Everything was ugly, plastic, stain resistant, beige. Kate had the baby in its sling, and Ben fought a wave of queasy ambivalence. He was attached to the baby, of course. He'd seen it a few hours after it was born, when it was still red faced and amphibian, and had felt the terror of a parent at its blind fragility; he'd held it a few times, and its tiny warmth had pacified and moved him. Now, at five weeks, it was uncannily perfect: black eyed and button nosed, a thoughtful mammal that peeped and frowned as if working out a problem and still lived in a world of self, a universe with only one conscious subject. The baby was a locus of magic, and Ben was not immune to the baby's spell.

At the same time, the baby was a locus of pain—not only because of José but because of Kate who couldn't really be a mother, who was clinically insane, who couldn't remember its name and would call it interchangeably Ryan or Salman or the nonsense syllable "Qued," who was terrified that someone would take it away (as someone should probably take it away), and whose way of coping was to act as if the baby were invisible to everyone but her. She didn't like people to mention it. She kept its face covered by its sling.

Sometimes Ben defied this and said hello to the baby and insisted on seeing it, with mixed results. Oksana's presence was an added complication. He decided not to risk it as Kate stood up.

Then the moment that always went through him. It was Kate. It wasn't just an awful situation, it was Kate—albeit paunchy and exhausted in the aftermath of childbirth, her dramatic black hair eliminated by a ponytail, her face gaunt and ordinary in the mean light. She moved stiffly, coming to greet them, and he thought, *They're torturing her; they're killing her.* But of course, she'd just given birth. Anybody might look that way if they'd just given birth.

With Oksana there, Kate didn't try to seem sane. Instead, she talked to Oksana as if Oksana were visiting from Kate's alternate universe, where everything was happy and nice. For Ben, it was gratingly narcissistic—Kate projecting her fantasies on Oksana, who was reduced to a prop in Kate's game of make-believe. But Oksana didn't seem put out when Kate asked about Oksana's documentary films or her organization that rescued mail-order brides. She just explained in her tuneless voice that she didn't do all that, she was a stripper. Then (fingernails down a blackboard to Ben, but apparently fine with Oksana) Kate looked stricken and apologized for making a world where Oksana was a stripper—as if Oksana agreed that stripping was awful and that Kate had made the world.

"I thought I could change it all back," Kate said, "but it doesn't really work like that. All the timelines exist now and can't be erased. I've made all these terrible realities. I mean, this one feels like it's terrible. Is it terrible?"

"It's terrible," said Oksana.

"I'm sorry," Kate said. "I wish I could fix it."

"Kate, you don't have to be sorry," said Ben. "It's not real. You didn't really create the world."

"I'm talking to Oksana now," Kate said. "Oksana doesn't mind if I'm crazy."

"Yes," Oksana said. "Here, we're in the crazy hospital. I don't come if I don't want to hear a crazy thing."

Encouraged, Kate described her latest delusion, in which she'd gone to visit Shakespeare in a dream and asked him how to cure her insanity. He'd told her to kill herself, so she'd obediently stabbed herself in the throat. She'd fainted on the stage—this was at the Globe—and had naturally assumed she would die.

But she'd stabbed herself through the front of the throat. Another patient here had made the same mistake, and he said she might have only nicked the jugular, or even just cut some bullshit artery like the thyroid artery. Then the blood loss would be minor. Some people even suffocated slowly from the damage to the trachea. It could take twenty minutes to die.

So now, in her dreams, she kept returning to that scene. The pain was unbearable and drove her to wake; she could only stay for seconds at a time. In one dream, they carried her from the stage. In the next, they'd made it to the outside stairs. It took ten dreams—ten nights—before she was bundled into her friend Southampton's barge to be taken to a doctor. All the time, she was in agony, choking, and cold as if her body were all bared bone. Then the following night. It came back and back. She couldn't escape the dream.

And, in waking life, she was plagued by visions of a post-apocalyptic city. It was a thing she'd seen in dreams before, but now it could appear when she just closed her eyes. She saw the burnt remains of the long-dead world; she felt its sticky ashes on her skin. In those moments she knew the apocalypse would come. The world would burn. There was no point in anything. Worse—everything she'd ever done had brought the world's extinction closer.

Here Kate paused and looked for a reaction. Her hand was stroking the fabric of the sling—the baby's back—in a mechanical gentling motion, and now Ben noticed she was still wearing his engagement ring. The last time he'd visited, she'd told him she didn't remember accepting the ring and said she'd always hated engagement rings. But then when he'd asked for it back, she'd cried.

Ben said carefully, "It seems like a dark vision."

"Not really." Kate made a face, as if Ben were being overdramatic. "After all, it's not news that we're destroying the world. We're obviously destroying the world."

"It's right," said Oksana. "It's true."

Ben said, "Have you told your psychologist about this?"

"I think you're missing the point," said Kate.

"The psychologist should know," Ben said, trying to keep his voice calm. "It seems like it could be a bad development."

Oksana said to Kate, "I think you shouldn't die in this dream. You dream instead that your neck heals, and it's better. You don't have any problems like this."

"No," Kate said. "Then I'd keep having the dreams, and every dream makes things worse. I've already erased my *brother*. I'm sorry, I know you don't believe all this."

Ben said, "So you realize this is your sickness?"

There was a pause like the pause of leaping over a chasm and the film going into slow motion, then Kate said, "No. I'm going to leave so I want to be honest."

"You're going to leave?" said Ben. "What does that mean?"

Kate's face became paranoid, her eyes bright with a chilling superiority. It was blatantly the face of a crazy person. Ben was physically affected. He was hit with a nausea that seemed to begin in his eyes.

He said, in the coolest voice he could muster, "When you talk like that, I have to be worried you're thinking of killing yourself. Do you see that?"

"No," Kate said in an odd, prim voice. "It seems like a bit of a leap."

"Then what do you mean by saying you're *leaving*? Does it mean you're going home to Ohio?"

Kate grimaced. "I'm not from Ohio. I've never been to Ohio in my life."

Ben almost went into his well-worn explanation about her childhood in Cincinnati. But then he saw Kate knew. She was insisting on her favorite delusion—the one where her parents had stayed together and they lived in Manhattan and were Kate's best friends—but she knew. He was blindsided by a wash of despair. The baby was stirring now, and it made him so miserable he was afraid.

He said hoarsely, "Your mother was going to come and take you home to Ohio. I'm just asking, is that what you mean about leaving?"

"You don't listen to me, or you'd know what I mean. I take your reality seriously. I treat it with so much respect, even though I'll only be here a couple of days. And you don't even listen."

Then his hands were in fists and he was saying, "My reality is *real*. It's everyone's reality. That's how we know what's real, Kate."

The baby stirred again, twitching in its sling. Kate looked down to it and said in a baby-softened voice, "Please don't attack me."

"I'm not attacking you. I want you to focus on getting better. If you aren't going to talk to the psychologist—"

"There's no point. It's a waste of time."

"It isn't," said Ben helplessly. "It's how you get better."

"No one really gets better that way."

"So how do you plan to get better?"

"I'm leaving. I'm leaving this history. I *said*." Then Kate sat back and was suddenly crying—crying and violently rubbing her forehead, as if she were trying to crush her thoughts. The baby bleated and kicked in protest. Oksana stared at Ben with a fixed, flat hostility.

He muttered to himself, "I can't cope with this shit. I can't. I'll go insane myself."

Then Kate leaned across the table and shouted, "So don't come back! I didn't tell you to come. You just punish me. You don't even know!"

Ben stood up, and Kate raised her hands as if warding off a blow. The baby earsplittingly wailed. He hated her so much at that moment, he was high on it. He could have thrown the table across the room. He could have broken a window with his head.

"Don't worry," he said. "I won't come back. I wouldn't want to stand between you and your psychosis. Have a great life as a mental patient. I'm sure you made the right choice."

He left—and was surprised to find Oksana had followed him. All down the bright corridors and then the dark corridors, she shadowed him, her sneakers squeaking on the wet floor. Outside, where the chewed-up junkies were still lined up in a miasma of cigarette smoke because the methadone clinic still hadn't opened, Oksana stopped him and talked for ten minutes, so intently her teeth seemed gritted against it. It was about Kate's belief that Oksana ran an organization that rescued mail-order brides. Oksana said she'd once been a mail-order bride, and she was beaten and raped by her shit husband, then she ran away and lived with other shits who fucked her; she had no money so it was her life. She was breathless, spitting the words. The junkies all listened with a quiet recognition; they listened as if they might like to join in. Ben kept glancing at them while she talked. He was too tired to listen properly.

At the end, she said, "What Kate thinks, it's beautiful. I wish I made this, for women like me. If I can help some person, even one person, I can maybe be okay. But I don't. Kate thinks I'm a good person, but I'm nothing person. I'm shit."

When she stopped talking, Ben pulled himself together and said, in his best sympathetic voice, "I know how you feel. Kate thinks I'm a good person too. Or she did."

"It's wrong," said Oksana. "You are not a good person."

Then she took off Ben's jacket and threw it on the ground. The junkies burst into applause. It wasn't clear if they were clapping for her outburst or for her bra. Ben was suddenly afraid of them. Afraid of Oksana.

She said, "I am ashamed I come here with you. You talking to a sick woman like it's an animal. You are evil. You are like Satan."

The junkies cheered again as Oksana walked off, with her naked back hunched and pink from cold. Ben tried to remember Oksana was crazy. He tried to think about how funny it would sound when he told Kate later. But no, he would be telling Alicia, who wouldn't understand, who would be horrified and pity him. Whom he therefore couldn't tell.

And the wind blew over the city (just a day like any other) and the sky was blue. Ben picked up the jacket but forgot to put it on. He walked to the subway with it crumpled in his hands and didn't know for a long time why he was cold.

That spring, ExxonMobil moved Ben to Houston. He fell out of touch with his New York friends. So it was Kate's mother, Ágota, who emailed to tell him that Kate had died in a hospital in Ohio. There had been a fire; she'd died of smoke inhalation. There wasn't any reason to believe she'd suffered.

22

And the city
     black and white
       its cinders and ice. The broken planet venting its innards in smoke. Rocks raining from inimical space. The husks of dead beetles that had gathered in drifts; the black eons beyond the world's end. Her brain all ash. It blew apart, became nothing but the skyline engraved on the skin of her eyes. Was a time where she was nothing. There was no one in the world. Couldn't breathe. And screamed:

Kate woke in Ohio at a bathroom sink. She was gripping the cold sink, in grateful tears, alive and not sorry for the things she had lost. She was real. There were people. She could breathe and there was air. She was at her mother's house and it was raining outside. She heard the rain and heard her baby crying in her bedroom. But she didn't think of going to him yet. She breathed.

In the corner of the sink, there was a white ceramic soap dish shaped like a stylized scallop shell. It had a soapy residue but held no soap. On the sink's other side was a kitchen sponge: a yellow rectangle with a forest-green scouring pad. It looked weather-beaten, and the scouring pad had a long white hair entangled on its surface. Beside it stood a bottle of apple-scented hand wash, translucent green with a white dispenser beak. It had a price tag on it, wrinkled from being in water but still bright red. It had cost $3.69.

How would you describe such objects to a person like Will Shakespeare? Had Kate made them, and if she had, should that make her proud or ashamed?

Well, she'd tried to save the world, when she'd thought about the world. It shouldn't matter that she was insecure and vain, that she didn't only want to save mankind, but to be the great heroine who'd saved mankind. That she'd wanted a world where she could matter—as Will wanted a world where he wrote great plays, as Alexander wanted a world where he conquered Asia. It was the nature of consciousness to care about itself. Put a consciousness anywhere in time, and it would spawn new worlds from its spasms of ego. Thus the ugly kitchen sponge and the government of stooges; the cheap hand soap and the death of the seas.

But now all Kate wanted was for Kate to be a person. To live like anyone, to die and forget. It was the only change she wanted in the world.

Behind the kitchen sponge was Ben's engagement ring, which Kate had taken off to wash her hands—a trite diamond solitaire she'd found on her finger one morning long after Ben had gone. Now she put it on and paused. The rain had stopped, but the wind was gusting harder. It sounded as if it hurt the windows. Her son had fallen silent and she felt an old panic, the urge to check that her son was still breathing. She could go to her son and never answer the door. Never answer the phone and never open her mail. She could hide in this small, dull life.

But as she thought of it, the doorbell rang.

She went downstairs, compelled and afraid. José was at the door. His rental car was in the driveway. He was ill at ease, too neatly dressed. His hair looked freshly cut. It was exactly as if it were the one real world and he were here to visit his son.

And she remembered a time in a different real world—in the world where the baby had been Oksana's, in the months just after that baby was born—when they'd rented a canoe and gone out on the lake. She'd sung "Tom o'Bedlam" while José rowed. It was a beautiful day, but José had been strange, making odd, nervous jokes that didn't quite land. He was troubled in a way that wasn't like José. In the middle of the lake, she realized. She said it out loud, and he stopped rowing and sat with his sweaty hands clutching his knees. She said, "No, you're another one. I know what you are." Then she talked and begged, but he stared and couldn't hear. He was away with the treacherous world.

And, as Will had once hated her, she hated José—or the stranger from the future who inhabited José, who was here to save the world because Kate had failed. She wanted to tell him he would also fail, and the world would burn and the insects die, and the blackened towers stand in lifeless space.

But he was suffering. The light shimmered over the lake. On the shore, children laughed and threw bread to swans. He was real. He was sweating and trying to wake. And in all the green world, there was no one else. Alone in this doomed and carefree world, he was feeling what she felt.

At last, she lay against him in the bottom of the boat and they stared at the sky until it passed. She sang "Tom o'Bedlam" to the dumb blue sky. And he said, "Don't go into the hospital in Ohio. If you go to the hospital there, you die."

For a while then, they were friends. It was the time when she was finishing the mural at Martin's. He would come and sit with her while she painted, and they would talk about anything but. Often, they discussed politics, always skirting the issue of where events led, of the future that presumably was preying on his mind. And that feeling of the two of them together in a room—he was real, and the deep well, the shadow of the world. He was her same height, and when they walked down the street together, they seemed to be coasting on the same level, buoyed by the same inexpressible thing.

She talked about her dreams, of course, although José never talked about his other life, his life in the presumably desperate future. But he did drop hints about what she should do. She should steer clear of politics; she shouldn't try to have a public career; she should lead a quiet, therapeutic life. He would involve her in discussions about how one person couldn't make any real difference, even if that person were a charismatic leader, and once he got it off his chest, he looked calmer. Kate didn't point out that she was clinically insane, that no one would mistake her for a charismatic leader. He was trying (she knew) to protect the future. He was trying to enlist her in protecting the future. For the same reason he would never say to anyone: *I time travel, too, and Kate's not crazy.* She had to stay crazy and obscure and insignificant. She knew and she agreed. It was the least she could do.

Still, at times she sensed what it would be like to be that destructive atom, the great individual who broke the world. Within it was nostalgia for the lost simple life in which she'd been a person who could live like anyone—as, until he'd dreamed of Alexander, Will Shakespeare had lived like anyone and died and been forgotten. So every world was a soap bubble ripe to be burst by a weaponized nobody, to yield the airy glory the bubble contained. And she saw how one could arrive at a point where that glory was the only thing left to want; when all one's human life was gone, the family vanished and the friends not friends; all the world become an alien hostility, a grave. She could say all that to José.

Their friendship lasted while she went to psychiatrists and while she was adjusting to meds. It lasted through the end of her and Ben's relationship. She woke up pregnant, and José was still around. In the hospital, he visited once a week. They did jigsaw puzzles in the cafeteria, José often holding the baby because he was predictably good with babies. She talked about killing herself in the dream, and José didn't say he understood, but she knew. And when he reenlisted, she took it for a sign he intended to be killed in Afghanistan for the same reason, to be freed from his dreaming self. It was a tacit camaraderie; they both knew what needed to be done. It was a bond not unlike love.

That phase came to an abrupt halt when she learned José was her baby's father. They'd never had sex—but they obviously had. It felt as if she'd been raped. Then a black lost time where the meds were too strong and she was crazy and the baby kept crying. She couldn't wake up or sleep; it couldn't last. It was a white pandemonium with the wrong past.

When she spoke to José again, it was a phone in the hospital corridor, with staff and patients wandering by. He was calling from a forward operating base in Afghanistan. It was just after the first use of tactical nukes, in which ten thousand civilians were incinerated, and José was strung out, not concerned with making sense. He talked as if he were calling from an apocalyptic future. He sounded like the voices in a crazy person's head.

He started by saying he was done with games. He would level with her, so she should take a deep breath. She should ignore all the doctors and ignore what people like Ben were telling her. She wasn't really sick, and there was still a decent chance, if she could just hang tough, if she could just not blink. He went on, sounding increasingly loony tunes, explaining what he called the "time travel thing." He said, in his time, people knew about the time travel thing. They believed it relied on the transmission of consciousness, which was now thought to be a subatomic particle with the ability to move in all directions through time. They believed that in the distant future—roughly a thousand years in the future—scientists had figured out how to bounce these particles between two people, past and present. When they did it, the phenomenon replicated itself, bouncing backward from person to person, so a chain of travelers was created, going deep into the past.

When José's people first discovered this was happening—when they discovered José—everyone was ecstatic, and José was treated like a cross between an astronaut and a wizard. His counterpart from the future appeared—a trans woman named Breton who was José's hairdresser. In her future life, she was a physicist, and so she gave public presentations about the principles involved in time travel. No one understood it (even Breton didn't fully) but everybody talked about it happily, incessantly. It was a time of headlong optimism; the frame of the world had changed. José and Breton were popular celebrities, feted wherever they went.

That soured when people learned about the negative effects. Apparently, whenever someone traveled to the past, whatever they did there was toxic for the world. It didn't matter if they murdered the pope or sneezed; when they woke, it had damaged the world. But the traveler, who'd started as a nobody, gradually turned into a colossus—a Shakespeare, an Alexander the Great. Somehow, these people turned history into a vehicle for their own wish fulfillment. They even worked together to do it, like a trans-temporal cabal or clique; one person would go back in time and immediately help the person before him, who would help the person before her—typically they saved each other from early deaths and steered each other into better opportunities—and they all became great while the world fell apart. It didn't matter what they thought they were doing. They did exactly this. It appeared to be an ungovernable impulse, or possibly a parasympathetic function, like breathing in your sleep.

Finally, this process had triggered an apocalypse. The devastated city Kate saw in her dreams—the one all travelers saw in their dreams—was believed to be a vision of the day when the time travel experiment had first been launched. The people who'd invented time travel were gone, their civilization erased and every living thing dead. Their experiment had caused the Earth to be destroyed many centuries before they came to be. What's more, the apocalypse seemed to be creeping backward, coming earlier and earlier. In fact, José had now stopped waking up in his own time. He didn't want to be dramatic, but he was terrified that everyone he knew was gone, his civilization erased and every living thing dead.

So he didn't want to tell her what to do, but he didn't want to hide things from her either. And okay, it was looking like she ended his world. She became important and it ended the world, *his* world. She killed everyone two centuries earlier. He of all people wouldn't judge, and she had time to think, and this was totally her decision. But maybe when she got to Ohio, she should go into the hospital there and just accept dying early. It sucked, but for the world, it was the safest choice.

He hoped it wasn't wrong to tell Kate this. He'd had a lot to drink but he thought she should know.

"It's fine," said Kate. "I'm good."

(She leaned against the wall and watched three mental patients passing, shuffling, in their NyQuil pajamas. She was heavily sedated, and José's voice made her nostalgic for Martin's house. She wanted José to go on talking. She thought if he talked a little longer, she might feel something about what he was saying; she might think of something helpful to say. The baby slept in his sling, her warm and constant thing. Her one thing. The phone was warm against her ear. At the same time, she was conscious that the hospital charged ten dollars a minute for incoming calls, and her mother would end up having to pay. But when Kate woke up next, it would have all changed. José might not have called, or it might cost nothing. It didn't really matter. Nothing could.)

He said, "Another thing. You have to give up the baby. You have to give him up for adoption."

"No," said Kate, and hung up the phone.

He called back two days later and started with the baby: Kate had to give the baby up for adoption, and he knew it was hard but it was what she had to do. "I'm not saying this for personal reasons. I'm saying this because I know how it ends." She hung up again and was trembling with rage. Of course she should give the baby up for adoption. And Oksana should have given Qued up for adoption. Ben's mother should have given Ben up for adoption. All babies should be given up for adoption, except there was no point. There was no safe place. What made José think there was any safe place?

Then she moved to Ohio to live with her mother and was trying to be okay. For the baby, for her mother, just in case there was something at stake, she was trying to be okay. But still she would drift off over a book and find herself staring at the blackened dead towers, the broken skyline glittering with ice, and wake up screaming with her mother at her side. Her mother would stroke her forehead and wasn't quite her mother; had changed, had coarsened. Then every night, Kate dreamed of dying in Southampton's barge, Will gripping her throat in his fright-red hands, Southampton weeping and shouting at the oarsmen—and she woke in Ohio, gasping and alone. In her bedroom window, the dull flat night. The yard was muddy, overgrown. The woods beyond were thinned by dieback; everywhere were rotten leaning trunks, bare crowns like patches of winter. Kate was sweating, disoriented. She got up in a panic and went to her son. Usually she found her son.

But three times she'd found a changeling baby looking at her with bright strange eyes. She'd done something in the dream and switched him; he was now the baby of an unknown father, or José's baby from a different day. He was always a boy, which didn't have to mean anything; a coin that came up heads four times. She didn't know if she knew his name.

She took the new baby unconfidently in her arms—and was his mother. He was hers. He had grown beneath her heart. It pierced her through, and she loved him absolutely—this boy who had usurped her boy, this avatar of boy who was all she had. And when he latched onto her breast, the faint, haunting queasiness of milk being drawn was a vow. She couldn't know anyone, but someone still needed her. She couldn't be anyone, but she could still love. And she would sleep on the floor beside his bassinet as she'd once slept beside Qued's bassinet with her friends, with Ben, in a summer when the forests were thick and green; in a year when the world still could have survived.

She'd told people not to give José her Ohio number, but of course he got it at last. When he called, he was already boarding a plane. She said, "Don't come. I don't want you to come." He apologized but said he would be there in the morning.

And she dreamed about the barge and she dreamed about the city. The last night passed somewhere else while she dreamed. Morning came, and she took a long shower. She prepared herself meticulously as if for a date. She faded in and out; in the city, in the world. And the doorbell rang and she went down the stairs, compelled and afraid, to confront José.

He said, "We need to talk. I have to tell you something."

"I know you've come a long way," she said, "but I can't deal with difficult things right now. So I'm going to ask you to just go away."

"Kate, I'm here for you. Just hear me out."

"I'm trying to keep my life simple. If I tell you not to come, it's because I need that. I'm making my decisions and you have to respect that. You said I have to make my own decisions."

"No, please listen. Something bad happens today."

"Is the world ending?"

"No, the world's not ending," he said as if that were a ridiculous idea.

"Then go. Go wherever you go. Please go."

"Can we both just accept that I'm not going to leave?"

"No. I'll call the police."

He stepped back but didn't turn to go. His face was stubborn. Kate had been standing in the doorway, and now she came out and let the door swing shut behind her. It was immediately colder. It felt like stepping into an arena. It felt as if battle had been joined.

She said, "I have to concentrate on getting better. You can't talk about taking away my baby and expect me not to be harmed. It's crazy."

Then she went on talking, her voice rising shrilly, while part of her was mortified and frightened of her voice. José listened grimly, impassively. The sky full of rain clouds, a heavy damp wind. An ominous shining in the wet grass. By the end, she was leaning back against the house and José was staring at his feet with a stiff, pained face. He would have cried, perhaps, if he were a person who cried.

She finished senselessly, "So that's why you should leave. If you don't understand, I don't know what to do. But I need to have some peace. I need that from you."

He said, "I know my phone call to the hospital was out of line. But you don't have to be afraid of me. I don't blame you."

"Okay. So you told me that. Now you can go."

He shook his head. "No, listen. You're going to have a kind of an amazing life. Try and look at it like that, 'cause none of this is your fault. If you live, you get to do all these incredible things."

"Stop it. I'm not doing anything. I'm not."

"You do. You become a grassroots leader. You spearhead this whole grassroots movement. I know it's hard to see from here, but it happens. I mean, you know I've got to try to stop it."

"I'm not a leader. I live with my mother. So if you came here to stop me, to kill me, whatever you came to do, you can just go away. All I want is to stay out of the hospital so I can raise my son. *Our* son."

"Kate. He dies."

A thrill of fear went through her, a physical jolt. In that first moment, it was sexual. She almost laughed from fear.

She said, "No. What are you talking about?"

"He dies. Our son. I couldn't tell you on the phone."

"Don't say that. Why are you saying that?"

"I'm sorry. That's why I came here."

She took a breath that caught in her chest. "But you're saying if I . . . I can stop it?"

José flinched. "I'm sorry. It's not anything you do. He just stops breathing. It's no one's fault."

"No. When does he die?"

José looked up at the windows of the house. Already she'd realized and turned to the door. At first she couldn't get the door to open. She was pulling without turning the doorknob, panicking. It felt as if the house was broken. Then she was through and going up the stairs, scrambling clumsily, using hands and feet. She was swearing out loud while she prayed in her head. The door of her son's room was open, and even the open door looked unnaturally still. The mobile over his bed was turning slowly although there was no draft.

She couldn't breathe. It was as if she were floating in the air over her own head. She went to him, and walking felt like falling. At the bassinet, she touched him gently but his flesh was wrong, wrong like a missed step. He was dead. He looked the same but he was cold. He was dead.

And the room was suddenly massive, contained all space, and it spun around her head. She heard José's footsteps on the stairs, huge. The light grew blackish. It trembled and eluded her and wouldn't hold still. The bright scene collapsed as if she shook it from her shoulders:

Then a time where she was nothing. She was no one in the world.

And she dreamed into the scene she always dreamed. She was lying on the floor of Southampton's barge. It was sunset already and the river was dark, but the sky above was still large with day. As she came into the dream, the pain opened wide. She breathed and dragged a thread of agony; her breath was a long knife that drew a thread of air. Will's hand still pressed a soggy fold of cloth to her throat: a numb blot. Southampton was crouching at her side, his white satin doublet smeared with blood, his narrow face alien with tears. Death's blackness seeped through the world, while the world was the same soft evening with all its pretty details: dim lights beginning to appear in the windows of the nobles' great houses on the northern shore, the rose petals strewn on the floor of the barge, the Turkish rug on which she lay. She wept for pain, though it made her nose run and suffocated her. She wept for the world and pain. In waking, the other pain waited and made a kind of balance that let her stay. And she wept as if balanced unsteadily, rocking, as the oars went through the time and pain.

And the wind blew over her tears, and they dried, and time passed rockingly on the water until the tears were gone. Emilia breathed dirtily, weakly. Her head lolled against Will's chest, and the sky was beautiful, after all. The world; she had loved it, after all.

Then a waterman's voice carried over the river. He was singing "Tom o'Bedlam," the sound coming hollow and pure in all that air. Emilia turned her eyes to the sound and saw a low drab boat, its occupant singing like a happy dog barking and letting his oars trail in the water. Then Southampton rose like a golden delirium—his long tresses flying in the air, his white gloves bright with blood that looked fluorescent in the woolen light. He screamed at the man to be quiet; she didn't understand the words he was screaming while Will laughed under his breath. The man sang on, oblivious. Perhaps he never guessed that the golden lord saw him. Emilia shut her eyes and heard:

> *That of your five sound senses*
> *You never be forsaken*
> *Nor wander from your selves with Tom*
> *Abroad to beg your bacon*

Then she was dying, and the water seemed to realize beneath her, and splash it to the air with the cut of the oars. The enormous day that fell like downpour. The whole sky of air that could not breathe. And she knew one last thing that didn't mean anything, that freed her from the changes of the terrible world.

23

Ben married Kate in Sabine's ghost town—strictly speaking, not a town, but an abandoned neighborhood in a depressed but still extant town. All the houses in the neighborhood had been foreclosed, then bundled into one large property in the hope of attracting a developer. It was in West Virginia, in an ex–coal region. For hundreds of miles around, the people were white, xenophobic, open carry, evangelical. Sabine had bought the neighborhood to test-drive a strategy for turning poor red states into swing states by talking to every single person there. She would repair all the homes in the ghost neighborhood and offer them at locally affordable rents. She would open free preschools and clinics. She would recruit seasoned activists and sympathetic locals. She would be a big éminence grise in a small pond.

She hired a contractor and grassroots organizers, then got distracted by the war with Iran. She was speaking at protests and having eggs thrown at her and writing op-eds and being called Iran Harridan by right-wing hacks. Credit Suisse fired her for damaging their image. Then the Save America Act was passed, and her assets were frozen because the State Department said she was bankrolling terrorism. That turned into a year of legal battles, in the course of which Sabine became a cause célèbre and a hate figure for the nativist right, and although she eventually won in court, she was sentenced to three months for contempt because, as she admitted, she was a cunt to the judge. She didn't mind prison, though (or so she told Ben in a letter from the correctional facility), because she got a lot of reading done and easily bought the other prisoners' friendship.

Meanwhile, in West Virginia, the contractors worked, and houses were demolished or fixed. The organizers settled in a nice Victorian (the town's former haunted house) and got the fireplace working and planted a garden, but nothing else got done. No free clinic: doctors didn't want to move there. No preschool: people wouldn't send their kids. The sympathetic locals didn't do anything but complain about the unsympathetic locals. Sabine started calling it "where money goes to die" and said it was a lesson to anyone who thought they could reinvent the wheel.

For Ben, the next phase began with a series of emails from Kate's mother. Kate had been living in Ágota's house for a year, but had now run away with an old family friend, a Hungarian writer of children's books with a history of preying (Ágota said) on vulnerable young women. Kate had been acutely depressed ever since her infant son had died of SIDS, and was about to be admitted to the local hospital, since Ágota didn't trust her not to walk into traffic while Ágota was at work.

Then Gabor (the family friend) came to visit, and he and Kate vanished in the middle of the night. Kate called Ágota from the road but wouldn't say where she was going. All she wanted was for Ágota to wire her money. Ágota went to the police, who treated her like a demented old woman. They told her they couldn't prevent her adult daughter from having sexual relationships. "It doesn't matter that the daughter is perhaps a schizophrenic," wrote Ágota. "It is I that must be crazy."

At the time, Ben was in Louisiana, interviewing former Exxon employees—now refugees living in FEMA tents—and editing the interviews for use in press kits. The aim was to argue for more aggressive action to protect Exxon's remaining installations in the Gulf.

The day he arrived, the Raza Verde had set fire to a string of oil platforms, and when the wind blew from the sea, the town was cast into a stinking, nebulous dusk. The tap water was contaminated, and bottled water was selling for twenty dollars a liter. Trees had begun to die, and no one had the money or energy to find out why. People had abandoned their homes, and apparently some had left their pets behind, since there were warnings posted everywhere about wild dogs. Ben's skin was perpetually sticky. His teeth were sticky from sucking throat lozenges.

The other guests in Ben's hotel were all reporters, FEMA workers, and military contractors, who congregated in the bar every night and drank until they passed out. To Ben, they all seemed like different species of vulture; they competed to tell the worst atrocity stories, made a game of drinking through their per diems, shared tips about local girls desperate enough to trade sex for bottled water. Only the refugees retained their humanity, and couldn't help raging inconsolably to Ben, weeping and telling him their life stories—although he was patently just another vulture with no power to do anything there but feed. By the third day, Ben burned out and began to find it all unendurably boring. He couldn't pay attention. Something had gone wrong with his mind.

In that context, the emails from Ágota felt ethereally harmless. Even the idea of Kate being ravished, which would have made him jealous the week before, now felt like a scene from a comic novel. Ben imagined Gabor and Kate as Humbert Humbert with an overgrown Lolita, fleeing across state lines to—as Ágota's final email revealed—Sabine's twice-abandoned West Virginian town.

There the emails stopped. He got home to New York and expected his depression to fade. It didn't. His second week back, he broke up with Alicia from a feeling that he needed to change his life when he couldn't really change his life. Another month went by. Every night he ordered takeout and drank a six-pack in front of the TV set. Three months in, he'd given up running. He'd stopped going out with friends. When six months had passed, he had headaches every day and chronic eczema on his hands. Often he threw up within a minute of waking; he kept a bucket beside the bed.

Then one morning he didn't go to work. He lay in bed suffering until ten o'clock, then threw on some clothes and went to Sabine's.

On the way, he had time to realize Sabine might not be there and to feel the anticipatory despair of being turned away by the doorman. But he found her at home, in a sea of boxes; she was being thrown out by her uncle, who was afraid the government would seize his assets. Two TaskRabbit kids were packing her belongings to be put into storage while Sabine, with brittle, ferocious cheerfulness, was listing the friends and family members who now wouldn't answer her calls. The TaskRabbit kids were starstruck, laughing besottedly at everything she said. When Ben came in, they stared at him with the instinctive mistrust of sibling rivalry.

Sabine said to Ben, "Look, you want to take a road trip? I'm driving to West Virginia tonight."

Ben's mind said *Kate.* He felt tremulous and blank. He said without thinking, "Yes."

There'd been a blizzard and Sabine drove recklessly at first, impatient with the slippery road. The car was a nondescript battered Hyundai; Sabine said when she used to drive a nice car, police would always stop her to shake her down. She'd once spent the night in a Maryland lockup while the cops tried to seize her Jag; they were trying to say she had cocaine in the car, when of course Sabine couldn't do cocaine; she was a motherfucking cardiac patient. At last they let her make a phone call, and Sabine called the governor of Maryland—the mother of her best friend from Yale. "White privilege is kind of my cocaine."

Then she talked about privilege, self-castigatingly, gloomily, and fell silent. Ben turned the radio on. They listened to a Christian station denouncing the Red Cross as Satanic. On the hills, billboards began to appear, which exhorted them to protect America and scolded them about the horrors of abortion. Meanwhile, the sun went down in fits and starts. Long after night appeared to have fallen, they would crest a hill and find another purple remnant of dusk backlighting the farther trees, while the people on the radio quoted Isaiah and assured each other that they, too, had at first found it hard to believe.

On the border of Virginia, they stopped at a service area. The area was going through a blackout, and inside it was pitch dark and achingly cold. The Cinnabon and Burger King staff (for whom this was apparently now routine) had set up LED hurricane lanterns and were otherwise acting as if nothing had happened. Customers carefully inched through the black expanse between the restaurants, admonishing their children to stay close and breaking now and then into nervous laughter. Sabine and Ben got the last cooked cinnabon and went back to share it in the car. There was a full moon and it was snowing again. Ben already felt happier.

Then driving again, and the mountains beginning, seeming to arise and help the car upward in reward for its long day of work. There was something tranquilizing about Sabine's shadowed profile in the chilly, close darkness of the car; the gentle light from the gauges on the dashboard; the feeling of being borne through a vastness. Ben stared out at the massed close trees until they opened out suddenly into a valley. At that moment, the lights came back on in a roadside town, and it appeared as a fairy constellation on a hill. He'd been assuming he would call his boss in the morning, that he'd be back at Exxon the following Monday. At that moment, he decided he wouldn't go back. He had some money in the bank. He could just keep moving. It didn't have to be about Kate.

When they arrived in the town, it was almost midnight. It had snowed here, too, and any sign of poverty was effaced; all the world was smoothed over, neat and white, and decorated here and there with Christmas lights. All the way through town, theirs was the only car.

They turned into the ghost neighborhood, and Sabine slowed down and made Ben admire the new playground and the children's library; she named the people living in the renovated houses and explained the affordable-rent scheme until Ben felt pleasantly quiescent and bored, like a child listening in on an adult conversation. At last, they pulled up to the organizers' house, a steeply gabled Victorian whose paint was peeling so badly it had the appearance of a molting bird. The front yard had been churned by thousands of footsteps, which parted around a little island of snow with a sign saying: PEOPLE'S AID OF WEST VIRGINIA.

They got out of the car, and the silence was so intense it felt like blinding light. Walking to the porch, they repeatedly slipped on the terrain of frozen footprints. The front door had a lopsided wreath and a novelty welcome mat with the message: HI, I'M MAT! Sabine opened the door without knocking. They came through a hallway littered with dirty boots and cheap umbrellas and into a living room where half a dozen people were drinking wine around a fire. Everything here was in disrepair: the banister had been torn away from the stairs; so many chunks of parquet were missing from the floor that it looked like an incomplete jigsaw puzzle; one window was covered with blue plastic, which swelled and drained with the changing wind.

There was a round of names and handshakes. Most of the people were organizers—earnest, puppyish millennials—but Gabor was also there, a fiftyish man with a receding hairline and a long white nose, who wore gold-rimmed glasses and a rumpled old suit, as if he were in costume as an Eastern European intellectual fallen on hard times.

Gabor got up motherhennishly and brought Ben and Sabine plates of bright red stew. The organizers chattered at Sabine excitedly; Ben

251

was suddenly too tired to take part and had to concentrate even to eat. All he got from the conversation was that Kate was out helping some elderly woman of the neighborhood put up Christmas lights. Then Sabine talked about her fair-weather uncle, gesturing with her fork, but suddenly trailed off mid-sentence, put her stew untouched on the floor, and announced she couldn't think about anything now. She was wasted; she was going to bed.

Ben went to bed too (he was afraid to see Kate) and slept deeply in the thrilled, luxurious way he'd slept when he was a child who could easily fall asleep in airplanes, and he would sleep suspended above the world, and wake up believing something supernatural had happened to him in the sky. Then the long cold morning; Kate was still out. She'd slept at the Christmas-lights woman's house because the woman was depressed because her dog had just died. Ben kept wanting to make a mean joke about it. It made him uncomfortably aware of being too selfish to do a thing like that. He also felt as if he ranked below the dog, since Kate now knew he was here; Sabine had called Kate's cell phone and told her.

One by one, the activists went out. Sabine went out, and invited Ben to come along, but Ben was waiting for Kate, while pretending he was tired and didn't feel like going out in the cold. Gabor was still in bed, and for a while, the only other person was an activist named Billy who looked about fourteen years old but had (as he told Ben) an MA in economics from Georgetown.

Then the doorbell started to ring, and the living room began to fill with locals. Three thirteen-year-old girls rang the doorbell and asked if they could build a fire; they huddled at the fireplace, whispering and giggling, pretending to be elves who were building a magical fire to summon a wizard. A strained-looking, bleached-blond woman came, who was angling to move into a renovated house; when Billy said she had to fill out an application, she stormed out, swearing about "red tape". An obese man came, who walked with a cane and was accompanied by a limping, rotund dachshund, to ask when the veterinarian was coming to do the free clinic; then he and Billy stooped over the dachshund, which shut its eyes gratefully while they inspected its teeth. And more people came and asked favors, asked questions, and groused about the "Democraps" in Congress and belligerently asked Billy how anyone could defend that corruption. They gossiped and invariably asked after Kate. They left notes for Kate, and one woman left a casserole for Kate, and a girl left a scented candle wrapped in faded American-flag wrapping paper for Kate. At one point, Gabor (who'd come down at one thirty, frowsy and barefoot but in his same black suit) informed the company that Ben was Kate's ex-boyfriend. Then everyone—the fireplace girls and the casserole woman and a man who was going through a box of donated shoes to see if he could find a pair that fit—looked at Ben with sudden fascination. The casserole woman asked if he was from New York, and the shoe man asked if he was Puerto Rican. When Ben said he was Indian, the fireplace girls said they'd seen a Bollywood film once and started to laugh uncontrollably, remembering the chase scene from the movie; they tried to describe it but couldn't get anywhere because they were laughing too hard.

For a while then, everyone told Kate stories, mainly about Kate making friends with improbable people and acting in improbable ways. Clearly, Kate was a local celebrity, partly by virtue of being half Iranian but also by virtue of being Kate. She babysat kids for free and baked birthday cakes for lonely senior citizens and exuded an infectious happiness, but could also suddenly collapse and cry all day. After all, she'd lost her child.

Then Gabor talked about how he'd brought Kate here from her mother's house, and Ben realized (or realized he'd already realized) that Gabor had never slept with Kate, and Ágota was crazy to assume he had. It was only three hours' drive from Ohio, and Gabor had known Kate all her life. It was no big deal to drive her here. What was strange was that he'd stayed on afterward, which Gabor explained as "a fit of inertia." The shoe man said, "Well, you found the right place for it. Nothing happened here since Noah invented the ark." The casserole woman said she didn't know why people had to have their inertia here; there were plenty other places to have their inertia in. The fireplace girls asked what inertia was, and the shoe man said when they got older, they would find out.

Then the shoe man left, wearing new hiking boots and carrying his old sneakers. The casserole woman left and gave the fireplace girls a ride home. It went quiet. The door stopped opening and closing; the room began to finally warm. Gabor went to take a bath. Billy went into the kitchen and started to chop vegetables for dinner. Ben built up the fire and thought of it as summoning Kate. He was happy in a tranquilized way; it was the heat of the fire and the bathwater running, the too-intimate particular splashes Gabor made in the bath, the pans banging in the kitchen and the big snowy world outside.

Gabor came back out, wearing a bathrobe that Ben recognized with a shock of affection; it was one of the identical cashmere robes Sabine gave all her guests, because Sabine's aunt once had a bathrobe company, and when it went out of business, Sabine got a hundred robes. Gabor sat in an armchair and stretched his bare feet toward the fire, then suddenly looked at the door. He pointed to it and said, "Kate," as footsteps thumped on the porch and the door squeaked open. Kate walked in, already smiling with sentimental eyes and looking for Ben.

She was wearing a shapeless parka, corduroys, and pink snow boots of Kmart quality. But she was herself, with her old shining candor; the way she used to put on a rumpled old bag-like dress and wear herself like jewelry. Not beautiful exactly, but wonderful to look at, her black eyes charged with a particular emotion no other person felt. She looked (she had always looked to Ben) like a queen disguised as a commoner to walk among her people.

When she spotted him, she shook her head and grinned, then turned to shut the door behind her. In those few seconds, the room had grown crisp with cold. Ben got up from his chair but didn't go to hug her. She turned back and didn't come to him.

Gabor said, "This is a moment of tremendous excitement."

Kate and Ben laughed without looking at Gabor. Kate said, "Ben, you want to come out for a walk? I have to go to church and ask for hay."

"Can't you ask God for hay anywhere?" Ben said.

Kate laughed. "Silly."

"I guess I should put on boots, then," Ben said.

Gabor said, "It was as if they had never been apart."

The sun was already setting; it was December and the days were short. They took a shortcut through the snowy woods. As they walked, Kate explained that she was asking the Baptist congregation for hay for a rescue cow; Kate's friend Misty had adopted this cow but couldn't afford the winter feed. The cow was from a nearby farm; she'd been about to be slaughtered because she couldn't give milk, because she'd had to have a radical mastectomy. Ben burst out laughing, then apologized and said that of course it was no laughing matter.

Then they talked about Sabine and how she couldn't stop trying to save the world, no matter how much the world hated her for it. They talked about the town as an example of Sabine's compulsive efforts to save the world. They talked about Gabor and the popular children's books he'd written in Hungary, which had all now gone out of print, and it was giving Gabor a crisis of identity. They talked about José and his job in Iran and how Kate had fallen out of touch with him entirely after the baby had died. Ben said he was sorry about the baby, and Kate cried a little, still walking, then said, "I can't really talk about it. It was obviously just an awful thing." At last, they talked about Kate's psychosis and how the symptoms had all gone away. Even after she quit the medication, her time travel dreams had never come back. Kate said it didn't feel important now. It felt like water under the bridge.

Ben said, "Are you still from a parallel universe?"

"Who knows?" Kate said. "It isn't really a question that comes up."

Then Ben wanted to pursue it, but stopped himself. They walked without speaking for a while, and the crunching of snow seemed amplified in the silent woods. The dusk had advanced; it was shadowy and frigid. It felt as if they were gradually being submerged in blue, even though there was no actual blue in the landscape. The only real color was the flashing pink of Kate's boots. They came out onto a narrow road and passed a series of clapboard houses with Santas and nativity scenes in their yards. Kate pointed out the church, another clapboard house that only differed from the others in having a parking lot, which was full. There were extra cars parked along the road. As they came to the door of the church, the congregation was singing, abominably badly, while someone played a keyboard badly. Kate got the giggles, and they paused in the snow while she leaned against the side of the church, pressing a mittened hand to her mouth. Ben grinned at her foolishly. He wanted her to keep on laughing. He didn't want to go inside.

At last she caught her breath and said, "I love this place. Don't you love this place?"

"It is pretty great."

"Are you staying?"

"Am I staying?"

"Lots of people end up staying. Or they keep coming back. You could keep coming back."

"Could I stay? If I wanted to?"

"Of course. You're one of Sabine's favorite people. She would give you a room."

Then he wanted to ask about staying in *her* room. He wanted to talk about Louisiana and how he'd come to realize he'd let her down. But he couldn't. He just stood in the snow, his feet growing numb, and looked at her face that was radiant with cold, while the congregation's singing jarred into silence.

At last he said, "I could help save the world."

"No," said Kate. "I think we could be happy. But there isn't any way to save this world."

Acknowledgments

First, I want to thank my husband, Howard Mittelmark, who read several early versions of this book and always had brilliant advice. He's a great editor, a great friend, and my sounding board on all things. Also, dreamy.

Paul Bravmann and Peternelle van Arsdale gave great and meticulous advice on early drafts of the book. I also want to thank early readers from Echo: Ellen Tarlow, Gail Vachon, Jim Baumbach, and Liz Margoshes.

Many, many thanks to my amazing editors, Peter Blackstock and Anne Meadows, for their invaluable help with the manuscript and all-around genius. My agent and good friend Victoria Hobbs always goes above and beyond, in addition to just being brilliant, charming, and all things wonderful.

Finally I want to mention my ex-husband and close friend, Robin Mookerjee, on whom the character Ben is very loosely based. Because life is awful, I can't directly thank Robin; he died, far too young, while this book was being written. While Ben is not Robin, and *The Heavens* is not about Robin's life, the pervasive sadness in the book is very much about Robin's death.

GROVE PRESS

Reading Group Guide

by Keturah Jenkins

THE HEAVENS

Sandra Newman

ABOUT THIS GUIDE

We hope that these discussion questions will enhance your reading group's exploration of Sandra Newman's *The Heavens*. They are meant to stimulate discussion, offer new viewpoints, and enrich your enjoyment of the book.

More reading group guides and additional information, including summaries, author tours, and author sites for other fine Grove Atlantic titles may be found on our website, groveatlantic.com.

QUESTIONS FOR DISCUSSION

———

The Heavens is a genre-bending novel that begins in an alternate version of the year 2000 where there is peace in the Middle East and the president is a woman; it then moves back to sixteenth-century England. Consider how the dual timelines affect your reading and connection to the characters. Why do you think the author chose sixteenth-century England for Kate's adventures in the past? Why do you think the author uses dreams to transport Kate through time?

———

Kate has believed since she was a child that she is destined to save the world, but her efforts to save it go tragically wrong. What makes her fail? What is the novel saying about political idealism?

———

The novel features real historical figures, notably William Shakespeare. How does this affect your reading of the novel? Is Newman's portrait of Shakespeare anything like how you imagine Shakespeare?

What does 9/11 represent in the book? In the 9/11 scene, Kate suggests going back in time to kill Shakespeare to make the world a better place—including preventing 9/11. If you believed that would work, would you do it?

Emilia seems to be fixated on "Tom O'Bedlam," a song about a man who becomes a mad beggar on the streets of England. Discuss the importance of the song to Emilia/Kate.

Do you think the reader is meant to believe Kate is really mentally ill? Does Newman answer this question, or is it left unresolved? Which answer do you prefer?

Discuss the evolution of Kate's relationship with Ben and how her experiences in the sixteenth century change their bond. What draws them together?

Discuss the changes that occur in characters like Sabine and Oksana. Have they really changed, or is it only the circumstances around them that are different? Do you think you would be a different person in a more utopian or dystopian world?

How does Newman achieve a post-apocalyptic mood in *The Heavens*?

Compare the characters of Ben and José. How does José serve as a foil to Ben? Are you surprised when he is revealed to be having the same experiences as Kate?

Sandra Newman has said there are five ways to describe her novel: historical fiction, time-traveling fantasy, political allegory, social realism, and a love story. Do you agree? Which genre worked best for you? How do the different genres develop throughout the novel?

Why is Ben so hostile to Kate when he visits her in the hospital? Is he a good man, a loving boyfriend to Kate, or as Oksana says, "not a good person" (pg. 227)? Is Kate right to forgive him at the end? In the end, do you believe he has changed for the better or the worse?

Discuss the ending of the novel. How does the resolution of the story address the many questions the novel presents? Is it a happy ending? If you could write the ending, what might you have done differently?

SUGGESTIONS FOR FURTHER READING

The Time Traveler's Wife by Audrey Niffenegger

Lost and Wanted by Nell Freudenberger

Hard-Boiled Wonderland and the End of the World by Haruki Murakami

Outlander by Diana Gabaldon

Kindred by Octavia E. Butler

The Bell Jar by Sylvia Plath

The Devil's Arithmetic by Jane Yolen

Days of Cain by J.R. Dunn